THIS TRAIN

JAMES GRADY

PEGASUS CRIME

NEW YORK LONDON

THIS TRAIN

Pegasus Crime is an imprint of
Pegasus Books, Ltd.
148 West 37th Street, 13th Floor
New York, NY 10018

First Pegasus Books edition May 2022

Interior design by Maria Fernandez

Library of Congress Cataloging-in-Publication Data is available.

ISBN: 978-1-63936-151-9

10 9 8 7 6 5 4 3 2 1

Printed in the United States of America
Distributed by Simon & Schuster
www.pegasusbooks.com

For all of us on this train . . .

"Meet me in a land of hopes and dreams. . . ."
—Bruce Springsteen

1

Nora kept her head down as she hurried up the stairs into Seattle's train station that chilly spring Thursday afternoon. She angled away from the main entrance's glass doors toward a brown steel slab Service Door. All that any sentinel looking down from the station's brick watchtower might notice was her *night-before's* home-chopped short and dyed chocolate-cherry hair.

She wore an unzipped burgundy leather jacket. A black purse/belt-pack. Black slacks. Savvy shoes. Pulled a clunking roller bag behind her.

Her cellphone unlocked the Service Entrance's brown steel slab.

An AUTHORIZED USE ONLY sign was bolted to the inside of that steel door that slammed shut behind her as she stepped into the station's vast main lobby. She surged to that particular square of the black & white tiled chessboard floor.

A dozen strangers to her went about their business across those black & white tiles inside that pale-walled ballroom. Sunlight streamed into the huge lobby through the far wall's glass portals to the waiting tracks.

Nora filled her cellphone screen with the station's security cameras' Live Feed showing her the same reality as her eyes.

The black square where she stood was a blind spot for the cameras.

She *tap-tap-tapped* her cell.

Blink and the seen in her screen became not what she saw with her eyes.

Yes, it was the same giant ballroom of Seattle's train station lobby. And yes, there were people hustling their lives over the chessboard tiles—

—*but* what the cameras now played and logged was yesterday's scene.

Nora roller-bagged her way to a lonely blue & red U.S. Post Office mailbox standing against a wall. Opened her purse/belt-pack.

That black purse held all her *not-much* cash. A charger. Pills. Six condoms. Red *and* pink lipstick. Deodorant, toothbrush, TSA-tiny toothpaste tube. Musk perfume. Black hairbrush—a round, grooved-handle cylinder of rubber bristles that couldn't brush blood-black hair back to the way things used to be.

She pulled out a new thin maroon wallet.

Slid out her Washington State driver's license.

She never liked that picture. Her natural Marilyn Monroe hair flowed fine, but her face strained in her usual 'Official Picture' expression.

She filled the wallet's slot with the driver's license she'd made last night after she'd scissor-slaughtered and dyed her blonde hair to chocolate-cherry. The picture on that fake I.D. showed a dead-eyed face above a name that wasn't hers.

Nora put her real license in a stamped envelope addressed to who she used to be in the studio loft apartment where vertical windows beyond the three desktop screens in front of her chair revealed real horizons where she wasn't.

She licked the envelope.

Lost herself in the taste.

Opened the lonely mailbox's slot.

Released the envelope of the true her into its darkness.

From behind her came a cellphone camera's *Click!*

She whirled—

—saw a pubescent peach fuzz boy with thick glasses lower his cellphone from taking her picture dropping the envelope into the lonely mailbox.

Only the two of them stood in that deserted section of the station.

"Wow!" said the just-made-teenager. "I've never seen anyone do that! Like, you actually *for real* mailed an old-timey letter!"

"Here's *for real*," said Nora in her husky voice. "We delete that picture and I'll let you take a more '*wow*' one *right now*."

The kid named Luc shrugged OK.

Nora let go of her bags.

Shed her burgundy leather jacket.

Mesmerized Luc held his cellphone between them. His back was to the pale stone wall. Her back was to the station's distant and distracted shuffling crowd.

Nora jerked her blue sweater up and over her face.

Cool air brushed the uncovered flesh of her front.

She heard Luc's cellphone *Click!*

Let her sweater drop. Lifted the cellphone from jaw-dropped Luc's hands.

Nora worked the algorithms of his unlocked cellphone.

"One image gone and then *really* gone, but you got your *for real*," she said. Put the cellphone back in Luc's hands. "BTW, it won't take pictures for two days."

She left him mind-blown against the wall by the lonely mailbox.

Slid into her burgundy leather jacket. Grabbed her roller bag.

Rolled all she had through the vast castle toward a sign that reserved wooden benches for Premium Passengers with Roomette Suites, Bedroom Suites and Superliner Bedrooms. A second sign pointed to a corral of yellow plastic chairs designated for Coach Passengers.

Nora sat on an empty wooden bench.

She still had time to run.

BAM!

A street door slammed open back by where she'd come from.

The ever-louder *slap slap slap* of sandals on the black and white tiles made him easy to track as he closed in on her. His gold and maroon monk robes showed no dots from the rain. He'd shaved his head to a smooth skull.

The monk marched straight to where Nora sat and in Iowa American said: "Do you know the gate for the four-oh-four train from San Francisco? I want to be sure my son sees me when he gets off."

"*Ahh* . . . I don't think he'll miss you in the crowd."

"I would think there'd be better signage."

Nora blinked.

"I mean," said this 21st century official monk, "I look around, and do I see proper, clear, definitive directions? *No* I don't, do I?"

The man in gold and maroon robes sandal-slapped away with all his *I*'s.

Out of nowhere came a middle-aged man wearing a gray jacket, khaki work pants, a denim shirt. He pulled a duct-taped roller bag. Strapped across his chest hung an army surplus messenger bag.

The messenger bag man headed toward the corral of yellow plastic chairs.

Looked down at his ticket as if he couldn't believe what he bought.

Rolled his duct-taped suitcase to the Premium bench opposite Nora.

His messenger bag *bonked* the bench.

He jerked!

Froze in horror.

But the young woman across from him acted like she hadn't heard a thing.

Nobody ever notices, he thought as he sat down. Now, *finally*, that's good.

"*Yip!*"

Never-married Constance, a stout *mature* lady in traveling clothes from her parents' dignified era before the Beatles, cradled that *yipper* rat dog in the crook of her arm as she marched into the Premium waiting area, paused in the black & white tiles valley between the facing-each-other wooden benches.

"*Yip! Yip!*"

"Mugzy!" scolded she who carried him. "Mind your manners! I'm sure she's a perfectly respectable young woman."

Constance and Mugzy gave Nora their backs and butts.

Constance saw a *mature* man clutching a messenger bag sitting on that bench. But even with his flecked gray hair, he was more than a decade away from that magic moment when The Government declared you "old" and mailed you a red-white-&-blue Medicare card to prove it. *No,* that does *not* mean one is old!

Constance sighed. Messenger bag man was younger—*OK, a lot* younger than her. She eyed his shabby clothes. Still settled on his bench across from the woman Mugzy had doubts about. Constance sat close enough to not discourage Mr. Messenger Bag and far enough away to be safe from his indifference.

Mugzy growled at four more two-legged beasts marching his way.

The 15-year-old daughter led her rolling suitcases family. Her eyes saw only more strangers who wouldn't understand. Who couldn't possibly know what she was going through. Her purse of secrets rode strapped across her chest like an outlaw's bandolier of bullets.

Striding behind the teenage daughter came the family's mom. Ebony hair swayed on her shoulders. The mom kept her eyes locked on her walking away daughter. Strained to see where she was going.

Trudging behind Mom came her 10-year-old son pulling his suitcase while bent over with the weight of his backpack. He raised his gaze off this castle's black & white floor tiles to search for the answer to the obvious question:

Are there monsters here?

Dad marched behind his family. Rear guard but facing What's Really Out There. Like he should. Like every Marine—any Marine—would. Ready to do what had to be done. Trustworthy. Loyal. *Semper fi.*

Semper fi fucked, he thought even as he hated himself for *ever* thinking that even though that *ever* was now.

His daughter marched them to the Premium passengers' wooden bench where a cherry black haired woman twice her age sat on the far end. His daughter dove into her cellphone as she plopped near that edgy woman. Dad made sure his son who tended to drift off to dreamland—

Not, no *NOT* on to some *"spectrum,"* Dad told himself.

—his boy sat down just like he should.

And their mom . . .

Their mom. His wife. The high school teacher. The ebony haired beauty. She settled on the wooden bench beside her screen-mesmerized daughter.

Just one minute, thought Mom. *Please give me just one minute.*

One minute without me having to think about—worry about—all the ifs.

Nora.

The messenger bag man.

Constance and Mugzy.

That family of four.

They were the first to arrive in the Premium seating section that gray Thursday April afternoon, but by 4 o'clock, a flood of travelers filled the rope-controlled corral of plastic yellow chairs designated for Coach passengers.

There were men. Husbands. Fathers. Brothers. That man in the rain. All sons of someone. All trying not to be lost.

There were women. Moms. Aunts. Sisters. The blurred face in a passing car. All daughters of those days. All striving to be who they were.

There were children. A boy clutching a stuffed monkey. A girl playing with Superhero action figures tied into a mega-millions Hollywood franchise.

There were people burned by a lot of sun. Pale clerks and techs. Cubicle and counter and warehouse workers. A ride-share driver. They breathed, they bled, they bred, they dead. They sold stuff, they bought stuff, they did stuff. They were people who had jobs and people whose jobs had them. There's a flash of lonely. A look of fear. A laugh in the crowd. A cough. A babble of octaves. There's silent sad and humming happy. And everywhere there's the tingle of *Let's go!*

Knifing through all that came a werewolf.

Silver hair. Cheyenne-worthy cheekbones on pale skin. Burning blue eyes. The werewolf wore a scruffy black leather jacket over a black hoodie, faded black jeans. His roller bag looked like nothing special.

As he rolled his way into the benches, Constance felt her heart twitter even though he looked like the *no-no* kind. She felt certain he also carried a *Not-old!* card of red-white-&-blue. He claimed the end of the bench to her right. Sat.

Mugzy nuzzled his snout out of sight in her arms.

And just as Constance was trying to figure out some casual greeting to send him with a prim but friendly smile, the silver-haired stranger spoke.

Not to her. Constance felt like he saw her only because The Everything of this the train station filled his steel blue eyes. Constance heard him softly say:

"And thus, we are here."

What does that mean? thought Constance.

She pulled into herself like she did when she heard something in church or coming out of the TV that she didn't understand or didn't *want* to understand.

Mugzy nuzzled deeper into her hiding embrace. Silenced his *yips.*

Constance glanced back toward the silver stranger who wasn't like the Main Street gentleman she'd hoped for or even a *no-no*. He was an *oh-oh*. Though she would *of course* speak to him if the rules of politeness so dictated.

Now he settled on her bench. Let his smile wait for what was coming.

What came was Brian Keller.

Bank president Brian Keller.

In his beloved golden cashmere coat.

Behind him trudged 'the little woman.'

She wore a prim pantsuit proper for her place in small town American life, dark ruby lipstick with none of the heat from the shade of red in Nora's purse.

Brian sighed and silently cursed himself for being too good of a guy, too good of a husband. Letting the wife talk him into this.

And so now here he is, but there's some old biddy with one of those damn yippy dogs hoarding up the middle of the bench, the only bench to sit on because—*Don't look!*—there's a whole family of *them* sitting over there.

"I thought this was the Premium section," he muttered to his wife.

Brian nodded to the bench beside the old lady with that yippy dog, told his wife: "You sit there."

She did.

Brain claimed the space between her and some guy hugging a shabby bag.

Wished he wasn't here. Wished he hadn't come. Today was Thursday. Chamber of Commerce luncheon day. Sitting down and standing up with all the right people. Pledging *liberty and justice for all.* Getting the low down and the down low. Not stuck on a wooden bench across from a family of *them.*

Black people, he thought. Or whatever we have to call them these days.

A whole family: dad, mom, daughter, son.

Sitting on the same Premium bench as some funky red hair woman who probably thought she was too good to walk in his wife's shoes.

Nora looked away from the cashmere coated banker.

Saw arriving icons of who she once thought she should be.

They were the Makes Sense couple of Nora's Millennial generation.

The woman kept her head up like she was still the Prom Princess *and* Student Body President who went on to Ivy League Phi Beta *wow* and a

Power Resume with a brilliant future. Sunlit auburn hair floated on her shoulders.

Her name was Terri.

Her white knight *hunk* strode beside her. Had smart eyes and a welcoming smile, wore just the right clothes. Had nature-built muscles from backpacking mountainous woods and whale watching off Oregon cliffs. Had a handsome face that got *hmms* from women whenever he arrived in a bar to meet Terri.

His name was Erik.

Erik sat on the bench next to the Black teenage girl.

Smiled straight ahead with a patience that gave no hint of *The Countdown.*

Terri slumped next to a cherry-haired woman her age.

Saw no bloody answers written on this train station's white stone walls.

Everyone in Premium *wowed* when they saw who next joined their group.

The new arrival paraded like a retired Baltimore stripper.

Witnesses could almost hear a sultry saxophone play *wah–wah–WHA, wha wha–wha whaa* as what Nora's *nana* would have called "a big girl" hip-swaying and chest-trembling clomped between the Premium benches, a strong neon pink nails right hand clutching an old-fashioned paper train ticket for Della Storm.

Slathers of pink makeup and matching lipstick conspired to hide Della's truths. Flowered hairspray made a cloud around her swirl of shiny black hair. A purple feather boa looped like its namesake constrictor around Della's neck.

Mugzy snapped his teeth at that purple snake.

That sent Della to a seat at the end of the bench beside the Black family.

Everyone was careful not to stare.

Well, except for the silver werewolf.

Mugzy growled at who he next saw striding into his herd.

The new arrival reminded Nora of a second-tier Hollywood star whose name she couldn't remember. Hair dyed the color of hay brushed to cover baldness. Handsome jowly face that surgically defied late middle age. Beady eyes making sure everybody saw him and how good he looked in his tycoon's suit.

That Hollywood clone sat on the bench by Constance. Her hand wrapped around Mugzy's muzzle so he wouldn't be rude to this obvious *gentleman*.

Hollywood paid no mind to Constance's smiles or Mugzy's trembles.

Let his eyes lick the two 30-something women sitting across from him.

Would have licked the teenage girl, but there sat her dad.

Plus, down *that* road he wasn't fool enough to go. Not these days.

Across from where Hollywood sat, of all the passengers, only the 10-year-old boy in the Black family noticed banker Brian's wife slip *something* into the pocket of her husband's golden cashmere coat.

Husband and bank president Brian didn't realize what she'd done.

No self-betraying smile escaped her ruby'd lips.

Then came Ross.

Last, actually.

Last came Ross.

Ross bummed a lift to the train station from Upstairs Amanda who believed she could always beat the clock.

Upstairs Amanda owned the Seattle townhouse where Ross rented the basement apartment, bonus cash for her because the marijuana dispensary she managed paid just fine, *thank you very much* everybody who'd gotten the commerce and cool of cannabis out of the local crime books.

Upstairs Amanda's tattoo-sleeved arms wrestled her car as they careened to the train station through this city with a science fiction skyline of construction cranes and looming skyscrapers for cyber tech corporate giants.

They drove under a bridge. Passed tents of tattered cloth and plastic sheeting pressed up against the concrete. Could be a woman, could be a man pushed an overflowing shopping cart. A rags-swaddled, sister-brother duo huddled against the Apple store's brick wall. Out there in the rain, a thin man standing on the center line of this major road held a hand-lettered sign—HELP.

As Ross's ride *whooshed* him where he had to go, he felt the familiar firm flatness tucked against his spine and wondered again if he should use a holster.

Upstairs Amanda slammed on the brakes. Her tires slid/stopped on the wet street in front of the train station with what she called "plenty of time to spare."

Ross bent down to lift his computer bag off the car floor by his feet.

When he turned to say thanks, she said: "Open your mouth."

He did.

She popped in a lemon drop.

"Is that . . . ?"

"Hundred percent," she said as the *officially cool* did back then.

Tucked a cellophane envelope in his maroon shirt's pocket.

"Later da-zzz-es," she said. "Maybe it will help you pull your triggers."

Reflexes brushed Ross's hand over the black leather jacket above his spine.

"And remember," said Amanda. "You wanted this gig."

"No," said Ross. "I *needed* this gig."

He hurried into the station with a lemony clicking in his mouth. Ran through the crowd as fast as politeness and his bouncing roller bag, side-slapping slung computer bag and what was tucked in his belt allowed. Ran past a corral of fellow passengers milling amidst yellow plastic seats to the Premium benches.

Flashed: *Everybody wants to go somewhere.*

Starts now, he thought. *This is the gig you got.*

Ross unzipped his rain jacket that hung low over his maroon shirt and faded black jeans. Pulled out his cellphone, held that device in front of his face—

—turned the phone horizontal to peer through its viewfinder.

Tapped the red button for VIDEO.

Ross moved like movie directors Soderbergh, Scorsese and Tarantino. Sydney Pollack and Patty Jenkins. Wes Anderson, Howard Hawks, Francois Truffaut, Alan Rudolph or any of the other great ones he'd watched for the *wow* and to absorb how to see. Ross sidestepped like Bruce Lee. Tried to keep his shot level. Curved around the Premium benches. Caught the faces of everyone there.

Whether or not they cared.

Ross slid his view screen/lens past those with whom he'd travel, a slow 180-degree pan to film where they all were supposed to go.

His screen showed the pale ivory wall of the train station.

A museum display about the Nez Pierce.

Glass-paned double doors for the gate to the gray afternoon outside.

A man clutching a machinegun.

2

Machinegun Man stepped further inside the train station.

Blue jumpsuit. Helmet. Ballistic vest. Machinegun.

SWAT, thought Ross. Special Weapons And Tactics. A government gunner.

"What are you doing?" barked a second SWAT warrior marching toward Ross. This gunner wore a blue cap with a communication headset, no machinegun but a holstered pistol strapped to his right leg: a SWAT boss.

Ross lowered his phone. Kept his smile. Kept recording.

"Being me. What are you doing?"

"Any particular reason you're filming?" The SWAT boss had a face of stone.

"I didn't think I needed one."

Oh-oh, thought Ross as he felt himself rise on a lemony cloud.

The SWAT boss marched close enough to grab Ross—

—stopped as cellphone fans stirred on the Premium benches.

A second SWAT machinegunner joined her comrade at the exit to the platform. A third paced back and forth at a different door.

Hurrying toward Ross and the SWAT boss came a hefty Amtrak stationmaster wearing a gold-braided blue cap and a straining white shirt.

The stationmaster reached Ross: "Everything's OK! These guys, they're—"

"Routine," intoned the SWAT boss, his eyes drilling Ross. "Training."

"Yeah," said the stationmaster. "Sure. It's always something."

A firm male voice called out from behind Ross: "Officer?"

The father from the family of four.

Standing tall, no sweat beading his black skin.

Ignoring everyone except the SWAT boss: "Is this area secure?"

The SWAT boss wore neither a name patch nor a rank insignia. He insisted his crew call him "L.T."

SWAT boss L.T. felt himself almost answer: "Yes sir."

L.T.'s eyes flicked to a *suddenly here* silver-haired civilian.

"Wahaaan!"

A plaintive cry.

Three heartbeats, then louder came: *"Whaaan!"*

The *ding-ding-ding* of charging bells . . .

. . . *WHAM!*

A shining blur whooshed into the station. Rumbling steel. Screeching metal. A hiss of steam. A shimmering shudder of metallic light settled outside at the depot platform. Two levels tall and nine cars long. Rows of windows like translucent scales ran the length of the cars parked by the depot platform. Blue and orange corporate stripes lined the skin of this steel-wheeled silver dragon.

A loudspeaker boomed:

"Amtrak train 779, the Empire Builder, has arrived. We apologize for a slight delay before boarding. Please remain inside the station."

SWAT boss L.T. gave a *Watch it!* glare to this nosey trio of passengers. Stalked to the guarded gate for the arriving train and through it to *gone.*

The stationmaster sighed. Raised placating hands to those three passengers. Lumbered to the check-in lectern in front of that gate leading to the rumbling, hissing, hungry beast.

In the Premium benches, banker Brian couldn't stand it anymore.

Brian *harrumphed* to his feet, shook himself to set his cashmere coat on his shoulders, stalked over to the action like the V.I.P. he knew himself to be.

Wouldn't look at the Black guy even though he'd been the one talking to the boss cop. Saw the merciless eyes of the silver-haired guy.

Ah, *no*, thought Brian.

That left the cellphone stud to get Brian's demand: "What's going on?"

Ross. The father. The silver werewolf.

They'd all seen Brian *not* talk to a Black man.

Ross's smile came slow and sly: "Consider the question."

The silver werewolf and the Black father shared a look.

"What?" said Brian.

"Exactly."

"*What*—No! *Oh no*, don't you fucking do it! Don't you twist me up with words! Just tell me right now: What the hell was going on with those cops?"

"Oh," said Ross.

Smiled: "Routine."

Brian blinked.

The silver-haired guy said: "It's always something."

The Black guy just stood there. Saying nothing. Doing nothing.

Brian stared at these three obvious citizens of Crazytown.

"This country," muttered Brian: "What the hell is it coming to?"

He marched back to the shuffling crowd at the Premium benches.

The silver werewolf in the black hoodie said: "Good to know that he cares."

Said to the Black father: "My guess, birds on your shoulders, Sir."

"Maybe after the next rotation," said the father, who let them hear nothing in his tone. Nothing.

Whoa, thought Ross. *They're talking about military rank. 'Birds' meant 'colonel,' one rank down from general. Or at least lieutenant colonel.*

My dad might have spotted that the father was military, thought Ross. *But then, he grew up when any American male might have ended up in uniform. What uniform? Army, Navy, Air Force, Marines? Each one makes it in different scenes. And the birds haven't come yet, so the Black father ranks as . . . a major.*

The werewolf said: "Do you see any insignias or badges or agency letters on the SWAT? Amtrak Police? Seattle Police? ATF? FBI? Homeland Security?"

He shook his silver head: "Maybe all that doesn't matter anymore. Maybe now it's all just *gonna shoot you on down.*"

"Your attention, please! Amtrak train 779, the Empire Builder, now ready for boarding. Have your tickets out and ready. *All aboard!"*

Ding! Ding! Ding!

The stationmaster at the ticket kiosk beckoned all ticket holders. His white shirt held a brass nametag stamped WAYNE FABER—not that anybody shuffling toward him cared about his name: Wasn't he only what he did for their train?

The older guy flowed back to get his luggage in the Premium benches.

Ross headed to where his bags waited.

The Black major's wife gestured from the Premium seating for him to stay put. Wait for the kids and her to come to him rather than trying to push his way through the crowd to get back to them and help with the luggage.

Banker Brian bulldozed his way back to his wife: "Got everything?"

She said *yes.*

He spun his fawn-colored cashmere coat in a half circle of force that knocked the man with the messenger bag back down to the Premium bench.

Brian pushed into the moving crowd as his wife closed her eyes with a sigh so soft that the bumped-down messenger bag man barely heard her.

"You!" yelled a woman's voice behind Brian.

Again Brian whirled.

The Makes Sense couple Terri and Erik dodged the spinning coat, rode its centrifugal force into the line behind Constance and Mugzy. Mugzy growled.

Spun-around Brian spotted the woman who'd yelled at him: *Her*, her with her two kids and husband *who*. Brian growled: "What did you say to me?"

"I didn't say anything to you . . . *sir*."

"Like hell! You yelled '*you*'!"

"I said '*U*.' That's my husband. *Ulysses*. I was calling out to him."

That wife knew she had to watch out for her husband as much as her kids in this fucking scene she'd had to play out 10 thousand times before, different dialogs and setups but always the same shit under What Was Being Said.

She shot her hand up and out, ordering her husband to hold.

It's OK, she lied. Knew he'd understand. Knew adrenaline surged in him. Knew his ebony face hardened. Knew that tension was akin to the fury that found Ulysses when he won his Silver Star and a second Purple Heart in Fallujah.

She gave Mr. Asshole in the cashmere coat *The Look* she'd used to stare down the angry, the lost, the manipulative, the lashing out, the troubled, even the few dead soul teenagers in classrooms she'd taught from sea to shining sea.

Brian shrank back, *harumphed*, whirled and filled his eyes with the backs of that Makes Sense young couple walking ahead of his strides *outta here*.

His ruby lipped wife leaned toward the messenger bag man. A human being who she knew her husband hadn't noticed he'd knocked down. Some ordinary guy from an American town who, like her, saw 50 in the rearview mirror.

"Sorry," she told him with experienced delivery as they moved into the shuffling queue. "My husband, when he's had a few or needs a few, he gets . . ."

"No," said the man with the messenger bag walking beside her.

She blinked.

"That's who he is," said the stranger. "Don't apologize. It's on him, not you."

Came her whisper: *"Me."*

From *behind* then *between* them came flaxen-haired Hollywood. He noticed the messenger bag man enough to move him aside. Checked out but didn't leer at the lipsticked too-old and too-plain bird pulling two roller suitcases.

She found herself behind the messenger bag stranger and Hollywood.

Walking behind them. Pulling two bags. Knowing how to do that.

The man who'd been filming scooted past her, his lightning-struck face locked on where the cropped reddish haired woman near his 33 years had gone.

The married woman's wistful smile watched him chase hope.

That young man slid into line behind the family of four her husband loathed and feared, all of them now at the kiosk where the white-shirted stationmaster took paper tickets or scanned cellphone screens to grant passage out of the station through the proper gate to the chilly April afternoon mist.

To the hissing silver dragon stretched along the station's wooden platform.

Hollywood stepped out of line. Stood on the platform. Watched the rest of the world board as he tapped a cigarette from a gold case. Gave it fire from a glistening lighter. Blew a puff of smoke like he was the dragon.

Watched the last two passengers bumble on board.

They had to pass an Amtrak attendant in dark blue pants and a white blouse, a blue company cap on her 40+ blonde head and a pro's smile on her face.

Bodacious Della, paper ticket in hand, pouty pancaked face, swished and swayed toward the waiting train—

—stopped, shifted this way and that to straighten the skirt that clung to her like a second skin. Wobbled a slow walk in those killer high heels.

Behind her and last in line came the silver werewolf.

He passed a paper ticket to the blonde Amtrak attendant.

"Hi!" she said. "I'm Cari! You're in Car 2013. My car. I'm your Attendant, here for *whach you wanna* and *whach you gotta*. You're ticketed for a Bedroom Suite, Cabin B, up those stairs straight ahead, into the train. Second level, go left."

"Left," said the werewolf who could have gone to high school with her dad.

He nodded down the long wooden platform. "What's *'right'* down there?"

Cari didn't blink: "The front of the train."

The front of the train.

Three cars beyond the one for Cari's passengers.

That first car to the right from hers had a rolled-down aluminum door in its center, clearly the Baggage Car. SWAT gunners paced there.

Then came the second passenger car before the locomotive, a regular passengers' car that instead of the train crew now housed SWAT troopers.

Past the SWAT-swarmed cars came the rumbling locomotive looking like a bullet toward tomorrow.

The passenger who was no way like her father smiled to Cari.

"So," he asked: "Those . . . *officers* down there. Are they by the Baggage Car?"

"Kinda looks that way."

"And—"

"*And* you're in this car, 2013. That's after the engine, a Crew Car where—then the Baggage Car. Then us, three Roomettes cars—coach seats on the first level. The Dining Car over the Lounge. Then the Observation Car and *shazam*: the rear window and off the train."

"You're on the train or the train's gone."

"All aboard," said Cari.

The silver werewolf saw Della reach the stepstool on the platform in front of Car 2013's open door. Hesitate. First that tight dress sheathed beefy left leg tried to rise to the occasion. Retreated. Lowered back to where it had been. Up went the right leg. Both efforts struggled and failed.

Hollywood stood only two steps away from helping Della.

He took a drag on his cigarette.

The silver werewolf reached Della's stalled backside just as Della wrapped one strong neon pink fingernailed hand around the shiny steel handles bolted along the sides of Car 2013's open door. That arm pulled and the opposite high-heeled foot pushed and up into the car went the everything of Della.

"I'll get your bag," said the black hoodie silver werewolf.

Della's voice rasped: "Aren't you just a dear."

"*Well*," he said, then did as he'd promised and said no more.

Those two passengers disappeared into the train.

Smoking Hollywood snorted with amusement.

A blast of steam.

A groan of steel.

Hollywood knew what Attendant Cari called out even though he couldn't hear her actual words. Women were like that to him. He didn't need them to say a thing to know what they wanted.

He sucked in a last big burn of *because he could*.

Blew out the cigarette smoke.

Saw the last of the SWAT guys board the train.

Flicked the still-burning cigarette to the tracks under the steel wheels.

Walked to the blue-uniformed blonde Attendant by the door into the train.

Hollywood nodded to SWATs on guard by the Baggage Car:

"All that down there is about some kind of big bucks."

"I wouldn't know," said Attendant Cari.

"Yeah, I suppose someone like you wouldn't."

He climbed up the stairs into her car.

Attendant Cari swung herself up and into Car 2013 while at the same time sliding the stepstool into its storage nook below the fire extinguisher cabinet.

She slid the heavy steel door in its slide-sideways path to a satisfying *clunk*. Yanked the lever centering the door from OPEN to CLOSED.

Thought: *We're all locked in tight now.*

3

Nora'd hurried past Attendant Cari's ticket check and greeting.

Did not "*not*" look at the SWAT gunners as she boarded the train.

Told herself: *Act like you're a regular person. Innocent.*

Bounced her roller bag up through a metal-walled door in the side of Car 2013. Climbed the interior set of switchback stairs to this sleeper car's top level.

Inside the train smelled *cleaned*. Pine-scented disinfectant. A blue carpet led Nora down a narrow corridor past windowed doors until the cabin G specified by her ticket appeared. Only cabin H waited beyond hers before the wall of the train car and steep stairs down to the first level and the Baggage Car door.

Her cabin felt like a revolver's chamber for a bullet.

A long window made the outward-curved, cream-colored plastic wall. A chair clung to that outer wall commanded a view of where the train had been. A cushioned bunk filled the wall to Nora's right faced where the train was going.

The back cushion for that couch/bed ran up the curved wall to shoulder height, where waited a second padded slab labeled: FOLD COT DOWN

Across from the couch/beds by the door rose a metal sink with a mirror.

Next to the sink stood a floor-to-ceiling tube hiding a metal toilet and a shower. Inside the tube perpetually glowed with a night vision blue light.

She parked her roller bag beside the chair bolted by the window. Took the grift's cellphone from her burgundy jacket. That phone ran the grift as smoothly as the laptop in her suitcase. She tossed the jacket on the couch/bed. Felt to be sure the black belt purse still hung on her right side where it always rode.

"Attention please!" A male voice boomed through the train speakers. "This is the Conductor. Welcome aboard the Empire Builder, Seattle to Chicago in only 47 hours on the rails, the last great train in America.

"For our Coach Passengers, in about 30 minutes, the Lounge car located on the first level toward the rear of the train will be open to serve snacks, liquid refreshments, and adult beverages.

"Dinner for Premium Passengers will be served between 5:30 and 7:00 in the Dining Car. Please confirm a reservation with your Cabin Attendant."

In the corridor outside her opened-door cabin, Nora spotted the purple boa swirl of the *could be* retired Baltimore stripper lumbering past.

Attendant Cari loomed in Nora's doorway.

"*Knock knock!*" Cari leaned in for privacy with the woman passenger of Cabin G. "Everything good in here?"

"Fine," said Nora.

"Which way you like it in bed?"

"*What?*"

"Your turndown to a bed. You want the top or the bottom? Bottom's easier."

"Sure," said Nora.

"Bottom bunk it is. I'll make it up while you're at dinner.

"Now," said Cari, "pillow by the door looking out the window or by the window looking toward the door? Most people want to face the window."

"Lay me down facing the door," said Nora.

They shared a woman's look. A knowing. A sentiment. An awareness.

Cari nodded: "You got it. When do you want dinner? Most folks go by 6:00."

"Book me for 6:15," said Nora, knowing that choosing a later time to avoid 'most folks' would make the train attendant curious. Or worse, suspicious.

Cari smiled away to serve other passengers.

A man's excited words in the corridor blew into Nora's cabin as she walked toward her still slid-open door: *"Isn't this great?"*

Nora heard no reply to that question. Slid closed and latched her cabin door. Didn't pull the curtain across the door's window to the corridor.

Sure, somebody out there could see in, but she could also see out.

The train whistle screamed.

A *lurch clunking surge* shook the train from the locomotive's cyclops eye to the window in the first level EMERGENCY rear exit of the Observation Car.

That rear window filled with a blurry view of tracks under the steel wheels stretching away, growing longer even as all else shrank. White shirted stationmaster Wayne Faber stood on the wooden platform watching the train leave as he telescoped into an ever-smaller image, *going going gone*.

The train *clackety-clacked* through a chain link fenced urban valley of steel rails and power lines and parked boxcars as it strained to get out of town.

Vibration shook the grift's phone in Nora's hand.

Her screen filled with Snapchat, a communication app favored by millions of teenagers in that era, one that Nora'd downloaded under a phony user I.D.

What made Snapchat perfect for the grift was that its messages vanished in cyberspace after they'd been read, gone like they never were.

Now phantom words in her phone commanded:

> Don't worry about B father.
> U fix the dipshit guy filming
> w/his phone. I'll work
> Mr. Nosey old man in black.

Nausea mushroomed through Nora.

Zed isn't supposed to be on the train yet!

Major Ulysses Doss, United States Marine Corps, slid his cellphone back into the pocket of his civilian blue shirt as the train rumbled out of Seattle.

His wife Isabella turned from storing the family's bags in this Superliner Bedroom suite. Brushed black hair off her *café au lait* face.

Saw her daughter Mirana slumped on one of the couch beds. The teen-ager saw only the screen in front of her eyes, not where they were or were going.

Saw her son Malik riding the chair bolted to the window wall, his face to the outside world flowing past, seeing some *where* no one else would ever see.

Saw her husband Ulysses slide his work cellphone into his shirt pocket. Isabella said: "Everything OK?"

"Gunny checked," he said. "No alerts out for this train or where it's going.

"I mean," Ulysses added, "beyond normal."

"Everywhere is *'beyond normal'* these days," said his wife. "Off kilter."

Isabella shook her head. Thought of her Cuban grandmother fleeing Castro's communist dictatorship in an overloaded fishing boat.

"Smart of you to text," she said. "I doubt the kids were listening let alone hearing. But still, some things don't need to be said out loud."

She leaned closer: "But just *some* things."

Ulysses got the message.

Turned from *her* and *them* to *the kids.*

Said: "How we doing?"

Malik smiled big and bright and true as he said: "Great, Dad!"

Mirana didn't look up from her screen: "'Doing like you wanted us to."

"Really," said her father Ulysses.

He stared at his high school daughter.

Countered her indifference with: "What have you enjoyed seeing most?"

Mirana insisted her family call her what her real friends did: *Mir.*

Mir shrugged: "Those SWAT guys, there were a couple *bae*s."

"What?" said Ulysses.

His long-suffering daughter moon-eyed him, sighed: "*Bae*—cute guys."

Whoa, she thought: Look at him flare up! *So* predictable.

Mir said: "What do you care, they're not your troops, *no sir*, loud and clear."

Then *like, oh my God what's the big deal!* Mir flowed to her feet with the athletic grace that won a silver medal in her school district's 400-meter dash. Tucked her phone in her right hip pocket. "I am *so* out of here! Taking a walk."

Mom said: "Good idea. But be back in time for dinner—you know when."

Through clenched jaws, Dad said: "Don't get in trouble."

"*As if,*" said Mir.

Then she was out the door. Truly gone.

But she left her purse.

5

Mir slid the door between her and her family closed with *whunk*.

The *clackety-clack* wobbled her from side to side.

You gotta learn how to walk on a train, she thought.

Looked left:

The corridor ran past other closed cabins, ended with the shut door between passenger cars. *Wasn't the food car down that way?*

Looked right:

A passageway between solid walls led to switchback stairs coming up from the car's first level, then that corridor angled beyond where she could see.

"Hello dear," said an old woman standing inside the open door to the Superliner Suite across from Mir's family. The old woman cradled that rat dog in the crook of her arm. Smiled. "*Please*: call me Constance."

"*Ah*, OK."

"And this," said Constance, "this is Mugzy."

The old woman used her free hand to wave Mugzy's front paw.

He growled.

Mir was pretty sure that wasn't *hello.*

"Mugzy: remember your manners. We're neighbors with . . ."

The 15-year-old girl wobbling in the corridor told Constance her name.

The name *she* chose.

"Lovely to meet you, Mir. Would you like to come in and have a chocolate?"

Mir blinked.

"Oh my, *yes dear*, I just realized that, too! Father always warned me: *Don't take candy from strangers.*"

A twittering laugh and a warm smile went from Constance to Mir.

"But we're not *strangers*. I'm Constance. And you're Mir. And neither of us is a little girl who can't make up her own mind."

Mir took a deep breath.

Gave *hard eyes* to Mugzy: *I can take you and the old lady you rode in on.*

Mir marched into the old woman's suite like everything was *solid.*

Heard her host slide the door shut behind her.

Wondered: *Did she latch it?*

Constance sat on the lower bunk beside a closed suitcase.

Lowered Mugzy to the blue carpet. Let him go.

Mugzy scampered toward Mir.

Rat Dog saw Teenage Girl.

Mugzy scampered back to Constance. Jumped on the bed beside her.

Mir suppressed a smile.

"Oh dear," said Constance as the dog snuggled against her. She'd flipped open the suitcase on the bed. "Now we have to be so, *so* careful. When Mugzy gets jumpy, men get like that even if they've been snipped, well, I'm afraid now I'll have to be a bad hostess."

"I'm sorry," said Mir: *"What?"*

"Well if I am proper, stand up to bring you chocolates, Mugzy will dive into the suitcase. Now that he smells what's in there, he'd push the closed lid open and dive into his own coffin. Dogs and men, what can be done.

"And something must be done, mustn't it Mugzy-wugzy? Because chocolate is so very bad for doggy-woggies even if they want it so very much."

"But we can't always get what we want," said Constance. She thought maybe that was from a song she'd heard way back before she stopped listening to music about things she didn't know or that never came true.

Constance held a box of French bonbons out to the teenage girl.

Mir slid a piece of candy into the O of her mouth.

Dark chocolate with smooth maple cream melted on Mir's tongue.

"Oh my God," she moaned.

"Yes, I know!" Constance popped a chocolate in her own mouth.

The old woman and the teenage girl . . . *giggled* is indeed what they did.

Constance said: "Don't you just love chocolate in the afternoon!"

Chocolate in the afternoon, thought Mir. *Like the title of a French movie.* She'd taken a film class. Wondered if she could touch the Big Screen.

"But not too late in the afternoon," said Constance. "And look at the time: It's after 5:00, so we're pushing it. One doesn't want to spoil one's dinner."

"This spoils nothing," said Mir. "Thank you so much."

Mir looked around this suite exactly like the one across the hall that comfortably held her whole family. Well, more comfortably than the roach motel outside of 29 Palms once when their Quarters orders got messed up.

She stepped to the center of the train cabin.

"Is all this huge place just for you?" she asked her hostess.

"And Mugzy. He's my constant companion. *Constance's Constant* as they say in my hometown just, *oh,* an hour away from here," she said as *here* changed with every *clackety-clack.*

"You're going home?" asked Mir.

"No. There are some legal formalities for me to sign in Chicago. *First* they said they would email them to me and I could electronically sign and it would be legal. Imagine that! Who would be foolish enough to take a computer's word that I am who I signed I was? And then it was overnight delivery. But overnight here, overnight there, that's at least three days, and the Travel Tips column in Sunday's *Parade* magazine that comes with my newspaper, only thing I really read, the rest is just topsy-turvy bad news that who can figure out, that column told about this heavenly train that takes less time for that trip. And when I checked yesterday, someone had just cancelled their reservation for this suite. Who knows why anyone would do that, but what wonderful luck for me."

Mir grinned. "So that's how you got out of town."

"My dear, I absolutely love my hometown. Lived there all my life."

"Living in one place your whole life." Mir shook her head. "I'm 15—almost 16—and I've already lived in 5 places."

"I just *knew* you were wonderfully unusual!" Constance beamed. "Are you going home to Chicago, dear?"

Don't know where I'm going, thought Mir, but she told her new friend: "No. Our school's spring break family trip. Visit relatives. Aunt Roma in Chicago."

Mir looked at one empty bunk. Then another lonely bed. Then a third. Put her eyes on the bed where Constance sat with an open suitcase. And Mugzy.

I won't be all alone with empty beds like her someday! No way! Never!

"I gotta go," said Mir. "Thanks."

"Come back anytime, dear." Constance sat on the bed, guarding her open suitcase, controlling Mugzy as her new friend walked to the door. "You're always welcome. And you'll be surprised. There's much more here than chocolates."

6

What if all that *isn't* weird? thought Mir, back in the corridor again. Shuddered.

Saw her family through the window of their suite door.

Saw her purse still on that bed where she left it.

Found herself back at the same damn question: Which way should she go?

Her chocolate detour had turned her round, so what had been *left* was now *right*. Still, one direction was where she'd have to go to dinner with her family, the other direction was a mystery.

The mystery way took Mir past the switchback stairs.

Around a serving counter with a smelly coffee pot and a sign about *free*.

Mir wobbled down a corridor past the alphabetized cabin doors.

Cabin A. Closed door, curtain covering the window.

Cabin B. *To be or not to be*, thought Mir. *Be what? Who?* The curtain over that cabin's door was closed.

Cabin C—*ah, see!* The curtain isn't pulled over the door glass and . . .

Cashmere Coat asshole has Cabin C!

Mir glared at who she saw through that cabin door's window.

Slamming my mom, thought Mir. You don't know how lucky you are. Dad *coulda woulda shoulda,* but he's too smart to be that dumb. You're a Big Stupid. Sitting there in Cabin C, White face all *duh.* We've got a Superliner Bedroom Suite. Got an *up* on you.

She heard her smarter voice:

Don't give him that. Don't think like that. Don't be like him.

Look at him facing the window at the gray lit world *clackety-clacking* by.

The Puget Sound bay to the ocean.

People tossing Frisbees over the packed sand beach.

A woman walking alone beside a narrow black road.

Bet cashmere coat just sees his pale reflection in every window.

His poor wife, thought Mir.

Jesus, look at her:

Perched on Cabin C's lone chair. Facing backwards. Not looking at him. Just sitting there. Like she's on a ledge above the long way down.

Mir wobbled on to Cabin D: No curtain covered the window in the door.

The *him* who videoed the SWATs sat on this cabin's chair like the trapped wife next door, but he's . . . He's writing with a pen in some kind of black book.

A pen! Who even does that anymore?

Still, Mir told herself, he's young enough that you can see he used to be someone like me. Maybe some of the SWAT troopers back in Seattle had been *bae,* Mir didn't know, she never looked, she just popped that one off knowing her dad was an easy target, but this *too old* guy, Mir had to admit he's some kind of *bae.*

But not her *someday* dream.

Wobble on, girl, she told herself. Just wobble the fuck on.

Cabin E. Open curtain, closed door. The man in there is *way* older than the *bae* guy next door, thought Mir, but younger than Constance. Holding on to his messenger bag. Sitting by himself. Staring out the window.

She blinked:

How many all-alone people are on this train?

Cabin F—

Whoosh slides open that door.

Mir froze as out into the corridor stepped an Ultimate Cool Woman, right down to her off-brand sneaks and back up to her auburn hair.

She's so lucky it's straight and won't frizz up! thought Mir as she stared at the Ultimate Cool Woman standing in front of her. Outta college—Mir just knew she went, and to one of the good ones. Mir remembered the hunk who'd been with this woman on the bench back in Seattle. Both then and now, Mir noticed *no rings* and figured this *wow* woman was not married but still traveling with her own *him*. No 'rents or rules keeping them off any train, so *romantic* and totally cool!

The teenager heard herself screaming inside her skull: *Come on, Mir, say something! Don't be a dork! You can do it. Say . . . say . . .*

The auburn-haired woman standing in that cabin doorway sighed.

Terri said: "I used to be you."

The spooked teenager hurried back the way she'd come.

7

Terri watched the teenage girl wobble her retreat down the corridor.

Stepped back inside where she was supposed to be.

Erik looked up from his laptop. "What did you say?"

He'd *of course* left her the best place to sit: the view that faced out the window the direction the train was *clackety-clacking*. Waterside houses and low brick buildings and boatyards slid past that glass.

Erik gave her that primo place while he sat closer to the door. Sat working his laptop on the padded cushion that converts to a bed.

The obvious *our bed*, thought Terri, though he asked Attendant Cari to also prep the top bunk for him to use *when*.

"So you'll be more comfortable," Erik had told Terri.

Just like him, thought Terri: Thoughtful. *Arrr!*

"I'm sorry, I didn't hear you," he said. "Like you didn't hear me before when I said this place is great."

Sorry, thought Terri. *He's always saying he's sorry!*

"So you were saying . . ."

"No," said Terri, "it's what I should have said."

"That teenage girl was out there. High school, looks like she's got it together. Got that *something's going on* in her eyes. And I should have told her *sorry!* I should have told her stay strong. Never give up hope. But . . ."

She stared out the train window.

"What's out there now isn't what we expected. What was promised."

Erik closed his laptop.

Terri knew he did that so she'd realize she had his full attention.

Not because there was anything in his screen he didn't want her to see.

Terri shook her head: "Remember 9/11?

"I was younger than her then. They hustled us out of school. Onto buses. Wouldn't tell us what was going on. We all thought it was another Columbine."

They felt the *clackety-clack* of the train they rode.

"I was going to fix that," said Terri. "Make it all work. Help position *this* and *that* just so. Then it all fell apart. Or blew apart. I don't know anymore."

"It's not all on you," said Erik who moved money around for his daily take. "You always do your best."

"Then maybe I should *really* apologize."

"If you just take a step back and see—"

"We're on a train. Step back all you want, you're still rushing forward."

Erik stood.

"It's going to get better," he said. "Trust me. There are big things in the works. And all you have to do to change the universe is breathe."

Terri's eyes closed.

"*Please no,*" she said. "I didn't get on this train to hear about *the universe.*"

Erik absorbed the sway of the train with the grace of a natural traveler. His hands cupped her shoulders—to *comfort,* not *control,* yet somehow that made her feel worse, not better, even as she felt warmed by such a kind touch.

"Sorry," Terri told him. "I don't mean to ruin this trip. I know you paid a lot for the tickets and I'm grateful, I am, I really am."

"I don't want you to be grateful," he said. "I want you to be happy."

The perfect thing for him to say. *Fuck!*

She slid into his arms, closed her eyes against his strong chest.

Erik said: "I love you."

She said: "I know."

Terri thought: *How long can I hide with my face pressed into his warmth?*

8

Ulysses stood locked in his stance after Mir stormed out of their suite.

"*So nice* when our vacation gets off to a fun start," said his wife Isabella.

She turned to their son Malik who was tracing *I'm not here!* lines on the lower bunk where he'd sleep that night, Mir having already claimed the top bunk because it was as far from her family as she could get and—*I hope*, thought her mom—because it was safer for her brother to sleep in the lower bunk since sometimes sleep rolled him out of bed/*plop* on the floor.

"Hey, Malik," said his mother, ruffling his hair, letting him know everything was all right even though his whole family acted mad at each other.

"How about some iPad?" said Mom Isabella.

Malik's eyes widened and he vigorously nodded *Yes!*

Dad who always wanted to know said: "What book are you reading now?"

Malik started to say: "*Sherlock Holmes* . . ."

. . . but Mom jumped in.

"*Ehh*," said Isabella, signaling she had more than what she was saying on her mind and in her moves. "I was thinking . . . How about a little video game time?"

"*Fortnight!*" cried Malik.

"*Pokemon*," countered his mother.

The 10-year-old boy said: "Pokemon is kind of for kids."

"That's not you, huh?" said Isabella.

A *maybe* shrug was Malik's response.

Reward him for standing up for himself, thought Isabella.

"So I'm thinking," said Mom, not lying about *what* even as she said nothing about *why*, "if you use your earbuds, we could go for 15 minutes of . . . *Minecraft*?"

In 30 seconds, Malik had the iPad found and its earbuds blocking out any distractions to playing the *said I could* video game.

Isabella turned from their mesmerized son to her rigid husband.

"You read a novel, your mind opens to the story," she said. "And that opens you up to your own story because you use your imagination, not your thumbs. Playing a video game pulls you out of your own life and makes you its data."

On a roll, Isabella said: "Same as with great music. Mingus plucking his upright bass. Adele stepping up to the mic. Hell, Mozart tinkling out of some piano or Denzell grinning on the big screen. Your imagination and thus your heart and mind *interact* with them. You only *react* to video games."

"So throw in earbuds," she said, "and now we can say what we gotta say."

Ulysses shook his head. "Sometimes what Mir says to us, what—"

"She's 15 and scared and that *plus* pisses her off."

"What's she scared of?"

"Of 15! Just like my father is scared of 70! Once you get there, no going back or standing still. And whatever's coming doesn't tell you how to do it good."

Do it good flashed through Ulysses like the *lightflash*-mushroom BANG! of an I.E.D. on a hot dusty road.

Do it good.

How can you ever know?

How can you stop feeling the heavy eyes of Marines who you sent into some shot-up sandy city hell splattered red with their lives lost or fucked up beyond all repair? How can you forget that man you shot who looked so much like you, had to fight not to shit yourself and later lost it sobbing over a latrine trench filled with the stench of what you ate that brought you there? How can you look in the mirror after an I.E.D. blast pressure/dust cloud *crumps* an APC two vehicles back and your first thought is *NOT ME!* DeathPain zings around your head and your heart and your cock and your arms and legs as you cover behind a stone wall built by shepherds a hundred wars ago and you're calling for air support where the fuck is it/what did you miss/what do you do now?

"*Hey, Major.*"

Was his wife talking.

We're on this train.

"*Now* is when you tell me what's going on," she ordered. "And we've only got 13 minutes of nobody listening left."

A deep breath rose and lowered her shoulders.

"Whatever it is," she said, "we're going to be OK, *U'* Even Mir."

His head shook.

"Is it about promotion?" said his beloved wife. "Gunny told me your only problem is that he doesn't want to lose you and he is Gunny."

"He is Gunny," said the Marine major whose sergeant ruled.

Ulysses told his wife: "If . . . If . . . Wherever the next promotion takes us, they'll probably need great teachers like you."

"Of course they'll need teachers. But it's never a question of need.

"Now," she said. "What do *you* need?"

All her beloved husband could give her were his sorrowed eyes.

She took him in her arms, snuggled against his shirt, breathed the skin scent of the wonder of him.

How long can I hide with my face pressed into his warmth?

Isabella whispered the words no military wife wants to speak to her husband: "Do you need to go to a counselor?"

"Why would I need a counselor when I've got you?" he said.

"You know what I mean," she said. Kept her voice calm, her words precise. "For PTSD."

"PTSD?" said Major Ulysses Doss. "That's not me. Hell, anyone who's been paying attention these days is going to end up with PTSD."

"I know what you're talking about," said the woman who loved him. "And you know what I'm talking about."

She felt his embrace tell her *he did* at the same time it said *not now.*

The train rocked them back and forth but they never lost their embrace.

And even as worries ached her heart, pride warmed her mind and she marveled at how strong he was. *Hard core Marine.*

She whispered the words they'd both chosen to live by: *"Semper fi."*

Felt him change. Come back from *wherever* to *here and now.*

Ulysses whispered: "What are we going to do about her purse?"

"You mean when are we going to tell Mir how after the third time you *accidentally* bumped it on the couch when she was on the front porch with Tasha, her purse finally fell over and dumped out what's in it?"

"I don't think that's the line of attack we should use," said the Marine dad.

"If we use any 'line of attack,' we lose," said the mom and high school teacher who'd *once upon a time* been a teenager.

Whump went their cabin door as it slid open.

In came Mir with cool air from the corridor.

"Oh gross!" said Mir as she spotted her parents standing there *practically grinding.* "I'd say 'get a room,' but here is all the train we've got."

Mir sat next to her little brother.

He kept his focus on the iPad, shifted closer to her (but not so close that he couldn't deny that he had).

Their parents broke their embrace.

Mir's eyes twinkled as she said: "Think of the children!"

"Never," said her dad.

Mir looked away and maybe did, maybe didn't see the *'made it through another one'* glance her parents shared.

Mir told her dorky little brother: "I used to play that game."

Given his earbuds, maybe he heard her, maybe he didn't.

Maybe he leaned on her just a bit more.

As Isabella said: "We should start getting ready for dinner."

R oss ignored his cabin's window showing the world he was passing as, through the open door, he watched to see what—*who*—would pass by him.

You've got a gig, he told himself as he sat on the chair by the window.

But how could he focus on *what was* when finally, any heartbeat now, *what should be* might wander past his cabin door on this *clackety-clack* train?

A glimpse was all he had.

A lightning bolt blocked by the shuffling crowd in Seattle's train station. And sure, he was *so* lemony stoned.

But he knew *stoned,* and this wasn't that. Wasn't just his imagination.

She was real—*this* was real.

He saw her. He saw *her.*

The woman with chocolate cherry hair whose intense lightning knocked him into a fall through the all of who he was.

Clearly an absurdity that defied rationality and screamed *beware.*

I'm too old for this, he thought.

Or maybe I'm finally old enough.

He'd watched the cellphone video he shot in the train station a half dozen times. Found seconds' worth of her images that the Chinese software Face++ could have bundled into a data package linkable to any social media or I.D. like a driver's license or a city police surveillance camera crouched on a wall above where shoppers and subway riders walk. But try as he might, Ross couldn't tell if the woman in the images he'd caught wore rings.

She could be married.

She could be engaged.

She could be in love with someone else.

She could find him repulsive, or maybe worse, boring.

Or not be interested in any man *that* way.

She could break Ross with her reality that had nothing to do with him.

He knew that was the fact of life.

The data of our daze.

He told the universe *fuck that*.

If all we are is data, then nothing matters.

There has to be magic in the machine. Or why bother.

And if you don't follow your dreams, they chase you like nightmares.

Motion in the corridor caught his attention.

Ross watched the coupled man and woman who were his age walk past his open cabin door. He'd been watching such couples walk past him since sixth grade. Such couples made him smile, even during the phases of the moon he'd put in being less than a *'good boyfriend.'* These days, seeing such visions of other couples' togetherness conjured his ghosts of *Long Gones* and *Close Calls* who turned out not to be *The One*.

There'd been his crush from sixth grade who, 16 years later, he'd looked up on line and sought out in the adult streets of the city where she lived, a charming reunion that should have burned itself out after a month, but became a logic of its own that locked them into its tragic year and real world costly collapse.

There'd been a *tried hard* cat-eyed woman who couldn't get past her view that no matter whether it was half empty or half full, the glass was cracked.

There'd been the blonde who'd smiled up at him from her demure sit on a house party floor and seared them together with whatever he wanted while both of them fought to ignore her crazy and pain from *what happened to her before* until one midnight jackknifed her up in his bed and pounded her fist on his chest in a power slam she didn't remember at dawn.

There'd been the gorgeous heavy-breasted *Of course!* who wore proper power suits, always spoke socially approved responses of what was officially thought, every day *processed* in her very professional office, insisted her-on-top and sought fellatio, only climaxed after he did, couldn't understand why he left.

And *yes*, there'd been the whip-lean woman who rose like a rhyme one day when his life was going strong and who accepted the bullet boulevards he walked. Embraced everything he did—

—except him, no matter all the months he spent mooning at her side as she let him take her places she would have otherwise never gone with no more offered in return than martyred understanding and a total of four polite kisses.

Nothing in his past was like the lightning that hit Ross now on this train.

That was what he hoped the couple his age had as they walked past his cabin door.

But oddly, that couple's *she* slouched on her way to the Dining Car, her auburn hair hanging limp past sagging shoulders. And that couple's *he* flashed Ross a look of paranoia that Ross sensed was about more than romantic rivalry.

He heard his peers' footsteps fading down the train car corridor.

Heard the *whunk-clunk* of a cabin door sliding open then closed down the corridor from the direction of the Baggage Car.

Clumping past Ross's door came the purple boa wrapped Della, who sent him a slow, pink-lipsticked *ta-dah* before parading on to the Dining Car.

He told himself: *You've spent too much of your life waiting.*

Ross tucked his flexible well-worn black moleskin journal inside his pants between his spine and the cinch of his belt, a feeling so familiar after all these years that he barely noticed it anymore, like a cop carrying his gun.

He tapped his maroon shirt pocket over his heart to be sure he had his pen. Heard the cellophane crinkle of his secret lemon drops.

Checked his look in the mirror.

Fuck it: I am who I am.

And everybody's stoned on something.

He walked out of his cabin. Slid the door shut. Knew he could not lock his cabin from the outside to prevent snoops or ambushers.

Ross was almost to the end of the hall of Premium cabins on his way to the Dining Car when he heard a door slide open behind him.

10

Brian turned his head this way, then that: *Here I am, stuck in Cabin C.*

That's my coat hanging on the train cabin wall across from this couch bed I'm sitting on. My coat. Beautiful golden cashmere. The color of a deer.

Been almost 50 years. Back when he was a boy. In the alley behind the small-town bank, his old man, Owner 'n' President showing his kid some anxious customer's offering shot dead and tied across the hood of an old Dodge. *Yeah,* there was blood. Buzzing flies. Glazed brown eyes on the antlered head dangling above alley gravel. But what haunted the kid for the rest of his life was the deer's beautiful gold fur and what his old man learned him then and there:

Don't be the deer.

Be the banker on the pink slip for the car.

Here and now, Brian blinked.

Look at her. Sitting there on the black chair staring out the window like there was something to see. Least she keeps herself looking decent in public, dark lipstick like a proper wife with a position and an image to uphold.

How'd he let her talk him into taking the train to the bankers' convention? Why'd she even want to come?

'Hell, give her one every now and then,' that's what he'd often tell the guys at the country club. She got his last name. Got to be Mrs. Beck. *Sue.*

"She would if she could!" he'd tell the guys and they'd all laugh.

Now on this train, he watched Sue take a brown paper sack from her purse. She pulled a pint of Scotch from the brown sack, poured *geez,* a couple inch slug of *kind of like the color of a deer* liquid into a clear plastic glass.

Said: "I don't know if you'll be able to get your wine with dinner tonight like the heart doctor said, so you better have a drink before we go to the Dining Car."

Wobbled toward him and—

Stumbled/thrust her hands out for a fall and the glass of Scotch splashed.

Half the glass of that oak-smelling liquid soaked Brian.

"What the hell, Sue!"

"Sorry! The train hit a bump, but you're fine."

She held the plastic glass with its remaining Scotch toward him: "No time to change your shirt before our reservation."

"I'll smell like—"

"—a guy who gets the good stuff."

Amber liquid trembled in the plastic glass she held in front of him.

Brian grumbled: "I didn't really want any in the first place."

"What you want and what you get are rarely in the same place."

"Huh?"

"Come on," she said, holding the glass to him. "We've got to go."

He knocked down the Scotch in one burning gulp.

Brian went first out Cabin C's slide-open door, looked left:

Some guy is stepping out of a cabin down the corridor, holding on to a weird bag like it's all he's got. He gave Brian a nod and got a short one back:

In the street, polite who you meet. Smile them into the bank.

Brian turned to his right: There was that phone videoing stud, obviously headed to the Dining Car. Looking back to see. Brian gave him a nod.

Steadied himself. *Good thing I only had one gulp of Scotch.*

He heard the wife shut their door. Maybe she gave that weird bag guy a nod, maybe she didn't. Nobody said nothing 'cause there was nothing to say.

Like always, Brian led, then came Sue and behind her, the weird bag guy, the three of them wobbling down the narrow aisle toward the Dining Car.

Is that guy behind us watching my wife's ass? wondered Brian.

Sway left/sway right, swish/swish, brush strokes painting *never.*

For you and me both, thought Brian to the weird messenger bag guy.

Brian didn't wonder: *What about for her?*

BAM! He popped a silver door open and led his parade into the Dining Car.

Check it out, thought Brian:

Down on the left, first table: Not a bad-looking girl. Nice auburn hair but a long face like she killed the cat. Boyfriend looks like one of those granola guys who don't know the real *what's what.* Still, he gets the girl, *go figure.*

Next down that way, taking up a whole table is that family of *them.*

Don't stare, he told himself. Don't let them start it up again.

The maître d' walked up to Brian. "Good evening, sir."

Looked past Brian, smiled to his wife and the shoulder bag guy: *"Ah,* Mister and Missus. We've got a couple seating choices for you two."

"No," said Sue, her husband turning to look at her as her gaze swept from him to weird bag guy who'd entered behind her. "I'm with . . . "

She let her words fade away like they didn't matter.

Brian quick-checked his options.

Saw a four-top table where the old woman and her rat dog sat, backs to the Dining Room entrance. The rat dog squirmed in that old woman's arms as she babbled at a Hollywood-worthy, business suit man sitting across from her. Brian couldn't get a good look at him. The broad with a purple boa wrapped around her neck filled the aisle chair alongside poor Hollywood so he was trapped against the wall of windows.

That table had one empty chair.

The closer table had its two window chairs filled by the silver-haired man and the cellphone filming stud who was just settling into his place. The just-sitting-down stud had his back to Brian. The silver-haired guy met Brian's gaze.

That table had two empty chairs.

OK, so they're from Crazytown, thought Brian. But they're the ones in the know. Maybe they'd clue him in. Without any of *them* interfering. Or having to explain *what's what* to Sue, have her mess things up with dumb questions.

Brian told the maître d', "Those two guys are kinda expecting me."

The maître d' shrugged. "We're all kinda expecting something."

Brian faced his wife: "Hey, you keep saying we should meet new people."

He nodded toward the table across the aisle with that young couple and two empty chairs, told the maître d' about his wife and Cabin E with a bag slung over his shoulder: "They'll sit down there with them."

The maître d' heard no dissentions, so he swept Sue and the weird shoulder bag guy behind her past Brian, their faces locked on where they were being sent.

Brian joined his two Crazytown buddies, sat beside the young stud. Glanced past the silver-haired man sitting across the table from him, caught his first full glimpse of Mr. Hollywood in the business suit sitting at the next table.

Whispered: *"Holy shit!"*

11

Oh, great: now this.

Terri stared at the half-eaten plate of chicken in a black-peppered cream sauce *con* fettucine pasta plopped on the train's Dining Car table in front of her.

The train kept *clackety-clacking.*

And *now*, with a swoop of his arm, the maître d' sent some long-time married couple to the table where she and Erik sat.

The matronly lipsticked wife whispered *"Sorry!"* as she pulled out the chair beside Terri. Sat where she could look back the way she came. See the table across the aisle with its three *just sat down* men who were assessing each other with stares Terri'd tracked all her life, from playgrounds in Ohio to the Floor of the Washington state legislature where she was a staffer.

The husband strapped into a messenger bag perched beside Erik like a rabbit ready to bolt out the windows full of evening light.

The meek wife raised her hand to catch the attention of a waitress.

"Excuse me." She nodded to the newest arrival at the table of three assessing males. "That's my husband."

Oops, thought Terri.

The waitress glanced at the shoulder bag man. "I thought—"

"Not your fault," said that wife of somebody else.

"If you'd like to move . . . "

"No, please, I don't want to be any trouble."

Of course you don't, thought Terri.

Watched those conservatively colored lips give a shy smile to the waitress, to Erik across the table, to the *not-her-husband* bag-strapped man, to Terri.

Then those lips said: "Please, would you bring my *real* husband one of those mini-bottles of red wine? Put it on his tab, but tell him . . . Tell him *one's enough.* No more. I'm . . . I'm just helping him follow doctor's orders."

"Certainly, madam," said the white-shirted waitress.

No one else said a thing about that.

The waitress told this table's new arrivals about the fresh fish.

"Whatever you suggest," said *Madam.*

The man who'd come to this table with her gave the waitress a *me, too* nod.

Erik grinned as the waitress walked away.

A great grin, conceded Terri. So real. So from his heart. So fucking *sincere.*

Erik said: "One of the cool things about this train is you end up eating with new people. Look at the four of us. Kind of like we're on a double date."

Terri pushed her chair back, headed toward the door with: "Excuse me."

"Ah . . . ." Erik blinked at the half-eaten steak on his plate. French fries next to a glob of ketchup. The silver can of Diet Coke beside his plate shimmered with condensation. He stabbed the steak with his fork, stuffed the chunk of meat into his mouth as he stood, grabbed his Coke can, shrugged apologetically to the older couple he left behind, hurried after Terri.

At their table, the shy wife in that *not-a-couple* tried an innocent smile.

"I hope I'm not intruding," she told the gray man who sat across from her.

"It's a small train," he said. "We should share, even if I don't know you."

"Mrs.—Call me Sue."

"Is that who you are?"

His question rocked her.

Such a simple question, she thought as steel wheels spun *clackety-clack*.

Could be answered with a simple sentence, she thought.

Like a prison sentence.

In that hurtling train, only he heard her whisper: "*Suzanne.*"

She blinked. Shocked at herself.

"My mom," she said. "She liked this song on the radio. Leonard Cohen."

He smiled: "Remember when we all used to listen to the radio?"

Said: "You're Suzanne."

"I'm trying." She took a deep breath. "Who are you?"

"Back where I lived, small town—they call me Al."

"So that's who you are?"

"My folks, my grandmother pushed them to, they named me Albert."

Only he pronounced it: "Al-*bear.*"

Continued: "My people were French. *Grand-mere* was in the Resistance against the Nazis before my G.I. grampa married her, brought her home. She gave me that name. Dad used to joke that before Grampa, she knew a man."

"If she was lucky," said the married woman sitting across from Albert.

Wistful as she said: "I got labeled when I was a little girl. And in high school, I was a majorette. Baton twirler. We had our names sewn on our sweaters. '*Sue*' was easy, short. Besides, everybody called me that. Knew me as that. Made me that. Wasn't so bad, but . . ."

"Wasn't you."

"Wasn't it?"

He shrugged. "We are who we gotta be. I got to be Al. Good old Al."

"You'll always be Al-*bear* to me." Not a *smile* of those ruby lips, a *softening.*
The waitress put food in front of them. Asked if they wanted wine.
Whatever's right, they told her.
Paid no attention to the color she brought them (white).
Ate their fish and drank their wine in silence save for the *clackety-clack.*
Until she said: "It's so nice to *get to be* quiet instead of *got to be* quiet."
He breathed the scent of the fish and the potatoes, the oil and vinegar salad dressing, a whiff of her warmth, her skin.
Her eyes widened as she stared behind him: *"What the hell is he doing?"*
Albert turned.
Saw *her husband* rise like a circus bear from his chair across the aisle.

12

No, no, no! nailed Nora to the chair in her cabin.

The phone she grasped burned new thoughts in her head:

Not like this! The grift isn't programmed like this! That Snapchat . . .

Zed isn't supposed to be on the train. Not *now.*

And he knows who I am! How I look! That's not how it's supposed to run!

But I don't know who he is. What he looks like.

She closed her eyes. Pushed her stomach out to force air into her lungs.

You're OK, she told herself. The grift is running lines of functioning data. The man cellphone filming back in the train station.

Just a bug in the system, she told herself. One that triggered the Black father, the silver werewolf, even the asshole in the cashmere coat. Triggered them into leaving their PPPs—Predictable Programed Parameters.

But we can't have a *break point* to stop and rework the whole grift.

Zed being on board *now*, since the first *All Aboard*: We were supposed to get on board at different times, different stations.

Call that a bug, too, Nora told herself.

Knew that Zed rewrote the code.

Had to assume there was a good *why* and that he's holding up his end.

The grift is still a *go.*

Had to be, she reminded her quivering heart.

And not just because . . . well, not because of any permutations of what could happen if she didn't log up to what she had to do.

Nora told herself to Keep It Together.

Less than two days to go before it's all over.

She sat in her cabin on the Empire Builder *clackety-clacking* to *then.*

This is my grift, she told herself. I am Primary Coder.

And what Zed said—not *ordered*: proffered, urged. Made sense.

The Black father was just a father. The cashmere coat asshole was just an asshole. But the other two glitching passengers?

Follow Protocol, Nora told herself: C.C.C.C.

Confirm Contain Control Contingencies. The 'four Cs' of 'foresee.'

B.O.P. Basic Operating Protocol.

Now outside her cabin in the train corridor she heard doors sliding open, sliding closed. Footsteps walking away. People leaving where she was.

A glance at her cellphone told her the time.

She pulled herself up from the chair to—

Looming outside the window of her latched door: a giant man in blue.

Nora's heart thundered: *Staring in at me, he's*—

Not SWAT blue, *no*, not them, he's . . . just the train Conductor.

Staring at Nora. Only the glass of the cabin door between them.

The Conductor gave her a nod. A confirmation that she was on his train.

Then he was gone, a blur of blue with barely any face.

He was just doing his job, thought Nora. Now do yours.

She glanced at the mirror above the metal sink.

Her right hand floated to her waist, her hip, to the black purse clipped there, and in the *clackety-clack* of that moment came the purse's opening *snap.*

Holy shit!" whispered banker Brian when he finally saw the Hollywood man stuck sitting at the next Dining Car table with Della, Constance and Mugzy.

"You know who that is?" Brian whispered to the young stud and the silver werewolf. "That's Fergus Lang! We're on the train with Fergus Lang!"

"Like a poem," said the stud.

A black moleskin journal lay waiting beside the stud's plate.

"Poetry's got nothing to do with this," insisted Brian. "He's a billionaire. That beats the shit out of poetry."

The phone Ross cradled out of sight under the table obeyed his thumbs, gave him 3,374 hits in a Google search of 'Fergus Lang.' Ross tapped the top link:

LANG NOT INDICTED IN BRIBERY,

FATAL BUILDING EXPLOSION SCANDAL

"I met him last year," Brian told his table mates. "After his famous speech. *'Make politics like business so politicians will mind their own business.'* Guy oughta run for office. Would have told him so, but it was a long line of hand shakers at the BAT convention."

Ross said: "*BAT*?"

"*Businessmen for America's Triumph.*"

Brian flapped his arms so these two guys would get the picture: "*BAT!*"

The silver dude said: "Like in comic books! *You're Batman!* A superhero!"

"Well, I . . . yeah," said Brian. "But not just me."

"So a swarm of batmen. Flying everywhere in the darkness. Batty men."

"We've got women, too!" insisted Brian. Nowadays, he knew he *had* to.

"Of course you do. All those bats flying around. Men *and* women."

"Yeah!"

"Any vampires?"

"Yeah—*wait*, what?"

A waitress stepped to their table bearing a mini-bottle of red wine. Unscrewed its cap and filled the waiting glass in front of Brian, who paid her no mind because he was busy craning his neck to watch Fergus Lang.

The waitress asked the other two men sitting at the table what they wanted to drink. The young one asked for a beer and surprised her by not being snobbish about his choices. The old one asked for red wine. Said it was his color. The waitress told them about the fish special. Her customers without alcohol sitting in front of them took her suggestion. But Mr. Husband Who's Gotta Have His Wine First ordered steak—"and make sure the damn thing is dead."

"Dead," said the waitress. "Sure."

Told herself: *It's the job you got.*

Walked away.

Ross asked the billionaire groupie: "So do you know Fergus Lang?"

"Well, we all know *about* him," answered Brian.

He raised his glass of blood wine as if in a toast, took a gulp, grimaced.

"American hero," said Brian. "Sure, his family money was big in phar-maceuticals, but he made his own fortune franchising pain clinics all through West Virginia and the Bakken oil fields. Some near Seattle out by the closed bomber plants. Hard work on those shut-down lines. Lots of customers. Before that, he was one of the first of the big boys to go all-in on private prisons.

"Now," said Brian, leaning in, "*this* I know for a fact."

The silver werewolf leaned in, said: "How do you know the rest?"

Brian shook off such nonsense. "What he's big on now is real estate. But not like the so-called 'smart money.' Selling or renting to the *bucks-up*. They're too much trouble. They got the money or clout to shop around, negotiate. Fergus makes his real estate moves at the low-end multi-family market. Those big block buildings stuck on the edges of the good neighbor-hoods? Those people. Watch out the windows, this train'll go past places like that."

Brian shrugged. "In banking, we now call those people *precariats*."

"As in '*precarious*'?" asked Ross.

"Well, yeah, but they're not all bad." Brian laughed. "Hell, if they are, what with selling pain pills and his prisons, Fergus's 'P-P's get 'em coming and going."

Wasted that joke, thought Brian when those two guys didn't laugh.

In fact, he realized, both of them acted odd as hell. The young stud looked like he wanted to punch something. The old guy sat there like a stone.

"But they're good people, *precariats*," said Brian. "Delivery drivers. Day care workers. Mailmen. Shelf stockers. Nurses. Teachers. House painters."

"Used to be middle class, now they're *precariats*?" said Ross.

"No, *yeah*, but . . ." Brian glowed from an acknowledging gaze that he *just knew* was beaming on him from his hero who sat at another table. "Some of his customers don't even need to pay him their whole due, long as they stay poor enough to be eligible so a cut of their welfare checks goes straight to him.

"Fergus," sighed Brian. "Man's a genius."

The old guy who Brian figured for a smart ass now didn't say anything.

"Maybe someday you'll grow up to be like him," said the young guy.

"*Nah*," sighed the hometown banker. "Fergus Lang, he's up there out of my league—though, you know, we shook hands."

Ross frowned: "What's he doing on this train?"

"Hell, everybody knows that," said Brian. "He's afraid of flying!

"Weird, huh?" continued he who'd shaken the hero's hand. "Afraid of being in the air, but cool as ice about pissing people off—even if those people don't know who it is they *should* be pissed at. Mostly, they should look in the mirror!"

"*Mirror, mirror, on my wall,*" chanted the young stud with some kind of *wow* in his words. "*Who owns you, reflections and all?*"

Brian shook his head. *Why do I always get stuck with the strange ones?*

"Still," Brian said, "him being here *is* weird. He's all alone."

"Yeah," agreed Ross. "No assistant. No bodyguard."

The silver werewolf said: "Things happen."

"*Yip!*"

"Oh, Mugzy!" scolded Constance at the next table. "Say *sorry* to Miss Della. Sorry you snapped that roll right off her plate, *yes you did!*"

"*Yip!*"

"You're right, Mugzy! We don't know where you're from, Miss Della."

"Where I wish I was now," answered Della's husky voice as she flounced the purple boa like it could take her there.

Constance turned her attention to the *fascinating* flaxen-haired gentleman.

"We just love your red tie," said Constance. "So *distinguished*, like I always say, and my cousin, not the one married to *you know who*, but . . ."

On and on she went. On and on.

Brian couldn't take it anymore.

Drained his glass of red wine in one long guzzle.

Pushed his chair back, rose—shrugged his shoulders tall, sucked in his gut, puffed out his chest, lumbered like a circus bear to the next table.

"Fergus Lang!" beamed Brian, extending his right hand that—after Mr. Hollywood sitting with two women and a dog did not reach for it—came back to tap Brian's own chest. "Brian Beck, President, First State Bank of Zenith."

Ross watched Brian hear Fergus Lang smile: "Yeah!"

Ross saw Fergus Lang snarl: "*Yeah?*"

"You probably don't remember me."

"Got that right."

"*Thanks!* Loved your speech at the BAT convention."

"Lot of people said it was the best speech ever."

Constance beamed toward the man in the red tie. "Why, you never told us you were a public speaker—did he, Mugzy-wugzy?"

"*Rarrf!*"

Della muttered: "Hard to get a word in between the yips and the yuks."

Fergus Lang pushed his chair back. "From now on, I'm eating in my cabin."

"Wait!" said Brian. "You're in Cabin A!"

"How'd you know that?" growled the ga-jillionaire who was not indicted.

"Stands to reason! Of course you are! Of course you would be." Brian shrugged somewhere between embarrassment and modesty. "I'm in Cabin C.

"I mean, we are. My wife, she's . . ." He didn't turn to look for *his little woman*. "She's around here somewhere."

"Good for you," snapped Fergus Lang. "I'm gone."

"I'll walk you there!" said Brian.

"Walk me where?"

"Wherever!"

"Fucking free country." Fergus Lang pushed his way past Brian, who heard his utterance as invitational praise and fell in step behind his departing hero. A young boy scampered in the wake of those two exiting grown-ups.

"Malik!" called the boy's mom. "Other way to the Observation Car!"

Malik caught the eyes of two men still sitting there at that table when they could be going to *wow*, waved to them as he hurried after his family.

Saw a woman with dark lips at a table with a guy holding a weird bag.

Gave them a wave as he scurried past.

Didn't see the fluttering wave he got back from her.

Ross heard the *whump* of the Dining Car door sliding open behind him.

Told his silver-haired companion: "I guess it's just us."

"Not if you're lucky," said the silver werewolf, staring behind Ross.

Ross turned to look.

Saw her standing there.

14

Malik! Other way to the Observation Car!"

That *made you ache to hug him* child scampered past Suzanne. Waved.

Her own hand fluttered a reply to his wave as her husband and his hero headed back toward the car of Premium cabins without a glance at her. That boy and his loving family left the Dining Car out the door behind her.

"Didn't see me," said Suzanne of the boy who'd noticed her.

"Doesn't matter if they see your wave," said Albert. "Matters that you made it."

"Do you believe that?"

"I try."

Clackety-clack. Clackety-clack.

Suzanne said: "I haven't been to the Observation Car."

"I've been there my whole life," said Albert.

She heard herself whisper: "Show me?"

15

Nora knew she had to contain the bugs in the grift.

And now she had the best chance she figured this train would give her.

Target acquired.

Target turning around in his Dining Car chair to see her coming.

He's sitting against the wall of twilight-filled windows.

Sitting across from—

Shit! Nora stared at two men sitting at a Dining Car table. Her target—breath-to-breath with the guy who Zed says he's kind of like . . . *assessing*, right?

Assessing, she told herself. That's all.

Here and now, she *assessed* those two buddying-up men as a P.S.S.

A Perfect Shit Storm.

We're 45 hours out of Chicago, thought Nora, 30-some hours *until*.

In front of her: Suzanne and Albert walked away toward the silver door at the rear of this Dining Car, the door to the Observation Car.

To Nora's left, a waitress cleared dishes off a table.

To her right, past her Target's table, Mugzy, Constance and Della worked on their dinners.

Mugzy spotted Nora.

Growled.

From where she stood, Nora heard flamboyant Della tell dog-cradling Constance: "Get your money back if you had him fixed."

Zed's silver-haired target waved to the empty chair beside him. That target flashed the perfect smile to create trust. Told Nora: "Come sit with us."

"Please," added her own *yeah, he's handsome enough* target.

Who is he? thought Nora. What does he know? What is he doing?

Nora claimed that chair.

Stared at that man sitting across from her.

He didn't 'smile,' he *grinned* as he said: "We—I mean, him and me—we haven't had time to introduce ourselves. I'm Ross. Ross Passos."

The silver werewolf sitting beside her said: "I'll be . . . Call me Graham."

Out of her mouth popped: "Nora."

Shit! she told herself: *Why didn't you use your handle for the grift? The phony name on your tickets and your new driver's license and . . .*

. . . and if it comes to proving who I am, thought Nora, I've already lost. So letting 'Nora' out . . . You can live with that. You can do what's gotta be done.

The maître d' carried one plate to their table, the waitress carried two.

The waitress frowned: "Where'd the man who was sitting here go?"

Silver-haired Graham said: "He jumped off the train."

"Or more likely," clarified Graham to the waitress's horrified look, "he just left the Dining Car. My guess is, he won't be coming back.

"So," continued silver werewolf Graham to the train staff, "you can give my friend Ross his ordered plate of fish . . ."

The maître d' quickly obliged. He was not a server. And if he acted as such, *well*, that was one more job corporate could cut.

Silver werewolf Graham turned to Nora: "What do you want?"

"Excuse me?" she said.

"I also ordered the fish, so we have that plus a steak that is truly dead."

Truly dead? thought the work-wobbling waitress as her arms ached with the plates balanced on them. *Who are you people?*

Nora said: "I eat meat."

"Thank you so much," Graham told the dinner servers. "And don't worry, we'll sign whatever included-in-our-trip ticket dinner bill you want us to."

"Since it's on this chair's bill," said Nora. "Could I please have a beer?"

Ross tried not to smile. Failed, but tried.

Nora used the serrated knife she'd been given to cut the burnt meat.

The waitress put a glass of cold beer by Nora's plate.

Ross surged into conversation before the beer in Nora's glass stopped trembling. *Well*: trembling from the clunk of the glass of golden brew on the white tablecloth between him and her. The *clackety-clack* of the train meant everything and everyone on it hurtled through this lemony time a-trembling.

Ross smiled: "So *Nora*, where are you going?"

"Chicago," she said.

"Me, too," said Ross.

"I kind of figured," said Nora.

Ross shrugged: "I can't get off before."

As if either of the others cared, Graham said: "I'm going to Chicago, too."

"Why can't you get off the train?" Nora asked Ross.

"I've got a contract," he said.

Graham seemed to sink in his chair.

Nora said: "A contract to do what?"

"Write an article for a travel website on how great it is to ride this train."

Fuck! thought Nora.

She stared at the black moleskin journal on the white tablecloth.

What has he already written?

"Ross!" exclaimed Graham: "You're *a reporter?*"

His voice carried all through the Dining Car.

"Used to be," said Ross. "Then the paper crashed. I lost my job and all of us lost a bulwark against bullshit from both ends of the political spectrum."

"Politics isn't a spectrum," said Graham. "It's a sphere around all of us."

Ross ignored him, told Nora: "This train ride's a *gimme*: no real reporting needed, just type the obvious platitudes, hit SEND."

"Why did you get the gig?" she said.

"Pity. From the guy who owns the travel website. He set it up, complete with sponsors. Besides pumping up the train ride, I gotta write pieces talking about how great a certain hotel is, the *wow-est* restaurant in the Windy City, why flying back to Seattle on a particular airline is the best way to wing it."

"So much for 'honest and objective' journalism," said Nora.

"Nobody pays me for that anymore. This is the kind of work I get now."

Ross grinned. "Until my poetry pays off big-time. And that's *so* gonna happen—*right?*"

The door to the Dining Car *whunked* open.

In marched two blue-uniformed SWATs.

16

Two blue-uniformed male SWAT warriors—no machineguns, holstered pistols—patrolled down the aisle between the rows of tables.

Commander L.T. led the way. He nodded to Ulysses, but other than that, kept his eye on the mission objective.

Walking two steps behind him came trooper David Hale, 23. First train mission run, determined to do it right, no errors—*no sir.*

Nora knew better than to make eye contact as those warriors sauntered to the galley, where the maître d' nodded to the waitress . . .

. . . who passed the SWAT warriors three white cardboard pie boxes.

SWAT trooper David Hale carried the white cardboard pie boxes in front of him like he was holding a bomb, while his hands-free boss L.T. led the way out.

Writer Ross watched the warriors leave. "That's a story I'd like to know."

"Yes," said silver-haired Graham.

Nora's brain screamed: *'Fuck both of you!'*

Her mouth said nothing.

The waitress loomed beside their table. "How we doing?"

Graham smiled proudly: he belonged to the Clean Plate Club.

Ross blinked: *When did I eat that much of my dinner? My appetite* . . . Oh.

Nora looked at the hacked-up slab of meat on her plate.

Should have eaten more, she thought. *I'll need my strength.*

But she said: "I guess I'm done."

"So let's follow those two blue-uniformed gunners," said Graham.

No! screamed inside Nora's skull.

The waitress wrinkled her brow. "Excuse me?"

"Why, with dessert," said Graham. "Like they're having. What else?"

The Dining Car waitress shook her head: *Some people.*

Told this trio of passengers: "Tonight we got key lime pie."

"If that's what they had," said Graham, "good enough for us."

Ross asked the waitress: "Who are those guys? Why are they on the train?"

"I just work here," said the waitress. "Three key limes, coming up."

She scooped up all their plates. Carried away her clattering load balanced with the *wobble wobble* of the *clackety-clack*.

Ross tore his eyes off Nora.

To show he was cool not crazy, to be polite, Ross asked Graham: "The father back in the station, you knew he was a soldier. Were you in the military?"

"I never wore a uniform," said Graham.

Nora frowned at the not-too-old man. "You said you're going to Chicago?"

"I'll ride to the end of the line."

The silver werewolf and the dyed hair woman locked eyes.

He smiled like there was no tension at all: "And you're going there, too.

"I wonder," he added. "Is it the *going to* or the *getting there* for you?"

Ross thrust himself back into the conversation: "Gotta be both."

Graham's eyes locked on Nora. "Maybe even more."

No sound filled that *hold-your-breath* heartbeat.

"Well," said Graham, sinking into his smile at this Dining Car table, "now that I know I'm riding this train with a poet-*slash*-reporter and a . . ."

He paused and Nora knew that was to give her *say something* space to fall into. When she didn't, when she revealed nothing, his pause became an odd smile.

Graham said: "I guess I'll have to watch myself."

Shrugged: "But who doesn't?"

The waitress delivered three plates of lime green filling pie slices twirled with a white swirl of the lowest cost artificial cream chemicals money could buy.

Graham grinned like a seven-year-old at his own birthday party.

"Pie is more than just an irrational number you can never nail down. Pie is our most American dessert. Sweet and sour from amber waves of grains and fruited plains, each slice different, all one grand *YES!*"

Nora and Ross both blinked.

"So," said Graham, filling his hand with a fork, "let's be patriotic."

He forked off the front of his wedge of pie, that sweet/tart taste of lime—

Mugzy lunged from his at-the-next-table keeper's arms.

The dog's snout plunged into the whipped cream on Nora's plated pie.

Frozen in a clackety-clack heartbeat:

Mugzy, muzzle white with whipped cream.

Graham's dagger-jabbed fork checked millimeters from piercing Mugzy.

Wide-eyed, jaw-dropped Nora nudged aside by that lunging dog.

Lemon stoned Ross seeing a *wow* that he could barely believe.

"*Yarp!*"

Mugzy scrambled back into his owner's arms at the next table, smeared her with the white evidence of his adventure.

"Oh my God!" cried Constance. "What have you done? Mugzy, are you OK? What kind of person hurts an innocent dog!"

Constance bolted from her table, rocked it precariously—

—and forced her companion wrapped in a purple boa to also stand.

"Sorry," said Graham. "I was too long in cobra country.

"On the bright side," he added, "I must still have it. Your little snatcher got away without a scratch."

Constance's jaw jerked up and down as if she were chewing on air. She cradled the one she loved. Fled.

Chuckles shook her purple boa wrapped tablemate: "Dinner *and* a show!"

Della *oh so slowly* walked toward the door back to the passengers' cabins.

Everyone at the table Mugzy'd attacked knew Della didn't want to catch up to the fleeing, whipped cream smeared couple.

The silver steel door slid closed behind that retreating parade.

Graham sighed. "Intriguing evening, but my time is for moving on."

He stood as he told the younger couple: "Now it's up to you."

"What is?" said Nora.

"What isn't?"

A smile, a nod, a glide to the door toward the cabins, whoosh and *gone.*

"Who was that?" muttered Nora.

"Yeah," said Ross.

She stared at the clunked shut door. "I should have thanked him."

Turned her blue eyes to the man who sat across from her.

"After all," she said, "it's not every day someone stabs a dog for you."

"The dog's fine. Your silver knight showed some restraint."

"I'm my own knight. Always have been. Always had to be—got to be."

She shrugged—realized Ross used that gesture, too: "Restraint can be good."

"So is pie."

Nora pointed at Ross's pie plate with her chin.

Pushed aside her own plate of mashed mush. "You haven't had a bite."

"And no dog mauled it. Want some?"

Her response was a droll *Really?*

"I wouldn't joke about a thing like pie," said Ross.

"Good to know you've got boundaries."

"Some," he said.

She smiled.

Took his fork.

That tool lifted trembling green gel and crumbling graham cracker crust, eased it between her slick crimson lips. They lovingly closed over what they'd been offered, slid cool lime off the penetrating instrument, then let her pull that smeared shaft out of her mouth.

Ross caught his breath. Kept his eyes on her. Took the fork—*their* fork. Ate a bite of that key lime universe.

Said: "Now that we've exchanged precious bodily fluids—"

"*Dr. Strangelove*," she said, naming his cited/their parents' era movie about atomic bombs ending the world.

"—I've got about a million questions," finished Ross.

Turned the fork with less samurai skill than Graham, offered it to her.

"Only a million?" She cut another bite. "You're lucky."

"I hope so."

"So what's your story going to be about?" Like she was just curious.

"Hard to say."

"I thought you said it was just a *gimme*."

"Yeah." He took a bite, passed her the fork. "But now it's more interesting.

"Those SWAT guys, I mean," he said.

No! she thought. Can't let anything like that happen!

"Like you said," she told him, "this is just a gig. Do it easy. Do it safe."

"Safe doesn't always work for me," said Ross.

She looked away from him.

Took a bite of pie.

"You pushed off the whipped cream."

Nora said: "I don't like it from a can."

"How about if it's real?"

She shrugged. Nodded toward what was left between them. "Last bite."

"Split it?"

"Just let it be what it is—and you take it."

So he did.

Nora turned her gaze to the window flowing with what was outside.

"Getting dark," she told him.

"Come with me," he said. "To the Observation Car."

"You want to show a girl the world?"

"No," he told her. "I want us to see what's there."

17

Malik swayed as he stood looking through his ghostly 10-year-old reflection in the Observation Car's curved wall of windows.

Beyond that glass he saw the sky full of gray clouds streaked pink.

Houses and buildings, but not close together, *country* not *city*.

More and different trees than in Seattle. Who knows their names.

No zombies.

No tattered clothes, no outstretched grasping arms, empty eyes, mouths agog zombies wobbling toward you like they're always walking on a train.

"Why are there so many zombies?" he'd asked Dad a few days before. "TV's got a dozen zombie shows. And movies. Lots of video games. Some of the books Mom says I'm not old enough for, zombies in there, too."

"Lots of zombies these days," said Dad. "People walking around undead. Starving for brains they don't have. Scared and scary. Dangerous and doomed.

"You know zombies aren't real," he added, but with a sad smile.

"Sounds like you think they are," said Malik.

Dad shook his head from side to side.

"So why are they everywhere you look?"

"People need something to *not* be scared of."

"Why?"

"If there's something to *not* be scared of, it's easier to live with real fear."

"We don't get scared, though, right, Dad? We're Marines."

"We get scared, but *semper fi*, we move on, we get through it."

Then his dad fell silent. Just stared off into nowhere.

But Malik didn't worry: he was *Dad!*

Now, riding on this *so cool* train, Malik thought: Yeah, we move—

Oh wow!

Best idea for a TV show or a video game or a movie *ever!*

Zombies On A Train

The Observation Car windows reflected imaginary zombies behind him staggering in the aisle between the two rows of individual chairs.

Malik reached out to touch that magic glass—

"*Oye, mi hijito*, be careful!"

"I am, Mom."

Curved windows made this Observation Car like a fishbowl.

With only us in it.

Wispy reflections of Mom and Dad and Mir sat in the row of cushy chairs behind him. The floor under his feet rumbled and rocked but he wore his good sneakers. *I won't fall. I'm not a kid anymore. You'll see.*

The train clattered past a motel with one, two, *three* parked cars.

A café with teeny-tiny people inside its yellow glow windows.

Can they feel me looking at them? wondered Malik as they blinked away.

Neon red sign: TAV RN. Parking lot, cars, then that sight slid into *gone*.

"What do you see?" asked Dad.

Don't tell him about the zombies!

Malik shrugged. "Lots. Nothing."

Mir snapped at their father: "Is that what you brought us here to see? Lots of nothing?"

Don't turn around, Malik ordered himself. *Keep watching outside the windows like you don't hear.*

Mom said: "Mir, you—"

"We're here for you to see where you are," interrupted Dad in that voice that makes you want to hug him *and* run away as fast you can, both at the same time. "Not look at your damn phone or pout about where you aren't or complain about where you get to go."

"*Get to?*" said Mir.

"Yes, *get to.* This train isn't perfect, but it's real. You're in it and can move around. You can see what's out there, this country—*our* country—troops and civilians gave everything, *give* everything for it. So figure you can at least look and see what's there, what's not."

"How can you see what's *not* there?"

Dad said: "You think! You imagine! You hope!"

"You, *you Dad*: what do *you* hope's *not* out there for us to see?"

In the same heartbeat that the Observation Car's door *whunked* open, from deep inside Dad exploded his roaring reply: *"ME!"*

18

Whunk closed the Observation Car's door sealing in two arrived strangers.

Suzanne saw that Black family up ahead, middle of the car, frozen in place.

Obviously, she reasoned, transfixed by a view of the world outside.

That twilight world *clackety-clacking* past those curved windows showed Suzanne a big box store with delivery vans on a giant parking lot. A Bail Bonds shack. A brick building with a giant logo painted on its side: SARC (Seniors And Rehab Center.) A chain link fence caging old school buses.

She nodded for Albert to side-by-side swivel chairs near the door.

He did. Kept his shoulder bag close.

My name is Suzanne said: "Train tracks seldom go through the best part of town."

"Not everybody sees the best part of town," was his reply.

"Is that what it's like where you're from?"

"I'm not from there, I lived there. Since third grade. Small town."

"What do you do there?"

"I'm not there anymore. I'm here now. On the train."

"Where to?"

"I get out at Fargo, North Dakota, tomorrow night."

"And then?"

"Then I buy a cheap car. Drive where I'm going. Where I was born."

"To your family?"

"All my family is all gone."

"So what's there?" asked Suzanne.

"The creek just past the edge of a town with a couple of trees in a big wide-open North Dakota nowhere."

"Why go there?"

Albert hugged his shoulder bag closer.

"What's in your bag?" joked Suzanne. "A bomb?"

"NO!"

She flinched back in her seat.

"I'm sorry. I just . . . Don't be afraid."

"Is that a bomb?"

"No."

Her shoulders relaxed.

"Wait." Albert shook his head. "That's the truth, but not the whole truth."

She blinked.

"A bomb is for *every*body and *any*body. What I've got is just for *some*body."

"What are you telling me? And why—*why* are you telling me?"

"You matter more if someone sees your wave.

"And you," he added, "you see me. So I owe you the truth."

"What's in your bag, Albert?"

"Why do you care?"

"You don't lie to me. And maybe I'm carrying a bag you just can't see."

Railroad tracks rushing out from under this train led to the setting sun. White electric light softened the new darkness in the Observation Car. Albert said: "You know those gas stations we see out these windows?"

Suzanne nodded.

"For 14 years, I've been the night man. The last gas station in town. Stays open to 10, me in there. Locked in the office and the garage bays. Smells like oil and gas, rags. Station's on the far end of Main Street. Most local stores are dead. There's a bar on each side of Main Street. A café that closes after lunch. Dinner, you're on your own or out to the truck stop next to the Interstate. The in-town gas station I work—worked—after 8:00, two customers is a big night.

"I spent years staring out those windows. Linda Leavitt drives past like she's still a teenager back in the 1960s when the town thought it was bound to grow bigger. That's what teenagers did back then, drive up and down Main Street. Cruising to see. Cruising to be seen. Cruising to be cool. Cruising because they could, going nowhere but *going*. Before my time. Before gas prices shot up and computers or big TVs came down in every house. Before there was less than nothing new left to see on Main Street. Now people cruise the Internet, going everywhere and nowhere. But I'd see Zane still going for his nightly walk. He used to be a mailman, retired but keeps walking, looking for what's to see. Moms and dads drive by taking their kids somewhere, sometimes to who got the house in the divorce. Sometimes you see somebody going somewhere that's not smart."

"Smart is never enough," said Suzanne.

"Tell me about it."

"You've told me things nobody else was ever smart enough to," she said.

"Maybe the smart thing was to say nothing. I used to be like that."

"You got a lot of '*used to be*s,'" she said. "I've got a whole lot of *never was.*

"*Never was* who I thought I was going to be," said Suzanne. "*Never was* who I'd wished I'd be. *Never was* who everybody thinks they see when they look at me. Mrs. Beck. *Sue.* The wife. His wife. His *she must like it* if she puts up with it."

"Comes a time when you're done *putting up with*," said Albert.

"Yes," she said. "Yes."

She took a deep breath. Asked: "What are you done putting up with?"

"Saying nothing. Being *good old Al.* Stuck where his parents' car broke down. Where they worked hard. Where I got to watch them die while I was waiting for some other life that never came my way. Good old Al. Knew him in high school. Sat in back. Now gets up, goes to work. Used to clerk the Mom 'n' Pop store before it closed. Then Johnny Bishop wanted to keep his gas station open late. Not for the money. Johnny keeps it open to keep his dad's business alive like his dad isn't. Lately, he kept it open to keep *good old Al* in a job so I could pay my rent on my one room kitchenette where there's nothing but me and the next day just like the day before.

"Even with the little ones," said Albert, "I can't put up with all that anymore. I don't want to end up as the guy who just used to be there. Didn't ever pick his *where*s or *when*s, his *what*s or *how*s, just kept being where he got put until he was gone."

"*Wait*: What '*little ones*'?"

"Ask around, that'll get you a chuckle. Good old Al and those crazy thingamajigs he makes at night in the gas station. Metal off broke cars, scraps he finds 'round town. Can't weld them in the gas station. Spark of flame in there, Ka-BOOM! No more Al or anything 'cept a ball of fire. And that would screw up Johnny Bishop's life.

"I never want to pass along my screw-ups. So I hammer and wrench, wire and glue, metal shears and file. Old Al, he makes these metal figures you can hold in the palm of your hand: '*Why, a lot of 'em you can kinda see some shape, some critter.*' He makes 'em and leaves 'em around town. Some up to the cemetery on gravestones, but that's OK, it's just Al.

"Sitting in the gas station alone at night, I'd look out at my small town and see some shape or notion. Or see it in the junk metal. Hammer out something as true to that as I can. Then I'd spot where it belonged. Wasn't mine anymore. I took what came to me, then let it go be."

"Is that what's in your bag?" asked Suzanne. "Some things you made?"

Whunk the door into this Observation Car slid open and into its dim light came that blood-haired woman and the guy who'd cellphone filmed everyone.

They walked past Suzanne and Albert without saying a word.

Walked past the family stirring on the other side of the aisle.

Took the last seats before the wall that was the end of this train.

Albert shifted in his chair and the bag *clunked* against its arm rest.

Suzanne whispered: "You're holding onto that bag for dear life."

"Not life," said Albert. "The choice you can claim with it. The last, the only real big choice I ever got to make."

"What are you talking about?"

"*How* and *where* and *when* I get to die."

Roaring vertigo spun Suzanne.

"I finally get to choose what I'm going to put up with. Get to be a guy who didn't just fade away. I get to be somebody who did something big with the *not much* he had. I get to go back where I came from and go out with a *wow*. Like realizing the secret shape in the metal and setting it free. Doing so without making a mess for people who've been decent to me and shouldn't be saddled by my going. I didn't get to make the shape of my life. I ran out of time and chances and ways to be. But I get to create my leaving."

"*What's in the bag?*"

"The big thing?"

Suzanne nodded.

"You want to know its mechanics?"

"I want to know what it is."

"It's a metal thermos rigged with a grip release trigger that shoots out a flame when you let go. The thermos holds two quarts of a mix I found on the Internet, kind of a napalm goo that bursts into fire. You unscrew the lid, pour the goo on what has to burn, grab the thermos, squeeze then let go of the hand grip, the flame ignites the goo and WHAM: fast, hot fire."

"Fire for what? Why?"

"When my boss Johnny's dad died, I helped him clean out that room at his house. Awful day. That's why I left nothing behind me in that town. The top of that old man's clothes bureau held a forest of pill bottles. I took a bottle of painkillers—like taking a pill can cure what really pains us. Grabbed prescription sleeping pills strong enough to knock out a horse or even a guy like me who can't sleep good most nights, all alone in the same damn bed. I only used 'em a couple times, but know they work."

"What are you doing?"

"Trusting you. Telling you my secrets. You can't stop me and if you try, that might not be a good move for everybody else on this train."

"Is that a threat?"

"No, it's how things shouldn't ever be."

"How should things be?"

"In Fargo, I buy a cheap used car. Buy cans of gas. Ride the car out to where I'm from. Pull a load of old boards out of deserted farm houses dotting North Dakota. Make a wood platform by that grove of trees where my family used to farm. Take pain pills. Take a bunch of sleeping pills. Soon as I feel all that coming on, I'll soak the old wood with gas, lay on it, unscrew and soak myself with the goo. Grab the metal grips on the thermos. That cocks the lighter. When I pass out, my grip goes slack, the lighter shoots its flame into the goo . . .

"*Whoosh*, a fireball. One moment of pure, powerful awe. That's my victory. A funeral pyre. Like Buddhist monks in the Vietnam war. An ultimate moment in my time that I chose the *when* and *how* and *where* and *shape of*. Whatever of me doesn't go up in smoke will blow away in wind, not get stuck in some hole in the ground under a stone nobody ever reads."

"Nobody will—"

"This is about nobody but me."

"And now me," said Suzanne.

"You saw my wave. Now please don't try to talk me out of killing myself."

The train *clackety-clacked* through the night.

"Be hypocritical of me to try to stop you from killing anybody," she said.

Suzanne shrugged: "I'm murdering my husband."

19

H er father's *"ME!"* explosion blew Mir away.

She couldn't breathe.

Couldn't lift her arms out of her lap in the Observation Car chair.

The train *clackety-clacked* on like nothing happened.

OH MY GOD, DAD! Can't even . . . Didn't know . . . Didn't realize . . .

Mom took his hand, but even she didn't know what to say.

Mir saw the train door slide open. Heard it *whunk*. Knew messenger bag man and the racist asshole's ruby-lipped wife found chairs at the end of the car.

Mir shook her head. Sucked in air.

Malik, poor little brother Malik, stood by the train windows: trapped.

Him. Mom. Me. And *oh* Dad. All of us . . . *blown away*.

Right here on this damn *clattering through nowhere* train.

"*Me*," said Dad again, only softer, sadder as he confessed: "I don't want to look out our American windows and see warriors like me. Or worse, *wannabes*."

The windows showed the world streaming past this rushing train. Street-lights winking on in graying evening light. Huddled houses. Convenience stores and the edges of towns. Over such scenes floated phantoms with combat boots and helmets and assault rifles.

Dad said: "I'm in the Corps to keep our country free from being run by warriors like me. That's why I wanted to take this train with all of you. To show you that. Our country. While it's still here. Not me driving, having to watch the road and the car and the crazies and *can't drives*. Me, here with all of you like I'm not so much of the time. The time that's all the time we got. Not transferring from post to post but . . . looking. Seeing. With you. With us all together. Seeing our country. I was going to stop feeling lost. Or gone. Or afraid. So much of the time, I feel like I'm not *here*, I'm in some other *there*. And I don't know what to do."

Isabella leaned closer to the man she loved.

Are Mom's cheeks slick? wondered Mir. *Are mine?*

Isabella said: "We're here. Together. We'll see what's what, figure it out."

Mir choked back a sob and—

OH MY GOD MALIK!

"Hey," sighed Mir as she slid from her chair, her arm gently circling her trembling 10-year-old brother—*hers, damn it!* "Everything's fine. We're OK."

He kept his wet eyes focused nowhere as his lower lip trembled and he stood at attention like Dad received from his troops. Malik fought the train rocking him, a sway he couldn't beat, but he fought it, he fought it.

Squatting down to his height, Mir gave him a crooked grin, used *that voice*. The one like they were on stupid TV. The voice that always made him laugh.

"Check the haps, little bro'. 'S all good. We're here. We're fine. We're cool."

We're not! thought Malik. Dad's face, Mom's crying like I'm not I'M NOT!

Mir shook him.

Just a little. And it didn't—

She shook him again.

He had to look.

Her goofy eyes, whacko grin.

"Hey," Mir told that boy who breathed easier under her touch, who watched her with a trembling smile. "Let's go back to our cabin. I wanna read you a story like when were kids, and the story—*oh*, the story: it's totally cool."

20

"Murder happens," Suzanne told Albert as they sat in the Observation Car of that train hurtling through the night. "But you know that. You're doing it, too.

"Better than getting it done to you," she said. "I realized that last Thanksgiving."

"I went to the truck stop for Thanksgiving," Albert told her. "Free piece of pumpkin pie with every turkey dinner."

"There were two pies on our table." Suzanne's dark lips curled more in a sneer than a smile. "Pumpkin *and* apple. We had eleven people for dinner and Brian only found a dozen *wrongs* that I did before the doorbell rang.

"Guests." Suzanne shook her head. "What a lie.

"So many lies. None of those couples or the kids whose parents made them come were our friends. We don't have friends. Least, I don't. The men Brian sees at the bank or country club, coffee cafes or bars, meetings and conventions—it's like they're all chess pieces.

"As for women," she said, "any of them in town who might have been my friend can't stand him. As far as other women in other ways, *well*, when I still cared about being married, even then I didn't worry about him and other women. None of them are stupid enough to want to go and marry him like I did!"

Thousands of nights before flowed in the darkness of the train's windows.

"*Want*," she whispered. "I barely remember *want*."

Call the curl of her ruby lips a *smile*. "All Brian wants is to *be* the boss in the cashmere coat. He doesn't want to *do* anything—including 'cheat' on me. Take his clothes off to . . . to *fuck* a woman? Be naked?"

A whisper deep inside her: *How can I say this out loud—how can I not?*

"I used to think he puts the pillow or his shirt or something over my face so he won't have to see me, but then I realized he covers my face so I can't see *him*."

Albert said: "You saw him."

No shook her head. "Took too long. Cost too much. Killed me.

"Almost," she corrected. "I'm not going to let him kill me. His life will suffocate me and make me live with that. But I'm not going to let him. If I do, I'm just as bad as him. Or worse, because now I know that's what I'm doing."

Her smile came true and soft. "Feels like the first time.

"People like me, we become nobody. I became no more than a twirler shortened down to Sue, so getting noticed by the son of somebody who everybody said was important, getting noticed by *Brian Beck*, even if it was just because he was back from college and *gimme* drunk at that Christmas break party where a terrified high school virgin finally got to go . . .

"What he did must mean something, *right*? So doing it again with him means more. So what if he's . . .

"But he's also the kind of guy you're supposed to want. *Somebody*. Guaranteed job. Money. Walks like he knows *the real rules* you don't have a clue about. You must want him. It must be real. It must be what they say it's supposed to be. So when you end up pregnant . . .

"You should have seen Brian's dad when he found out," said Suzanne.

"Mad?" said Albert.

"No. And that should have scared me. He just smiled. That cold, empty smile. Because now he had his son locked up. Brian never had imagination or brains, the guts to go for more. But once there was wild spunk in him, so maybe—*maybe*—he might have tripped himself free of Daddy.

"But not with a knocked-up, underage girlfriend who could put the law on him. Big Daddy had to—*got to*—save him with a pre-nup and a Justice of the Peace. The grandbaby bump of my belly moved into Big Daddy's house. Brian landed at a desk on the bank floor outside the glass walls of his father's office.

"Brian was happy as hell. He was who he'd been born to be."

A glow lit her face.

"That's the heart of it! He's all about his gets to *be*. And that means I never got to *do*."

"Don't you have a kid?" said Albert.

"Sometimes the only good you ever got to do dies without ever being born."

Suzanne kept filling the silence of everything she'd never said.

"Sometimes the one good thing dying kills your chances to do it again. Not ever. No babies. Not with anybody, and who'd want somebody like that?

"Before they lowered Big Daddy into the ground, he put Brian behind the bank president's desk and in his own castle.

"But still stuck with that stupid Sue who can't do anything right. Always something wrong. Always my fault. Always gotta be where I gotta be. Don't talk to them. Don't care about that. Don't volunteer at the grade school, that's too much mixing it up with regular people for the wife of him. Don't. Just be there like you're supposed to and *don't*."

"Don't stay," said Albert.

"Ten thousand times I thought about that. If I leave, so does Brian's coverage of my parents' Assisted Living fees that Social Security won't and their blown-to-dust working class life can't. That lifeline for them gets cut off with any divorce. The pre-nup Big Daddy's lawyer had us sign. My bottom line reads *zero*. Zero bank account. Zero education. Zero skills."

"Twirling doesn't count?"

Made her smile.

"No," she said. "My life is one big *no*. The most pitiful thing about that is how easy a life it is. I got a roof and walls. I never go hungry or cold or wet. I catch a bug, I can call a doctor who'll fix it and even give me pills to flatten out my blues.

"But Brian's flat-out the bad guy in the blues and hell, country song, too.

"He hates things like that family sitting over there. Their skin isn't his, so if they're equal, if everybody's equal, what does that do to him being special?

"*Special* is all about him and his '*biz buddies,*' the chess pieces. He thinks they're all so smart and always *right*. Whitewashed windows up and down Main Street and boarded-up houses all over town nobody wants to or can afford to buy—that's all somebody else's fault. The government's, whatever that is or whoever *they* are—and *they* better cut his taxes and pave the road to his bank and guarantee its bailout if something goes wrong and that *wouldn't* be his fault, *no*, never any fault of his, so he should never have to pay."

She stared into forever. "And I live in his box until I trade it for a coffin."

"Happy Thanksgiving," said Albert, harkening back to where she started.

"'*Pass the turkey.*' That's what Brian said at Thanksgiving. Mashed potatoes, gravy, stuffing, cranberry sauce, corn and two pies. And he was going to eat it all. Like he'd eaten my whole life. Like I was a baked bird on a plate.

"You know those moments when you finally *get it?*

"Like: *What was I thinking? Why didn't I see this before?*

"That Thanksgiving food smell hit me and I knew there was only one way to save my life. I couldn't just leave. Or kill myself. Killing me is what he was already doing, one insult and one *in the box* day at a time. He had to keep me in there so he could keep being Mister Big in the cashmere coat. He'd fight for that and bottom line, he'd win—

"—*if* all I tried to do was escape.

"I had to beat him. Take *me* back from *him*. Jump off the serving plate. Break out of the box. Change the '*bottom line*' and make him pay. Make him *pay*. He's all about *be*-ing, so the only way to beat him was to make him not *be*."

"Because it's you or him."

"That's the way it's set up. I can't change history. I don't write the rules."

Clackety-clack. Clackety-clack.

"Murder," said Albert. "How?"

"Right in front of you and everybody else."

Suzanne couldn't—then *wouldn't*—stop her ruby-lipped smile.

Even shared her smile with '*that family*' as they walked past. The holding-each-other-up parents didn't look at her. They knew who she was married to. The teenage girl slumped past shepherding her little brother, but *ah*, he sent his shy smile to the nice lady he'd waved to before.

Whunks of the train car's door, that family was gone.

We're almost alone, thought Suzanne as she heard Albert breathe.

Her eyes narrowed toward the young woman with the oddly home-dyed taillight hair and the man who clearly adored her, the two of them sitting at the far end of this Observation Car hurtling through the dark night.

"When are you going to kill him?" asked Albert.

"I already am," said Suzanne. "I have been since Thanksgiving.

"Remember how he trapped me? *Brian got drunk.* That's how I'm killing him.

"Thanksgiving dinner, I kept filling his wine glass. He stumbled into the wall walking the departing guests to the door. When I whispered my apologies, they 'realized' what they saw.

"Bank Christmas party at the Holiday Inn. Him holding court to a huddle of trapped employees. I brought him a Scotch he hadn't asked for. Picked the wrong kind. Then it was—

"Oh my God, it was like being a twirler! I lifted my wine glass—someone made a toast. Soon as Brian downed his drink, I apologized. Fetched him a double of the right Scotch. I knew he'd tell everybody in earshot how *Sue screwed up again*, then make a big deal of drinking the 'right' Scotch. Few more tricks like that, he was getting drunk on his own. So drunk he threw up in the bartender's garbage can. Everybody who worked for him saw. Nobody forgot.

"Did you know you can order liquor online delivered to your front door? Our credit card company knows. Those records say he's been downing several bottles a week. Must have been rain that soaked the brown paper sack on top of the trash cans. The sack tore when the garbage men grabbed it. Empty booze bottles fell out and broke right in front of them. They know who lives in that house. They love to tell tales on the fat cat banker who everybody knows. But nobody knows what gets poured down his sink.

"I pour booze in him every chance I get. I stammer excuses for him for things and behavior no one thought twice about before I apologized."

Suzanne leaned closer to the man sitting across from her.

"Brian woke up two weeks ago. Didn't have a clue how the right headlight and bumper on his company car got smashed the night before. Weren't they fine when he fell asleep beside me and snored through the night? No glass in the driveway, so who knows what he hit driving home after that country club dinner meeting where everybody was drinking.

"When I went to the body shop to pick up the car, the mechanic told me not to worry, the local police hadn't found any collision damage anywhere in town—which means the cops knew about the headlight. Maybe the mechanic gossiped to them about what I'd told him when I brought the damaged car in.

"I knew I had it made when a church lady in the grocery store patted my hand and gave me that supportive *we all know* smile before she shuffled away, her good deed done for the day.

"So our hometown thinks I'm married to a drunk. He always was an asshole. Now he's a drunk. Seen it before. So sad for Sue, but what can she do?"

"Kill him."

"Him being a drunk is going to kill him," said Suzanne.

"Here," said Albert. "Now."

"I didn't know that until Valentine's Day," she said. "Hearts and flowers."

"Like some Country & Western song," said Albert, who kept the gas station radio on when he worked all those lonely nights.

"Was in the coffee shop where Brian and his biz buddies go every weekday. When he left for work that morning, he couldn't find his cell phone. I waited until I knew he was at their everyday 10 A.M. coffee. Got his phone out of the drawer I hid it in. Drove the car he lets me have to Main Street. Walked in all apologetic to give it to him. Let my lips tremble when I said: *'You were really . . . tired when I went to bed last night, you must not have seen it under the living room couch.'*

"I stood there and smiled while he came up with how I must have kicked it under there, so it was all my fault. I knew they all knew. Or thought they did. I stood there while he slapped me on the ass—just teasing, old married couple, no big deal. He kept his hand on my ass so everybody knows this is his, she likes it.

"*That's* when I heard Teresa and Bev. They're our town's two reigning widows. They were sitting two tables away for morning coffee. Staying late because they were making Valentine's Day cards for all-alone people who are stuck up at the County Nursing Home.

"Teresa's telling Bev about a second honeymoon her son Louis took *'all the way from Seattle to Chicago. Tell you, Bev, us old gals wobbling on that fast train they call the Empire Builder, two stories tall, we'd like to fall down and break our damn necks!'*"

In the Observation Car of that train, Albert said: "Like spotting the shape in scrap metal."

"What did we do before computers?" said Suzanne. "I found videos online about the Empire Builder. Our top story cabins. Those flights of narrow stairs. Even safety videos. How to open the train car doors—four latches and one lever. But there's a keypad lock on the wall. If you don't know the code, the lever won't flip, so that *perfect* way for his fall off the train was . . ."

She smiled as she finished that thought, saying: ". . . *out.*"

"When he announced that he was going to Chicago for the banker's convention, I used every trick to convince him that taking the train was elegant. Special. And that taking me with him to handle all the hassles like always would free him up to be important.

"In the Seattle train station, no one saw me slide mini-bottles of whiskey into his cashmere coat pocket—darn things didn't fall out when he was walking to the train like I hoped. But other passengers smelled Scotch on him and know the train staff tried to help me control his drinking at dinner. And everybody back home knows that Brian is a not-so-secret falling down drunk."

Alfred said: "When?"

"After dinner tomorrow."

"After Montana," said Albert. "When we get to North Dakota."

"And before you get off the train to . . . Before Fargo."

"You have to . . . "

"All I have to do is get enough dinner booze in him for witnesses and a blood test. Then get him to the stairs at the far end of our top-level car that nobody goes down because the only thing at the bottom of those stairs is the door to the next car, the Baggage Car, and it's locked.

"All he has to do is stand at the top of those stairs. His wife right where she's supposed to be—behind him. All those years of pushing grocery carts."

"What about those SWAT cops? They're somewhere on the other side of that down-the-stairs Baggage Car door."

"I didn't know they'd be on the train—who did? But they're not here about me. They mean I have to be more careful, but I can't let them matter."

"If somebody sees you . . . "

"Nobody's seen me my whole life," said Suzanne. "I'll risk it. Work with it."

The train *clackety-clacked*.

Suzanne was glad Albert didn't ask her *The Obvious Questions*.

Albert said: "This is the train we're on."

"Yes."

They stood and walked out of the Observation Car to their assigned beds.

21

Nora felt the train propelling her forward, ever forward, *clackety-clack*. Gotta do this.

Gotta get what I need.

Gotta keep Ross off the grift.

BAM! She popped the push pad to open the door out of the Dining Car.

Needed three pounding heartbeats to carry her suddenly oh-so-heavy body the two steps to the door into the Observation Car and what could be seen.

BAM! She popped the black push pad so the door slid open to the destination necessary for what she had to do.

And NO: she wasn't thinking about him at all, not *that* way, not like this was some James Bond movie or one of the better porn websites. He was just a guy named Ross. Just a man. Sure, maybe he was a swipe right on Tinder or Match, a hot connect or a cool commit. So what? What matters is the grift.

You gotta live your choices, she thought—she *told* herself.

Choices were why she had stood in her cabin before dinner, her black slacks taut over her half-moon hips as she leaned closer to the sink's mirror.

Reached into the belt/purse.

Pulled out two tubes of lipstick. One shiny and new. One smudged veteran.

The new tube painted the lips in her fake driver's license pink.

Can't help it: I gotta be a little of me if I wanna sell the lie of who I'm not.

She slid out the thick red shaft tapered to a curved tip. Puckered her too thick/too wide mouth. Stroked the shaft's sticky smear like slick blood back and forth over her soft lips.

Put both lipsticks back in the purse clipped on her right hip.

Pulled out the rubber-bristled and plastic-handled black brush.

She brushed her *never like this before* hair.

Put the black brush back in the belt purse, pulled out a finger-sized glass tube. Got off its cap with a one-handed firm grip, the stroke-push of her thumb.

Saw no fingernail polish.

In her old life, she always wore colorful, even whacky nail polish so her fingers wouldn't disappear from view as she keyboarded.

But now, the grift, this train, she wanted no one to notice her hands.

Never used this scent, thought Nora as she'd thumbed the glass tube, sprayed herself with one hiss that was definitely enough. Sprayed herself again, a drench of musk perfume.

She lifted up her blue sweater, shot a quick cloud somewhere up there.

Had to—right? Had to cover the betraying sweat of sheer fear.

She put the perfume bottle back in the belt purse.

Her unvarnished fingertips brushed the condoms.

Won't need them. Won't want them. Won't. Just won't.

She clipped the belt purse around her waist like a seasoned gunslinger.

Stared at the shape in the mirror.

Bra or no bra?

Told herself: Him and the cellphone peach fuzz back in Seattle. You'll hook him by giving him just a look. You talk *it* out of him. And him out of any dangerous *it*. All you'll do is charm. He'll do what you need because he'll want to. And you'll walk away clean. No big lie to him. No big lie to you. Nothing personal.

Nothing more, Nora told herself.

She reached under her sweater. Unsnapped her bra. Sent one arm up its sleeve to slip out of that bra strap. Sent her other arm to do the same. Lifted the empty black bra out from under her blue sweater.

Nora'd locked her focus on the image in the mirror.

Saw her dyed hair. Saw the swellings of her sweatered-only breasts.

BAM!

Now she's through the sliding open silver door into the Observation Car.

With Ross walking behind her.

Making her wonder.

Wonder what he's looking at. What he's seeing.

Nora spotted the cashmere coat asshole's wife and the sad man with the messenger bag.

She looked away from that nervous couple.

Looked deeper into the Observation Car, the carpeted aisle running between two rows of padded, swivel black leather chairs for passengers to look out and see where they will have been.

To her left, middle of the car she—and Ross behind her, *Ross's behind her*—middle of the car they were about to walk past, Nora spotted that family of four. Saw them locked in shock about something that couldn't be the grift.

Nora stopped by the last two chairs before the stairs down from the Observation Car to the last locked door looking out at what was rushing away.

She told Ross: "Here."

22

They rode in the Observation Car's shadowy *clackety-clack.*

Never once looked out those windows.

Ross said: "I don't even know your last name."

"The name I gave you is the last name I have," said Nora.

"That's some clever bullshit."

Nora shrugged. "More interesting than those SWAT guys."

Silently screamed:

Shit! Shit! Shit! You fucked up. Don't talk about it. Put that in his head.

Find out what's in there now.

Shrug.

Keep it deniably *not* double entendre. "I've never been with a reporter."

Ross didn't miss the beat. Tried to look like: *'I heard it and I don't care.'*

But Nora sensed his hopeful heart.

Even as all he answered was: "These days, I'm just a snoop for hire."

"*Snoop?* Is that a journalism specialty?"

"Should be in the definition of journalism: *snoop, scoop, serve.*"

"Are you an investigative reporter?"

"Every reporter is an investigative reporter, if they're doing the job right."

"Yeah, no, *bullshit,*" she said. "I read books. Watch movies. I know there's some investigative reporter *thing.* I want to know if that's you. What it is."

"What it is. *What it means*—there's this song—"

"Drive By Truckers, *yeah,* that doesn't tell me about you."

"How do I start?" said Ross. "I can say that you—"

"Don't *you* tell *me* about *me!*"

Ross blinked.

"Tell *me* about *you,*" she said. "And what's an investigative reporter."

Clackety-clack, clackety-clack.

Ross nodded at these windows of night without taking his eyes off of her.

Said: "Regular reporting is about either the forest or the trees."

She shrugged. "I get what you mean."

"Investigative reporting is about who owns the land."

"Oh."

Then Nora said: "Do you write everything in that little black book you've got stuffed down the back of your pants?"

"It's too big to stuff down the front of my pants."

Nora didn't flinch or roll her eyes.

Kept his eyes on her face as he shifted and twisted and reached and settled back in his chair with that black moleskin journal in his hand.

He set it on the table between their chairs.

"The journal is mine," he told her. "Where you take notes for reporting, you have to be able to share it with your editor. It's about that job, not you. But sometimes life makes you cross that line.

"Like if you're standing outside the yellow tape crime scene at a midnight street murder. The homicide cop you know beckons you under that tape. Suddenly, you're part of somebody's dying and somebody else's doing.

"Yeah, you'll *good reporter'* note-take the details like 'sprawled' versus 'curled' corpse in case you get the space to give them to your readers.

"But what comes to you is a poem about the blue night silent with heartbeat red lights and ghosts of nevermore from that sorrow in a Seahawks jacket sprawled on the pavement now darkening with the spill of him."

"Jesus," whispered Nora.

"But the crime reporter's notebook you carry—even today, reporters I respect, lots still go paper, trying to keep it real. Something you can touch and is more admissible in court. Probably everybody after us will dictate or click their notes into *devices*. But a classic reporter's notebook is like an old-fashioned steno pad. Pale lime green sheets of paper and tan cardboard flip covers. And you can tear a page out.

"So if *reporter me* gets a hit by a poem, later I tear out the page, Scotch tape it or transcribe, hell: rewrite it in my *poet me* journal."

His eyes dropped from hers to that black book on the table between them.

"For this *gimme* assignment," he said, "no notes really needed, why bring a notebook? But there might be a few things I want to log. Since I always carry the journal, 'cept when I'm strapped as a reporter, might be a few things about all this written in there, but it's mostly just the scrawls of who I am."

Nora said: "Can I see?"

"Once your poem hits someone else's eyes, it's not yours anymore."

"Won't you share with me?"

Nora sent her unvarnished hand to pick up the black journal.

Ross's hand stopped her moving flesh.

Both felt that touch.

Both pulled back.

Ross thought: Risk it. You want to risk it. You're *dying* to risk it.

Picked up his journal, thumbed pages.

Not the poem that rose up in him when he boarded the train.

He opened the journal to a poem from before. Held the black book in her lap so she couldn't page through it to what he'd written as this train started its *clackety-clack*. His hand brushed the warm tops of her black-slacks thighs.

The page on the left, lines crossed out, jots of words, black ink, a red line.

Inked black, printed letters on the journal's right side cream-colored page:

L.T.N.

We live and we die
and in that wind you must choose
how you light the night.

"*Hiaku*," he said. "A 5-7-5 of syllables in three lines, no more, no less."

Ross said: "Some rules let you be free."

Nora shook her head.

Meant it when she said: "You should be doing this instead of . . . *this*."

"I've been poor before," said Ross. "There's no romance there.

"So I'm like lots of us, *our generation*," he told the woman with the embers red hair, with glistening sky eyes, with slick red lips he yearned to see smile. "We hack it in the gig economy. Take an Uber and drive one, too."

"Lucky us," said Nora. "We can afford to have dinner delivered by some other hustler. Why not? After a ton of student loans and low bid gigs, we'll never have enough money to buy a dream house or do more than sport our tattoos."

Ross said: "We just keep churning and yearning."

Nora felt herself nod. *He gets it, maybe he gets it!*

"Our parents inherited the rat race," she said, "but at least they were going somewhere. Us, we're like mice in a maze, running hard to nowhere."

"And us Millennials, 'our' most powerful political leaders are two White males older than many of our retired parents! We're the squeezed generation. We're between what was supposed to be and what was never going to happen."

"Everybody's always stuck between yesterday and tomorrow," said Ross. "You're just on this train now."

"Yeah," she said. "I know."

"Knowing what's going on doesn't always matter," said Ross. "Or make you able to change *what's what*. I know I don't have a choice about being a poet."

Nora said: "What about the gig you've got about this train?"

"First I thought a no-thought, type-it-blind puff piece like my client wants."

"Only at first?"

"Now I think there's a lot more going on. What it is—"

Ross's *a song they shared* smile interrupted him. "*What it means*, I don't know yet."

Nora said what she had to answer: "Like what's going on here."

Breathe deep, thought Nora. You can do this. You . . . want to. It's just using the same notebook. Later you can tear out that page.

Ross said: "I was talking more about the SWAT team and the Baggage Car."

"Boring," she told him: "Inconsequential. There's always a SWAT team and there's always baggage and that's not our car."

Motion broke their gaze: Ulysses and his family leaving.

Turn back and Ross felt *zeroed* by Nora's eyes.

"Who are you *really*?" he said. "I want to know."

"*No* is what you want?"

"Stop it. We already know you're smart and funny."

"Full stack."

"What?" said Ross.

Give trust to get trust, thought Nora. That's all I'll do. Tell him truth without telling him facts. That's what I want to tell him. What I've got to do.

She gave him a shrug. "Developer speak. You want *the full stack*. All the code. All the data. The right language to write the program.

"I'm a web developer. Programmer. I work gigs outta my studio apartment. Rock three screens for clients who I never meet in flesh city. I use a handle so—"

"Handle?"

"Identifier. Work name. Hides my *who*. I could be a woman. Could be a man. Could be a they. Could be a really fucking smart monkey. Hard for you to dictate *who* I've got to be if all you've got is a handle."

She shook her head and felt the unfamiliar tousle of her dyed chopped hair.

"The first computer programmer was a woman. We ruled programming for decades until the boys figured out it was big bucks. Then it became something 'just women' weren't talented at, so don't let them get in the way of progress.

"So fuck that," she said. "It's handle time.

"My handle doesn't always free me up from the creeps. The come-ons. The hands and body brushes when you're riding the elevator. The boss who tells you *how things are*. The V.P. for Outsourcing who lets you know. The colleague's *what are you wearing* text. The creep in the workshare complex two glass fishbowls over who's always staring. My handle can't stop that, but it helps cut down on the smiles you fake, the smiles you sell yourself, the smiles you sword."

Ross interrupted: "I want you to have the smile you want."

Nora stared at the starry-eyed man trapped sitting across from her.

Told him: "Don't make up who you think I am. Not with your head. Not with your heart. Not with your cock."

Whunk went the exit door down at the far end of this car.

Gone were the ruby-lipped woman and messenger bag man.

"We're alone now," said Ross.

"We're always alone. We're never alone."

"Programming," said Ross. "It's like you find stories and poems, too."

"Sure. We can handle that. Let's make this just a story you found, a poem."

"No," he said as they rode through this indigo darkness.

He reached out. Took her hand.

Said: "The poem found me."

She replied: "Not here."

N ora led Ross through the corridors of this train rumbling the night.

Out of the Observation Car.

Through the cleaned and deserted Dining Car.

Through three train cars of Roomette cabins.

Into their sleeper cabins' car.

There, halfway down this train car, standing at the door to a Superliner Bedroom suite: the American warrior named Ulysses.

Looking into his ticketed quarters.

"Let me give you guys some privacy to get ready for bed," Ulysses said to his wife and daughter and son who all pretended not to be worried for him while being glad he was leaving them alone so they could *let it go*, breathe some relief.

Ulysses lived his combat eyes.

Check right: Toward Ulysses down this train car's aisle came that taillight-haired woman and the cellphone filmer, his face aglow with hope.

Don't get in the way of that.

Major Ulysses Doss, USMC, left faced and marched toward the front of the train, that lucky couple coming behind him.

Ulysses walked past the set of switchback stairs down to Level One.

The wall of low windows on his right flicked dark slashes of moving night.

He guessed one of the cabins on his left must be the couple's objective.

Reached the cream plastic sheathed wall at the end of the car.

Walked down the steep stairs to Level One.

Now this would be a nasty fall, thought Ulysses.

A computer keypad waited beside the sealed silver steel door with a blacked-out window leading forward in the train toward the locomotive. White letters on the blacked-out plastic window read:

BAGGAGE CAR

AUTHORIZED ADMITTANCE ONLY

Makes sense. Seems secure. The SWAT team is next car up.

Ulysses turned back the direction he came, but now on Level One.

He opened the train's schedule in his iPhone.

Less than 40 hours before we get to Chicago, he thought. Now we must be near Leavenworth—Washington, not Kansas. Not the fort. Or the prison.

Walk on, he told himself. Hit a black pad and went into the Empire Builder's next car. Marched one wobbly step at a time down the aisle between seats filled by strangers hurtling *clackety-clack* through that American night.

Oh what's out there! thought Ulysses, feeling all the sad trips he'd made to hometowns big and small where he dress uniform stood with sobbing families and friends in front of flag-draped coffins of men and women he'd commanded. Cemeteries of dreams destroyed for dreams believed. All that was out there in the American night for this train to rumble past.

Past painted homes for dads and moms divorced once, maybe twice.

Past houses of kids sorted and slotted by politicians & barely paid teachers & standardized tests & helicopter parents & dollars instead of these new generations experiencing war hero President Dwight Eisenhower's 1950's strategy of *everybody learns everything so we can be better and beat the bad guys* or pre-9/11 President George Bush's motto of *no child left behind.*

Past neighborhoods dotted by group houses for 30ish someones who'd escaped from their parents' basements to rented rooms.

Past sagging houses full of *beg to work every shift* fathers & mothers who share macaroni & cheese dinner with their children, the family computer prioritized to job pleas and queries to *do it yourself* medicine sites to *please keep us out of/can't pay for* hospital boxes or county nursing homes with handcuff-friendly railed beds.

Past lights glowing in mansions on hills where the children go to private (taxpayer subsidized) schools to learn how to use their parents' connections.

Past way, *way* down that potholed road, where no lights burn in the cracked window squats of the forgotten.

And through everything out there, Ulysses swore he felt internet webs not *connecting* but *caging* keyboarders in Data They Wanted. Data that Gave Answers. Data that confirmed They Were Right and They'd Been Wronged. Data that showed them *its* way. Gave them a community of other woke warriors clicking revelations of Alternative Facts and *'no question that'* and *'everybody knows'* and *'people are saying'* disclosures from screen ghosts who asked "true" Americans like them to assemble for what surely will be like an online game where they will be anointed as superheroes who win and level up to . . . to . . .

Where's all that going to? Ulysses asked himself as he rode a train hurtling *clackety-clack* through the twinkling stars heart of it all.

Ulysses shook his head as he walked this train's aisle.

This is us.

And we're all on a train.

A blanket over a closed-eyes woman with a corner beauty shop haircut.

Two students slouched in their cellphones' glow.

A bald Vietnam War era man nodding in his seat.

A mom with a baby in a sling and a slumped-in-sleep second-grade daughter on the mom's tired arm.

The pro football-sized, blue-uniformed Conductor who stepped aside to let Ulysses pass, but let that passenger know Whose Train This Is.

Snatches of conversation come to Ulysses.

One middle-aged woman telling another: *". . . and Steven, the guy Doug's marrying, he's so nice and he runs that appliance store out on . . ."*

One man telling the guy sitting beside him: *". . . so my cousin'll help me get a job on the city crew. Figure no computer's gonna steal ditch diggers jobs."*

A burning eyes middle-aged woman telling the stranger ticketed beside her: *"So forget about what Big Media and the Deep State try to sell you, if you want to know what's really going on, you gotta . . ."*

Up ahead sat a man with a silver chain around his neck. *Like dog tags.* Ulysses walked on, never knew that this now-civilian's 5-year-old son needed to wear medical alert tags at all times, so dad got his old service tags out of the bureau drawer, wore 'em all the time to make that seem natural.

Up ahead: two women lean across the aisle to whisper while beside the older woman, kindergartener Becka sleeps with her head against the train wall.

The older woman saying to her across-the-aisle fellow passenger on this train: *"And get this, they tell me that Becka's mom, my niece, she's Number 3,917 out of 4,149. One year—4,149—Don't worry, Becka's asleep!—all those overdose deaths. More people killed like that in our one state than died on 9/11."*

The younger woman who lived in a home where the TV was always on shook her head. *"And you know what they're doing about that? They got a new drug for 'opioid constipation' they'll sell you at the drugstore."*

Ulysses walked up the aisle between these the two women, who leaned back into their seats to let him pass.

As Becka, eyes closed, slumped beside the older woman.

Becka, her head pressed against the wall of this train.

Becka, shuffling through Kindergarten but better fed, cared for, loved and safe than during her 11 months In The System.

Becka, who worried whenever a car crunched gravel that *they* had come to take her away again.

Pressed against the wall Becka rode with this train rumbling her skull.

After Ulysses passed those two women, they leaned back across the aisle.

He heard the older woman say: *"Why are we all getting high to die?"*

Ulysses hit the black door pad BAM! and walked into the next car.

Where he heard a man with a hard worker slouch tell the gray-haired woman who could have been his mother: *"They're all some kind of crook."*

"We're all some kind of crook," said the gray-haired woman. Wistful.

"But they get elected to be better than that. They promise they will be. Then, turns out they're all just always new crooks with new scams. Fuck 'em all."

"All of them is all of us."

Yeah, thought Ulysses: *All of us.*

The *good news* daughter going home to her family.

The son going to woo the wrong woman he'll marry and cry over.

The regional manager on her way to explain the restructuring.

A suit & tied salesman who's Black like Ulysses.

A Latino family akin to Isabella.

A rust-skinned man Ulysses didn't recognize as a *Gros Ventre*.

A man with a bushy beard dressed in religious black—Jewish, Amish, one *ish* or another.

Two women in head-covering *hijabs*.

A man sleeping in a high school letterman's jacket he wore to his buddy's funeral 47 years after they took different roads out of their hometown.

A local hardware store owner on his way back from forging a clever honest deal with a fellow Main Street visionary back up the line, both of them kicking in buckets of their coming rainfall profits to local *feed our hungry* groups.

A white-haired man taking two girls who call him *Grampa* on their first/ maybe last train ride so they'll remember it and him all their lives, *yes they will, please let them remember.*

Some of us, thought Ulysses, me and my family, we got damn lucky *and* worked like hell to afford upper-level cabins. But lots of us can't afford what we need. Yet we're here. Bought or bled our ticket.

Can't you see that? he asked unseen eyes outside this clattering train. *How can you* not *see that? We're all on a train."*

His silent pleas counted cadence for his walk through the train cars.

End of the train, lower level of the Observation Car, he looked out the EMERGENCY EXIT door's rear window at the night flowing away into *gone.*

Climbed switchback stairs, walked through the Observation Car back the way he'd come and there she was, standing outside the closed door of their cabin:

Isabella.

How'd I get so lucky to marry her? thought Ulysses.

She saw him coming. Met him before he got there. Nodded him back to the end of the car where their whispers wouldn't disturb anyone.

Isabella leaned against the metal bulkhead of the train car. Let its vibrations tremble through her body, *clackety-clack, clackety-clack.*

Gave him all the space she could to hear what he had to say.

He leaned on the wall beside her.

They didn't turn to look at each other. Saw nothing else.

"It's not PTSD," said Ulysses.

Isabella waited.

She felt him shake his head as he said: "I keep thinking."

"You're good at it," answered Isabella.

"Nuremberg Conventions."

She waited.

"We won World War II." He shook his head. Knew that she knew what he said next came with a smile. "Not *just* the Corps, everybody. Everybody in our country, from every uniform to every woman on the bomber assembly lines to every farmer who did twice the work of before, every shopkeeper who donated blood every chance she got."

"That was way back before our dads' day," she said. "Back in our days of at least *officially* all together and great."

"The rules we insisted on then are still the rules we claim today. Out of the death camps came The Nuremberg Convention. *Just following orders'* doesn't hack it."

Ulysses turned so his right shoulder pressed into the steel wall, so he could see the face of the woman he loved as Isabella turned to give him all her eyes.

"Never used to think about it as much," said her husband. "Worry about it so much. But now, these days, keep reading about better people than me following their conscience out of government service . . .

"We just ended a Forever War we've been fighting since I've been in the Corps. Now I'm looking out those windows and praying not to see me. Nuremberg being right and good. How *crazy* is running wild all over our country. Remember the Chief of Staff who had to break protocol and rank and assure China that our government was stable just before a pissed-off Presidential election and that we weren't going to nuke them? What if I get an order I shouldn't obey? What if Command orders me to give it to my guys, my troops?"

The woman who knew Ulysses better than anyone else on this planet said: "You'll do what's right. And that's everything. More than any order."

They leaned together, forehead to forehead.

Wobbled on the train, *clackety-clack.*

She turned and led him to their quarters and their family.

Closed the sliding door behind them.

24

R oss slid closed the door to his cabin.

Made sure the curtain was shut over the door window.

My bed. Turned down by Attendant Cari. White sheets, blanket. Pillows.

Nora stood near the lone chair that held his bags. She kept her back to Ross as she faced windows to the river of night.

"Latch the door."

She just *said it.*

Her transparent reflection windowed over the darkness clattering past. She turned to face him.

Ross said: "I want to believe this."

"What do you want *me* to believe?" She took a step closer.

"That I've never been this guy."

"That you've never been alone in a room with a bed and a woman?"

"I've never been lucky enough to be anywhere with this real."

She shook her head. "I'm just me. Here. Now."

Ross said: "Why me?"

She stared straight at him. "We're on this train."

"Is that all this is?" he said. "We're on the same train?"

She sensed him pull away: "You're not supposed to go all *no*."

"I want to be more than just the man who's here."

She stepped close enough to touch.

He could smell her musk perfume. Feel her breath as she said: "I want to be with who you are right now. Maybe that's all we get, but we've got that."

His hands floated up to cup her face, they flowed into that first kiss . . .

. . . *YES* electric fire, her lips opening and the tingle of her tongue, her arms circling around him, pulling him to the crush of her body.

Ross felt the thunders of his heart like the *clackety-clack* on the rails.

She pulled back, her mouth and face smeared blood red with their kisses and for an instant Ross worried that—

She pulled the blue sweater off over her head.

Her breasts. Their heavy fullness. Proud nipples like top hats. Like eyes staring into his soul.

Nora took his hands in hers.

Filled his grasp.

Yes, and *oh* the stiffening, the weight of her in his waiting hands.

Off came shoes, clothes.

She dumped her black purse on his shelf. Its contents spilled. Her perfume bottle. Cellphone charger. Lipstick tubes. A black rubber hairbrush. Condoms.

They used what they should.

On that narrow bed. Pressed together in naked warmth. He kissed her mouth. Heard her whisper '*Yes!*' as he kissed her neck, her breasts, her trembling stomach and down, *oh the smell of her!* Kissed down to where she'd shaved her hair to hide its true color. He twisted off the bed to kneel on the floor and swirl her around, her thighs spread on his shoulders for a surging eternity—she cried out, words, who know what they said/they knew every sound as—

WAIT.

Every sound.

Kneeling on the hard carpet, her legs muscled over his shoulders, his existence a wondrousness of taste and smell, there in the thrall of that with her . . .

What's that sound?

Knocking on a cabin door out in this train car's corridor?

Muffled: "*'ister ang?*"

Nora cried out/pulled Ross onto the bed, a tangle of flesh, he's on his back/she's *ahh* enveloping/on top of him, thighs gripping his sides, his hands filling with her breasts just the right squeeze. Her head arches, her eyes close.

Beyond her—*look*:

The glass of that train window captured their reflection, her astride him.

Slap slap slap of flesh on flesh, *clackety-clack* of wheels on steel.

Fire grabbed-released them *Yes!*

They slumped into their embrace.

Clackety-clack. Clackety-clack.

Then, *oh then*, they stretched and curled and cuddled. Him on his back. Her cheek pressed over his heaving chest as they filled his narrow bed.

Ross had to ask: "Did you hear something?"

"Besides my heart exploding?" She raised her face to look at him, bent it to kiss his calming chest. "What more was there to hear?"

Her hand shot up to block his response.

"*My heart,*" she explained, "was just, *you know*, passion."

"Just sex."

"Yes. That's what it was. Just sex."

"And you're OK now? Your heart?"

"*Ba-boomp. Ba-boomp.*"

"That's good, because it sucks when there's a dead girl in your cabin."

"Who are you?" asked Nora. "Alfred Hitchcock?"

"More like *Rocky*." Ross shrugged. "I used to be a boxer. In Philadelphia."

"If that's your *what*, then Philly's your obvious *where*. Still, why boxing?"

"We all get hit. But there are rules in the ring. Poetry."

"Wouldn't it be nice if everything had rhythm, rhyme and reason that—"

"That made sense," said Ross.

"That you could work," said Nora. "That you could make happen *better*."

"Hundred percent," he answered.

Outside in the hall, Ross heard a door slide open, *clunk* closed.

Nora rubbed her cheek on his chest.

"You're hearing things." She nodded to beyond the cabin door. "Out there."

"That's who I am. I can't shut that off."

She whispered: "You can try."

"Then who would I be? Here, now, with you: I want to be me."

They kissed—*he* didn't kiss her, *she* didn't kiss him—*they* kissed.

Of that he was sure.

Nora said: "We could be your story—don't use my real name!"

"*Your real name?* I don't even know your last name!"

She shrugged. "Doesn't matter. You could write this story in your sleep."

"But I'm awake."

"So you like trains?" she said.

The bluntness of her dodge made him blink. "*Ah* . . . Sure. How about you?"

"Once you get on, you can't just get off."

He sent a frown to the ember-haired angel who lay on his heart. "You OK?"

She gave him a smile. "I'm on this train with you, how could I not be OK?"

They kissed and his body wondered.

And they shifted ever so slightly for comfort.

"What poem are you writing now?" whispered Nora.

He was certain he knew beyond any shadow of a doubt that what she wanted to know was the *forever* in his bones.

"Told you," he said. "The poem is writing me."

Nora looked away. "You're not supposed to be here now."

"Of course I am."

He leaned more on his left side so they lay face to face, loin to loin.

She whispered: "Tell me a joke."

"*Knock, knock,*" said Ross.

"Who's there?"

"*I don't know.*"

"I don't know *who*?"

"*Me, either.*"

Beat, then Nora burst out laughing and he joined her and it was *oh*, so good.

"That was terrible!" she said.

"Did you ever try to be funny on demand?"

"One time in high school . . ."

But the sound of her words faded when he glanced past her face, looked down the full length of her, saw the curve—*oh*—the soft pink curve of her ass.

The thought of her warm flesh cupped by his right hand made him tremble.

Nora said: "You still with me, cowboy?"

"Sorry, I was just . . . "

"You're inching your hand around like you don't know what to do with it."

She followed his guilty gaze to the curve of her hip.

Nora's deep breath drew his eyes to hers.

And she said: "Would I be here like this if I didn't want you to touch me?"

25

Erik sat in Cabin F's lone chair as the train rushed over steel rails through that first night. A rainbow caressed his face from the computer on his lap.

His eyes flicked off that screen.

Stared at the cabin's lower bunk stretching just beyond his reach.

Terri.

Under the sheet and blue blanket. On her back. Eyes closed. Lips parted.

Terri.

Who got back to their cabin after dinner and scarfed down a sleeping pill.

Who let her heavenly auburn hair splay on the lower bunk's white pillow as she slumbered away from this universe.

Leaving me here, thought Erik.

Alone.

Watching her.

And what she'd better not know.

Erik triple-checked his laptop screen's Mission Status Reports.

RECON: Comprehensive & Complete.

ALPHA TEAM: Geared Up & Locked In.

BETA TEAM: Prepped & Ready.

ALL TEAMS LINKED.

Erik smiled: Now all we need to do is get to Chicago without anyone realizing what's going on.

26

Ross and Nora lay naked on his bed.

The train rocked them. She kissed him as he lay on his left side, his back against the train cabin wall, his left arm trapped under yet around her neck and her bare shoulders as she lay on her right side and her breasts rose and fell, rose and fell, his right hand cupping the soft warm curve of her ass.

She pulled back: not *no*, but *slow*. "So if all this *were* going to be a poem, how do you imagine it would be? And what would you do with it?"

She needs to keep hearing it, thought Ross. It's like she's looking for something else. "This isn't a poem. This is us."

"We could be all that and more. We could be the *gimme* story for your contract gig. A sweet, reader-loved *Romance On The Rails.*"

"Good title," he said.

"See what I mean? You. Me. That couple—the wife with those dead red lips. That family. Those other two travelers our age who look so utterly normal and hip. You've already done all the reporting you need to do."

She nuzzled her cheek against his, her warm whisper filled his ear. "You don't have to report *everything*."

"To be good enough for you, I've got to do the best I can. For everything."

Her eyes looked away. Then searched his face. Her words were a whisper. *"Touch me."*

His hand, his lucky right hand, cupped the soft full of her breast.

She whispered: "Wait."

Nora swung off the bed.

Wobbled, and they laughed at the fall that didn't happen.

Nora's naked hips thrust toward him *oh* as she scooped their clothes off the floor, dumped them on top of the chair holding his gear, put her purse on top.

She turned out lights.

Left on the soft glow over the mirror above the silver metal sink.

Sank out of the shadows to press against him on the bed.

And *oh*, their us: mouths wet and hungry, kisses deep and long, his hands full of her breasts, her pulling him down to mouth her nipples, their strokes on loins that belonged now to both of them. Ross didn't know time or the towns outside in the darkness this train rumbled through, knew only her, knew only their turnings on the bed—

Bang!

His arm, her leg—what difference. They'd tumbled off the bed. Bare feet on the *wobble-wobble* floor. Stood naked and clinging to each other. Bumped the cylindrical bathroom. That door swung open. Out of that metal tube flowed its nighttime light to color their entanglement of flesh with hues of blue.

A heartbeat of clarity took Ross outside of himself and their passion.

He knew the blue lit *them* on the bed:

Him on his feet with his back to that swinging door, behind her as she knelt jackknifed over in front of him, his loins slamming into her raised hips, his right hand holding them together, his left hand stretched above him to grab the upper bunk ledge like it was the ladder to heaven, hearing her moan *yes yes yes* and glancing down her smooth back to the mop of her electric brakelight hair on the jumble of white sheets near the window that showed their blued reflection . . .

. . . seeing her face pressed against white sheets, her cheek slick and wet. With tears.

OH!

Afterwards.

Their heads on retrieved pillows. The tangle of white sheets and blue blanket pulled over them. The train car windows full of *who knows where* rushing past them in the dark night.

"Why would I be crying?" She gave him a light kiss before his lips could find an answer, told him: "You can use the bathroom first."

Swung out of his way. Stood. Swept her hand to the still open and drifting back & forth metal tube door.

Can't argue with that, thought Ross.

Once he got inside the tube, shut the door, her suggested urge became the streaming deed as it would have *last thing* before he went to sleep alone.

But what about tonight? he thought.

He felt no embarrassment as he flushed the toilet. Washed his hands.

Opened the door and found her sitting on his bed:

Totally—*Yes! Not dressed to flee!*—naked.

Nora held a plastic water bottle toward him, cap screwed off.

"I figure that after . . . *well,* now you shouldn't mind sharing," she said.

Her swollen red-smeared lips smiled: "Precious bodily fluids."

Ross hadn't realized he was thirsty.

"There's not enough left to save," she said. "Finish it."

He did.

She stood, walked toward the heart of the cabin's blue light.

"My turn," she said.

Into the tube she went, the door clunked closed.

Options flooded through Ross:

Lay on the bed—NO: just sit here. Don't be silly, stretch out. Under the sheets? On top of them? Move back against the cushioned wall so she knows you've left room for her. And could there—yes—would there be three times?

The bathroom tube opened. She stepped out. Closed it and cut off the blue light so only the pale glow from above the sink's mirror lit this cabin.

"Hey," she said.

"Hey."

"How are you? I mean: how you feeling?"

He laughed. "I don't know where to start."

She slid into bed beside him. Filled it with her warmth. Pulled up the sheet.

Asked: "What *do* you know?"

He started to say—

Her fingers pressed his lips. "Can we just lay here in the dark without words?"

She cuddled onto him like she'd been there a thousand times before.

Ross felt her rise and fall with his breaths, Springsteen's angel on his chest. He let his eyes close as the train rumbled, rocked them together like in a cradle.

And he was thinking not words, she didn't want words, she's here, *clackety-clack, clackety-clack* and everything, everything, every—

27

haking side to side.

Rumbling darkness.

Awake, Ross realized he was awake.

Sprawled naked under the covers in his bed on a rumbling train.

Alone.

Morning sunlight streamed through the cabin's windows.

The bunk above his head hadn't been pulled down from the wall.

The tube bathroom: Door closed. Silence inside.

No one came out of the tube bathroom to electrify his life with her smile.

Last night I just . . . crashed. The lemon drop. The tension. Spent energy. Crowded bed. She wanted to let me sleep. Needed to sleep herself. So she left.

Not *excuses*: logic.

Everything's fine.

"Good morning," he whispered.

Inhaled the ghost of her musk perfume.

The scent of them.

Where are we?

That's what he wanted to know. In every way.

Ross flipped away the bedcovers. The cabin air chilled his nakedness as he barefooted the carpeted floor to stare through his windows at the vast *out there.*

The mountains of Montana.

An eagle soaring in that winterish gray sky glanced down at this train.

Saw a silver dragon *clackety-clacking* over black steel rails through a snowy mountain pass.

Ross's window looked out across the mountain pass's quarter mile wide V, a gorge carved by some river a thousand feet below and a million years ago. Across that long fall rose fortresses of stone. Crags the size of cities. Pinkish-red outcroppings of rock bigger than sports stadiums. Clouds of crystalline white fog drifted through those snowed slopes of Christmas trees fearing fires to come.

Ross felt those silent snowy mountains breathe as he stood naked and chilled in front of the window in his cabin on a train chugging toward the sky.

No seconds to waste, Ross showered and shaved in the wondrously strange blue lit bathroom tube. Brushed his teeth. Grabbed the same clothes he wore yesterday—*sniff test* passable and fastest to put on.

Phone: where's . . .

On the window ledge.

Wish I'd plugged it in before I passed out.

He used his thumb print to unlock his phone: Still had a 29% charge.

He stared at what he held in his own hand.

All Ross had to do to be *everywhere else* was tap his screen.

Ride the train you're on.

That line shot through his skull made him smile.

Look for his black journal.

There!

By the sink where she must have put it on her way out the door.

Wait: Did she look at it? Read it while he slept?

Did she read the poem I wrote as the train pulled out of Seattle?

His flash of *if so* violated anger flipped when he thought: *She cares!*

He read what he'd written.

Read it again, then again.

Wouldn't—didn't—change a thing.

Ross figured that since he'd already lost those heartbeats away from her by being his *poet who*, might as well use his *reporter who* to revel in their first memories for a few more heartbeats.

He put his pen in his shirt pocket with the cellophane lemon drops. Tucked his journal down the back of his pants. Pulled his cellphone out of his black jeans' right rear hip pocket. Swiped and tapped his screen.

Video he'd shot at the Seattle train station of her and everyone else just before he filmed the SWAT machinegunner . . .

. . . was gone.

28

That Friday morning some 30+ hours from the train's final destination, the Dining Car's breakfast buffet offered silver metal warming trays full of scrambled eggs. Link sausages and bacon. Hash brown potatoes. Packets of ketchup. A pyramid of pastries. Cups of yogurt. Plastic forks, knives and spoons. Orange juice. Metal flasks of cream, low fat and whole milk. And coffee, urns of coffee.

Travelers who wobbled the narrow *clackety-clack* aisle from their cabins toward that feast passed seated strangers who held glowing screens.

That Friday's morning train's top tweeted and clicked-on news stories:

- The death toll in that week's school shooting reached 19: 11 middle schoolers (5 boys, 6 girls), 3 teachers, 2 responding police officers, 1 janitor, the 17-year-old shooter—an alum—and the random mom driving past the middle school who got her skull shattered by one of the gunman's wild bullets.

- A Super Bowl stadium sized chunk of the polar bears and penguins' snow white Arctic shelf broke off the continent and sank *melting, melting*, into the sea.
- A cosmetic crafted, TV programmed socialite famous for her bodacious booty got her picture taken for the ba-jillionth time.
- The concentration of wealth in America hit a high not seen since The Roaring Twenties starring Al Capone And His Boyz Of Noyz, with the 400 richest Americans like Fergus Lang now owning more of the nation's riches than the 150 million adults in the bottom 60 percent of the population, many of them lucky to land in banker Brian's new class of *precariats*.
- One of every nine American children was going to bed hungry.
- A car bomb in a country 73% of America's citizens couldn't find on a global map killed two U.S. advisers—Army Special Forces, not Marines.
- Raids by both one of our rival countries and one of our official allies locked up dozens of pro-democracy dissidents and honest reporters.
- A government scientist was "troubled" by reports of a new virus.

We're on a hurtling train where everywhere else feels like a distant dream.

Or so was the common consensus—*adjusted for articulation*—of everyone on board the Empire Builder that Friday morning.

Suzanne didn't spill a drop of the two cups of coffee or a crumb off the two plated croissants she carried back to the table in the Dining Car where she sat on the aisle next to her husband and across from an empty chair. She could angle her head left as if paying attention to Brian or looking out the snow-ivoried windows at the flow of time . . .

. . . and fill her eyes with the man sitting opposite the person she'd married.

"Brian," she said, "this is Albert."

Saying it *right*.

Brian grumbled: "Hey, Al, how you doing?"

Watched this, like, *random guy* sitting there with a weird bag looped over one shoulder say: "I'm fine."

Brian gave the guy a chance: "You know anything about those SWAT guys? As we were coming in here, a couple of them were packing out bags of donuts."

"I like donuts," said that loner guy.

What a dummy, thought Brian.

Suzanne caught the attention of the maitre d' with a flutter of her hand and a trembling smile of her ruby lips.

"Can I help you?" he said.

"I'm sorry to bother you," she said, "my fault probably, but when I was getting our breakfast, I couldn't find any tomato juice for my husband."

Albert watched that man in the story frown.

Suzanne's laugh was nervous and shy.

"You know," she told the maitre d', "like for a Bloody Mary, but we don't need vodka."

"Of course, madam," said the maitre d'. "Let me see what I can do."

As the maitre d' walked away, Brian said: "I don't want any tomato juice. Or that French roll thingy."

"Sorry," said Suzanne. "My mistake. *A-gain!* But, *oh dear*: Don't embarrass yourself now and tell that poor man who's going to a lot of trouble to get what he thinks you want."

"*Wow*," whispered Albert.

"Yeah, I know," said Brian. "She does that kind of thing all the time."

Brian saw *his Sue* give this guy a polite smile.

"Would you like a croissant, *Al-bear*?" she asked.

"Yes," he said. "Please."

Just Sue giving that guy a flaky roll pulled Brian's eyes away to what was going on across the Dining Car aisle.

Shock slammed Brian's face as he spotted that black hoodie silver-haired whacko werewolf sitting at a table—and talking to three of *them*!

Graham sat on the aisle next to Isabella.

Her husband wasn't there. Their kids sat across from the nice old man.

Graham nodded to a family laptop on the Dining Car table.

". . . and that holds the defining sound of your generation," Graham told the teenage girl and her kid brother. "The *clickety-click* of keyboards."

"For me," said Graham, "for my generation, for *us* . . . helicopters."

"Our dad rides helicopters!" said Malik. "He's the C.O. of helicopters!"

"That's *uber* cool." Graham grinned with his allusion: "But we're *talking about my generation*. Our sounds.

"Sure, rock 'n' roll is *the* birth sound of my generation. Lots of our poets picked up guitars. The best of those songs are about every *us* in every time ever, but back then, those stories coming first to my *'us'* generation for free over the car radio on soft summer nights . . ."

Graham sighed. "But the defining sound of my generation, kids in junior high or high school when JFK rode into Dallas and no more than a few years out of the Army or college after Nixon skipped town in a Marine helicopter—"

Marines did WHAT with a guy named Nixon? thought Malik.

"—and then Saigon fell, for us, defining us, *sure*, there were *marching feet*. But what cut *us* into *who we are* was the *whump whump whumps* of helicopters."

Isabella smiled as she sat in the breakfast buffet by the cool glass of the Dining Car window watching and *watching over* her babies—her *kids*, though Mir was more a woman every day and Malik had a freakish *something* beyond his nine years: *Look at them doing so well in an adult conversation!*

Casually, *gently*, Graham said: "Talking with you 'young people' reminds me of that kind of redheaded woman on our train. You know who I mean?"

Mir shrugged. "We've seen her."

"Yeah," said Graham. "I worry about her. She talk to you guys?"

No one at that table told him *yes*.

"Hey," said Graham, "it's harder for you and your generation—for that woman's generation, too, and her friend."

"The reporter," said Isabella, with no real concern. Then.

"Yes," said the man who could be a grampa. "Did you chat with him yet? I can't wait to find out about what he's figured out about all that's going on."

Teenage Mir said: "Why is it harder for us than it was for you guys?"

"You've got us and what we did and didn't get done to put up with," answered Graham. "You're going to need a hell of an app for that."

Graham blinked: "Ever notice how '*app*' is '*ape*' with a '*p*' for *power* shoving out '*e*' for . . . for whatever. *Essence*, maybe. Human essence."

Yes! thought Malik. *Somebody else sees things other people don't, too!*

"Watch the apps," Graham told the kids who weren't his blood. "You gotta *grok* who's clicking the keys. Don't be just data for Big Brother."

George Orwell, thought honor roll student Mir. *1984. SO long ago!*

Are they talking about me? thought Malik. *Am I going to get to be a . . . !*

He blurted: "Who's Big Brother?"

"More and more," said Graham, "*he* is *us*."

Malik said: "I hope I still know stuff when I'm *way* old like you!"

"*Malik*," said Mom with her *watch-it* frown.

Graham smiled away Isabella's worries about her son's candor.

"Little Man," said Graham, "when you get old, it's not what you forget, it's what you remember and what you see coming."

Mir *humphed*. "Whatever, your *you* stuck us all on the politics line."

Isabella said: "Kids, we don't talk about politics in public."

"Yes," said the *certainly* safe but intense old man, "but then, well, *public* is what makes politics. Atom bombs, global climate change, the 'Net making everywhere *everywhere*. Anonymous keyboard clickers becoming influencers because they say they are. The screens we choose choosing what we think is real. Now everything is our *polis*, public space. Every transaction of power is politics. Where you stand decides what you'll see. You know how people still talk about *liberal* or *conservative, left wing* or *right wing?*

"May I?" he said to Mir as he lifted the cord for her earbuds, stretched the cord out in a line on the breakfast's white tablecloth.

Should I shut this down now? wondered Isabella. *No, the kids need to learn how to handle what's out there in this world.*

Besides, I'm here with them. How bad could this get?

Graham touched one end of the cord: *"Left wing."*

Touched the other: *"Right wing.*

"And Mir, you say we're all standing trapped on that line, right?

"Way back," he told them, "brave men like your dad—women, too—they fought long and hard and so many of them never came home from fighting one evil extreme tip of this cord we call politics, the tip of the *right wing* called Nazis."

Graham touched the other tip of the lined-out cord.

"Then a little while later, more brave Americans like your dad fought and died battling the other evil tip of this cord, the tip called the *left wing*, communists, commies in Russia, Korea, Vietnam, the Berlin Wall.

"You know what both evil tips of this cord have in common?" said Graham.

Mir thought *maybe* she knew.

Malik shook his head *no*.

"Both tips of this politics cord are run by a big boss—a Big Brother dictator. And both ends of this politics line love prison camps. Do you know the difference between a *right wing* Nazi prison camp and a *left wing* Commie prison camp?"

Malik and Mir shook their heads *no*.

"The guards' uniforms."

"So that," said Graham, "means this."

He pulled the *left wing* and *right wing* ends of the line called *politics* together so they touched—and the line became a circle.

"Left and right extremes become one and the same, except for the uniforms and slogans. So you gotta know where you really stand. Because politics is what you *got to*, what you *ought to*, what you *want to*, what you *get to*."

Graham sighed. "And I should probably get going."

Gave Isabella a shrug. "Sorry to be that stranger on the train who rambles on and on. These days, seems like I'm losing my social skills."

Isabella smiled at the odd older man. "You socialize just fine. And I bet that your whole life, you've been doing it more and easier and better than you think."

"Maybe," he said. "I mean, it's not like I've been locked down in Solitary."

Isabella blinked.

"Well," continued Graham, "except for that one time.

"And that was more like a hospital, so . . . "

He shrugged. "No worries."

29

Isabella fought the urge to scoop her children into her sheltering arms as they sat at this Dining Car table with the silver-haired, fire-eyed man. Malik still had his awe-struck smile, but Mir's expression now radiated *stranger danger.*

Ulysses loomed beside this table where there was no chair for him.

Sensed tension in his family. "What did I miss?"

"Ah, Major," beamed Graham. "My guess is you don't *'miss'* much.

"Like when we were back in Seattle," continued Graham, as if he knew he had only seconds to ask: "Have you found out anything about that SWAT squad?"

Ulysses said: "Why? What are they to you?"

Graham smiled. A friendly smile.

Told the Marine: "I'm just a curious old man with time on his hands. And who's doing what, who can do what, *well*, such things fascinate me.

"But now," he said as he stood with what teacher Isabella recognized as deceptive awkwardness as he pretended to be just a senior citizen struggling to get up and get by: "You should have your chair I was just keeping warm."

The smiling Graham met Ulysses' command stare.

Said: *"Love the family."*

All of whom watched the silver-haired stranger head toward the buffet with the cadence of old guy's rock 'n' roll playing only in his skull.

The Dining Car door opened with a *whunk*.

30

Della clomped into the dining car as fast as her high heels allowed.

Coming after her, bouncing in his constant companion's arms, Mugzy fixated on the swaying purple boa wrapped around Della's neck.

"Oh my," called out panting Constance, "you are . . . hurry . . . morning coffee, aren't you, Miss Della! *Ohh*. I'm like too out of breath keeping up."

"*Catching* up," corrected Della. "Hellhound on my trail."

Behind her, Constance yelled: "I'll grab us a table, yes we will, Mugzy."

Constance wobbled past where the man with that cashmere coat, his wife, and Mr. Messenger Bag sat. "Good morning! How are we today?"

No one answered her.

Della reached the buffet two steps after Graham. That serve-yourself space was crowded. Those two strangers circled and sidestepped, didn't bump into each other though Della's high heels kept wobbling their wearer into Graham's way. Della did her best to keep her back to Constance's words and waves.

Like the sledgehammer swings of the gandy dancers who built the steel tracks for this train, again the Dining Car door *whunked* open.

In came Nora.

She felt all the eyes in the Dining Car lock on her.

Thought: *But he's not here. Not yet. Maybe not coming and if he doesn't . . .*

Act normal. Act like nothing's happened. Like nothing's going to happen.

Constance shouted to the younger woman standing by the closed door. "Come in, dear! There's nothing to be frightened of."

Constance leaned toward Brian, Suzanne and Albert to gossip about Nora.

"She's shy," claimed Constance. "Last night, Mugzy growled. So naturally, I went out—and found her walking around the dark train. She looked like she'd seen a ghost and *well*, who can blame her, she *wouldn't* talk about it *at all*."

Constance sighed. "Ghosts are such personal things."

She waved at her candy buddy Mir.

Mir waved back.

Nora stood by the door trying to absorb everything.

"Yoo-hoo!" said Constance.

Paranoia raced Nora's eyes to her right.

"Come sit, dear!" called out that woman holding a squirming rat dog.

Nora kept her face empty.

The door behind her opened with a sledgehammer *whunk*.

31

Ross saw her standing there.

Saw her turn around in that aisle of white-clothed tables and see him.

She wore her blue sweater and black slacks, the same morning-after, night-before clothing choices he made.

Did I ever really see you naked? thought Ross.

On this train in the morning mountains of Montana, they now faced each other like two cowboy gunfighters.

He knew she knew he knew—*what?*

And thus—*Damn it!*—she knew she had no better option than Zed's.

For the grift. Ross's sake. For her.

And none of that is a lie, she told herself.

Everyone in that Dining Car—

Brian, Suzanne and Albert huddled at their table where the maître de set a plastic glass of tomato juice with a celery stick pointing toward heaven.

The Doss family sitting across the aisle.

Constance sitting at her table trying to control Mugzy.

Della turning from the buffet beside Graham who seemed to pay her no mind, ignoring even her prodigious breasts millimeters from his arm.

—everyone in that Dining Car watched Nora and Ross step one . . .

. . . step two . . . .

. . . step all the paces needed to meet just out of each other's reach in the aisle between the white-clothed tables beside where Constance and Mugzy sat and the table where a wife was murdering her husband.

"Please *please*," Nora pleaded to Ross in front of God and everyone.

"Please," she said, "we needed to talk, I . . . I'll get us coffee, get you . . ."

Nora whirled and hurried to the buffet.

Left him standing there in front of all those watching eyes.

Ross's heart slammed his ribs: *What should I do? What should I do?*

Clackety-clack, clackety-clack.

Banker Brian stared at the young stud standing by his table who looked like he got hit by a train instead of riding this one.

He spotted the silver werewolf walking toward the younger man.

Plus, *that* family sitting across the aisle was stirring. Going somewhere.

Don't want to get trapped *anywhere* with them! thought Brian.

"I'm going back," he told his wife Sue. "Mr. Lang—my buddy Fergus. He's smart. Eating in his cabin. I'll check in on him. See if he needs anything."

The strange man with the weird bag said: "What could he need?"

And then—*Wouldn't you know it?*—the wife stopped Brian: "The maître d' just brought you that tomato juice. I know you don't want it, but . . ."

Her hands curved over that Styrofoam cup to *obviously* adjust the incline of the celery stick as she continued: ". . . a good businessman closes his deals."

Brian didn't waste time arguing. Downed the whole cup of *weird-burning* tomato juice.

Brian stood . . . wobbled—*Whoa, what was that?*

He caught his balance as Graham walked past.

Heard the silver werewolf smile at Ross: *"Charge."*

Ross watched Graham walk out, banker Brian trudging in his wake.

He saw Ulysses' family headed toward the Observation Car.

Heard the major's wife say: "Come on, let's go see our America."

Suzanne and Albert waited for the military family to clear the aisle, then excused themselves as they walked past Ross.

In the galley, Suzanne said *"Excuse me?"* to the maître d' whose gaze dropped to the red-stained white Styrofoam cup and napkin balled around something in her hand.

She said: "I don't know how to work your recycling."

The maître d' reached and took the napkin crumpled around . . .

Is that an empty mini-bottle for vodka? thought Ross.

The maître d' knew exactly what he held. "Thank you, I'll take care of it."

Standing at the buffet, Della watched Suzanne lead Alfred to the Observation Car.

"Yoo-hoo!" Constance waved her free hand at Ross, who stood there watching that odd middle-aged couple go. "Young man! Please join us."

Mugzy growled.

"We have a perfect chair for you," said Constance. "Sit right there next to Miss Della—she's getting buffet, though it's taking her an awfully long time, isn't it, Mugzy-Wugzy."

The dog panted.

See where this takes you, thought Ross.

He sat like a boxer in the chair by the windows full of snowy mountains. His eyes watched Nora. Saw only her back. Her curved moon hips as she filled Styrofoam white cups with what she'd promised.

"Such a nice girl, isn't she, Mugzy?" Constance smiled. "We'll all have to introduce ourselves when she returns, won't we?"

"Last names and all." Ross's tone was flat. "What a good idea."

Constance glanced out the window: "Do you know where we are?"

Seeing only Nora, Ross said: "I thought so."

Constance said: "I thought—*oh!*"

She was smiling when Ross turned to see why she'd yelped.

"My ears just popped! Must be the mountains." She leaned forward to tell the young man: "*The body knows.*"

"Knows something," said Ross.

Mugzy snarled.

"It's beautiful out there." Her nod led Ross's eyes to the windows.

"We're getting into Glacier National Park," said Ross, naming America's beloved swath of mountains, rivers and lakes that since 1966 had been losing its 150 glaciers from the late 19th century to rapidly increasing melting so that April morning, only 26 shrunken hills of ice remained, all of them doomed to disappear before Ross was officially scheduled to die.

"Oh, lovely," said Constance.

Smiled: "Speaking of lovely."

Nora shuffled toward the table, a cup of orange juice trembling in one hand, a cup of steaming coffee in the other.

She eased the cup of orange juice toward Ross.

"I didn't know what you take in your coffee," said Nora. "This one is mine."

"Yours. Mine. Good to know."

She didn't meet his eyes.

"I take my coffee with cream, milk," she said, like that was important. "I'll go make—get yours, but here: Drink some orange juice."

That white Styrofoam cup of orange liquid drew closer to the tabletop.

No smile in Ross's voice: "So you'll replenish my precious bodily fluids."

Nora's smile trembled with tension and—

Mugzy lunged.

Lapping *three*, *four*, make it *five* tongue slurps of orange juice before his attack knocked the cup from Nora's hand and splashed juice over her. That white cup bounced on the table as Mugzy's companion human pulled him away—

—and bumped Mugzy's back into the other Styrofoam cup Nora carried.

Hot coffee erupted from Nora's grasp. Scorched her hand. She yelled.

Mugzy barked and thrashed in loving arms that fought to hold him tight.

Ross was out of his chair reaching to . . .

Too late to do anything as two spilled cups rolled on the Dining Car's table.

"What did you do?" cried Constance.

Nora, hands dripping, orange juice stains on the blue sweater above her heart and streaking down toward her navel, yelled: "Wasn't me! No! I . . . I . . ."

The maître d' hurried over.

Nora shrank from the scene of the crime, her hands dripping.

The train whistle blew.

Brakes squealed steel on steel.

The Empire Builder shuddered.

Slowed.

Stopped with a hiss of steam.

The train loudspeaker boomed: **"Whitefish, Montana. This station stop, Whitefish, Montana. Nine minutes to** *All Aboard.***"**

Constance sheltered her beloved in her arms. Buffaloed from that wet table. Shoved past the clumsy young woman who'd *clearly* caused this catastrophe. Lumbered past the fussing maître d' and the waitress wiping dry the table and the stunned young man. She charged out the door toward her suite yelling: "Come, Mugzy! This place isn't safe!"

"No," whispered Nora.

"No," said Ross, reaching toward her as she shrank from him. "Forget about that, it's OK. We have—Tell me—"

She blurted: "I've got to go. I . . . Clean up, I've got to get cleaned up."

She fled out the door toward their cabins, gone.

"Your table's wiped and ready, sir."

Ross blinked at the maître d'.

Who told his passenger: "Why don't you have a cup of coffee?"

Ross followed the maître d's nod, felt that official follow him to the buffet.

The train whistle blew.

"All aboard!"

The Empire Builder lurched.

As steaming brown liquid streamed from the buffet urn into his fresh white Styrofoam cup, Ross told no one, told the world: "I take milk in my coffee."

Bodacious Della clumped past him, snapped: "Like the world gives a shit."

Ross sat at the cleaned table by the window holding that cup of coffee with milk as the train rumbled out of the mountain town famous for fun-times skiing, snowboarding and snowmobile machines with *Varrom!* engines echoing over a white landscape sporting wild Christmas trees and a huge lake, that idyllic cozy incomes town where in the basement of the public library, "Aryan Nationalists" had recently shown a movie that insisted the WWII death camps' holocaust many Montanans witnessed, fought and died to stop was an elaborate *never-happened* hoax—and that Something Should Be Done.

Ross held his cooling coffee as he sat at that table while the train *clackety-clacked* out of that town, through green forests and open pastures, land still mountainous, but now the train had crossed the spine of America, heading east.

He muttered: *"What just happened?"*

Left the Dining Car.

Walked through the train.

Neared his designated car where he knew Nora's cabin—

A woman screamed.

32

In the Observation Car on the Empire Builder eastbound that April morning, Suzanne huddled with Albert in 'their' chairs, the shoulder bag cradled on his lap as her ruby lips whispered: "How much time do we have *until*?"

Albert said: "Eight hours, more or less. Depending on when . . ."

"When I get him to the Dining Car," said Suzanne. "What about you?"

"I get off at Fargo. Sixteen hours. So I'll still . . . be around to help you."

"You don't have to do that."

"Nothing better left for me to do."

"That's a Hell of a thing," she whispered.

"Hell of a thing."

That military family sat at the opposite end of the Observation Car.

Ulysses sat on his family's perimeter.

Just be here, he told himself. Let go. Watch. Don't worry.

Mir nudged her mom to come back to their suite with her.

"Like," said the teenage daughter, "no way do I shower in that cabin all alone with the *clackety-clack* so loud nobody would even hear me scream."

Her mom's mind raced: *Yes, please let me come and hang out with you!*

But Isabella was too savvy to show such excitement.

Shrugged: *Oh, all right, sure.*

Malik barely knew what they were doing as this domed glass tube Observation Car filled his eyes with awe.

Silver werewolf Graham sat across the aisle from all of them. Sat on the south side of that eastbound train. Sat in the middle of the car. Sat facing the direction the train *clackety-clacked.* Sat facing the door out/door in. Sat in something akin to zen as he rode trying not to think about where he'd never been.

Only those seven passengers rode in the Observation Car that morning as it lone whistled out of the mountains and into a vast ocean of golden prairie.

Malik spotted his first Big Empty wonder as the foothills flattened to rolling earth caged by weathered gray wooden rails.

Oh wow!

Half a dozen spackled gray and chestnut brown *real horses,* no bridles or saddles, *palunking* over the golden prairie, eating grass, raising their heads to watch the silver dragon roar past the pen that kept them from galloping free.

But look! A frisky brown colt trots away from the herd to chase our train!

Mir and Mom told Malik "See you later!" as they headed back to their suite where neither of them expected anything to be going on except the shower.

Dad told Malik something about how they were near a town called Browning. How the train was passing through "an Indian reservation," land that belonged to a tribe called Blackfeet.

So are their feet like mine? flitted through Malik's imagination.

The train rumbled across a black iron trestled bridge over a blue river into a town called Cut Bank. Dad said *those are stockyards*: fences around churned brown bare earth holding *actual cattle* like hamburgers come from and—

Oh My God!

A puffy dead cow lay between the train tracks and the stockyard fence.

Are those flies buzzing around her face?

Malik hurried down to the middle of the car, peered out the other side of windows at the cluster of houses this train was *clackety-clacking* through.

Sitting-there, black hoodie Graham—who'd eaten breakfast with Malik's family and so was OK, *right?*—said: "Looks like just another nowhere town."

Malik shrugged. "We're here."

"That we are, Little Man. And maybe *way back when*, there were a lot more people here. Maybe the high school was full. Maybe they had dances. Lunch room tables pushed aside. Smells like . . . hormones and hair spray. Out of town guys, they'd come. Shy. Awkward. Risk it. Ask that local girl, blonde hair, ask her to dance. She'd smile *yes*. Walk you out onto the dance floor and *oh, man*: she'd hold your hand, intertwine her fingers with yours like nobody ever had or ever would again. Like an angel with your same pimples. You dance one dance. Find out her name: *Mitzy*. Then that song was over. She'd smile. Walk away."

Malik said: "Where did she go?"

"Where did they all go, Little Man? Where did all the Mitzys go?"

Malik shrugged.

Felt Mom and Dad's eyes on his back making sure he was OK. *Why wouldn't he be?* He was with the family breakfast friend Graham.

"Look!" cried Malik, pointing out the windows.

Space aliens!

More than a hundred white steel tower invaders 10 stories tall and topped by three *huge* slow-spinning white metal blades occupied the golden prairie.

"Windmills," Graham told him. "A wind farm."

That's what you think, thought Malik, but he didn't contradict the adult.

Major Ulysses Doss, USMC, *Dad*: "Malik, come look."

On the northern horizon far beyond the tracks rose three cobalt blue *humps* the size of what most people would call *mountains* but here were labeled mere *hills*, the Sweet Grass Hills.

The first one is best, decided Malik. Like a muscular 9 on its flat side.

On the far end of the Observation Car, Suzanne flicked her eyes from that adorable boy, found Albert's sad smile.

Albert whispered to her: "There's something I want you to have."

He unsnapped a clasp on his shoulder bag with a *click*.

Shallow gasps through her ruby lips.

Click as Albert unsnapped the second clasp.

Her heart pounding so hard the whole train shook.

Albert lifted his shoulder bag's flap.

Suzanne saw the shiny metallic gleam of a thermos.

Albert reached inside the bag, brought out his closed fist. Held his fist toward her. Turned his hand over, palm to the sky, his fist opening to offer . . .

A tiny silver metal bird.

"Spotted it in the twisted steel of a wrecked car's bumper," Albert told her. "Used shears, ballpeen hammer. The bumper stunk like burned metal, gasoline, but knocking *this* out of *that*, smell went away. Got the wings to V. Get the balance just right, it stands on its two legs and tail."

Her open palm floated up beside his.

His free hand transferred the silver bird to hers.

The touch of their hands. Their skin. Warm flesh.

Suzanne heard Albert's words.

"Was gonna put it in a tree by the creek before . . . you know. But now that feels wrong. Feels like a waste. Feels like it belongs with you, 'n' maybe down the road, when it's just you . . . Something to remember. Something to let be."

Suzanne heard the *clicks* of his shoulder bag closing.

Sensed Albert stand.

Heard him say: "When you need me for . . . I'll be there."

Saw him turn and walk out of the Observation Car.

Held a silver bird in the palm of her hand.

33

Erik eased open the sliding door into their cabin. Saw Terri slumped on the unmade lower bunk where she'd slept alone the whole night before.

She was dressed in her loosest *proper for work* tan slacks and baggiest of tattered pink political sweatshirts that covered her heart and her breasts he ached for her to want him to see, to touch, to kiss, to—

The white Styrofoam cup of coffee trembled in his hand.

Erik lied to himself that the trembles were just because of the train.

Quick glance!

Across the room by the wall window showing the train's emergence from the rule of the mountains on that sunny Friday morning sat Erik's zipped-shut computer bag, still positioned at that certain angle and draped under his jacket that he 'somehow' had not taken the time to hang up like he always did.

His laptop inside its bag. Just riding the train. Undisturbed.

Not that he worried even if Terri would have stirred herself to use or snoop on his laptop while he was out of the cabin. She didn't know his password.

All we've got to do is make it to Chicago.

Terri's eyes refused to look at Erik when he came back into their room. She stared at her cellphone screen even though she had nowhere to swipe.

"I brought you coffee," said Erik.

Terri didn't look up from her screen to see him standing there.

"You said you didn't want me to bring any breakfast back for you," he told her as she still didn't look at him, "but . . ."

"Oh. Yes." Terri sat straighter and out of her slump.

Took the carry-away cup of coffee he'd made with her preferred dose of cream and just a shake of low-cal sweetener.

She saw him nod to the cellphone in her hand.

"Anything new?" he said, having already sat in the Dining Car and read what his phone's screen told him was *The News*, right down to the bodacious booty celebrity's latest sigh of nothing.

"Is there ever anything new?" muttered Terri.

"Everything big doesn't always make the news."

"Everything *is* the news." Terri's voice was flat. Distant. "We've lost control of how things used to be. Of the boxes. How to stack life's everything. How—"

A woman screamed.

34

R oss ran toward the woman's scream.

Passengers filled doorways of this train car. *His car.* Pulled back at the crashing approach of his charging feet, the blur of his running shape.

Call bells went *ding*.

Constance stumbled into the train car aisle. Her trembling right hand fluttered back toward the open door of her suite.

In there . . . on the floor . . .

Mugzy.

"He's dead!" cried the woman who loved him.

The rat dog lay twisted, legs thrust out from his contorted body, lips pulled back in a lock-jawed sneer. Black eyes wide open.

Ross crouched beside the dead dog.

"Don't touch him!" Erik eased into the suite and also crouched near the corpse. "I mean, be careful. What if he's got something contagious to people?"

"No," sobbed Constance. "Mugzy-Wugzy and I went to the vet day before we got on the train and he said, the doctor said, he said . . ."

Memory drowned in her wail as she staggered back into her suite while Ross heard Attendant Cari proclaim: "It's OK, folks! Nothing to worry about."

Cari called for backup with her hip-holstered radio.

"'We all die sometime," Ross told Erik as they rose to stand corpse-side.

"BUT NOT NOW!" wailed Constance. Her face flooded with tears as Ross's face flushed red with embarrassment for having too loudly spoken the truth.

"I'm sorry!" said Ross.

"It's OK," whispered Erik beside him. "It's what we're all thinking."

Ross exchanged names with this man who'd probably die about the same time as him—barring global environmental collapse/toxicity, raging war, plague, political turmoil, prison, cancer, DNA failure, or some random-or-not bullet.

Ross saw Erik's disheveled pink sweatshirt girlfriend outside the suite.

The Conductor moved past her, stepped into the suite, grunted.

"Gotta maintain," the Conductor told Cari.

SWAT's L.T. muscled into the death suite without asking permission.

L.T.'s eyes lingered on Ross, who'd given him trouble back in Seattle.

The Conductor shook his head at L.T. "This isn't your thing."

The SWAT boss did his own look/see.

Muttered: "Yeah, we don't pick up the dead."

The grieving old woman sobbed and sank onto a bunk against the wall, her back toward the ceaseless forward of the train's *clackety-clack.*

"Good luck," L.T. told the Conductor without noticing the trainman's scowl.

Then SWAT moved on.

Constance sobbed on one lower bunk.

Ross and Erik sat on the other lower bunk facing her.

Mugzy lay on the floor between them.

Still dead.

"What do I do now?" said Constance. "Sit in the house Daddy left me? Turn on TV? Watch who I'll never get to be? Mugzy, if he's gone, what happens to me?"

The train *clackety-clacked*, the windows filling with a golden prairie sea.

> *Dogs die on the tracks.*
> *Dogs die on the train.*
> *These are our stacks.*
> *This is our pain.*

Ross yearned to reach for his belt-tucked black journal to capture that poem. Wondered if he dared make *Dead Dog On The Empire Builder* part of his gig's article. Knew that would never survive his boss's DELETE key.

Someone outside the suite brought something to the Conductor.

The Conductor turned to his grieving passenger: "Ma'am, we're all sorry about what's happened."

"So sorry," said Attendant Cari.

"We'll work out the details with you," said the Conductor. "Help any way we can. Honor your ticket, of course. But right now . . . There's one thing we got to do."

From behind the Conductor's back came a black plastic trash bag.

"No!" whined the tear-streaked woman. "He's not garbage!"

"Wait!" said Ross. "I got this."

He rushed down the train car's empty aisle to his cabin. Slid his door open with a *whirr* and the hope he'd find *her*, but *no*: his cabin was empty.

Attendant Cari had folded his bed back into a black leather couch.

His black nylon computer bag bulged with his laptop, cords, pens, two tattered paperback *noir* crime novels he'd long loved and just scored from a sidewalk FREE table, an anthology of poets he hoped to be worthy of someday.

Ross emptied his bag of all that.

Made it back into the death suite just as Erik asked: "Why Shelby?"

"'Cause it's coming up," said the Conductor. "Shelby, Montana."

"Because it's a crossroads," said Attendant Cari. "Since cowboy days. Got the east-west highway. Got the north-south Interstate, too. Only 87 miles to an airport where you—*she*—can catch a plane. Good people in Shelby."

"Not killer tough like it was in my dad's day," said the Conductor. "They was good then, too, but, blink of an eye."

"Times change," said Cari.

"Do they," said Ross.

"Hate to ask," the Conductor told the younger men. "But you two . . ."

"You two got a good touch with her," said Cari.

Talking like the tear-stained Constance wasn't in the room.

Erik and Ross nodded *yes, sure.*

"Ma'am," said Cari, "these two gentlemen will help you. But again, it's your choice, as far as the health codes let us give you. You can either get off in Shelby with . . . Or you can ride the rest of your ticket."

The broken old woman stared at the corpse. "I can't leave him."

"OK then," said the Conductor.

Ross flipped open his shoulder bag.

Erik unbuttoned and shrugged out of his shirt, a *Come Together* T-shirt the only thing now covering his rippling muscles. Erik slid his outer wear under the body and helped Ross ease that wrapped sorrow into the laptop bag.

"Don't got much time," said the Conductor.

"Buzz if you need anything," said Cari.

As they went out, Mom Isabella and teenage Mir came in.

Mir embraced Constance. Sat on the bed beside her. Held the old woman against her strong young shoulder.

What can you say for something like this? wondered the teenage military family member who'd already had to worry about those questions far too often. *How can I help? What should I do?*

Her mom Isabella said: "We'll help you pack."

She too well knew about when death came to someone's quarters.

As the train *clackety-clacked.*

35

Malik's eyes turned from that tiny silver bird in the ruby-lipped woman's hand to the Observation Car windows as the train chugged into a new town.

Look! Malik silently yelled.

Out there on a hill in the middle of town, *wow*, it's like . . .

A sand-colored castle four stories tall!

That flag-flying sandstone brick castle was the county courthouse built by President Franklin Delano Roosevelt's WPA federal dollars as part of his "bubble-up" from local America rather than "trickle down" from the skyscrapers of Wall Street plan to save the country from The Great Depression.

Malik didn't care.

He only wondered: *Are there ghosts in there?*

Oh, *wow!*

Zombies On A Train . . . *plus* . . . Ghosts In The Castle

This trip can't get any better!

Closing in on the town, half a dozen tracks ran parallel to the rails riding this train east. Lines of parked freight train cars filled those tracks. Some of those huge rectangular cargo carriers showed sliding doors for Woody Guthrie hobos. A few of those freight train cars were rusty gray. Some of them were reddish brown. But what Malik mostly saw were dozens and dozens of freight cars exactly the same, colored gold and logoed with huge black letters:

CHINA TRANS . . . CHINA TRANS . . . CHINA TRANS . . .

"Your attention, please! This stop, Shelby, Montana. Shelby, Montana, this stop. We'll only be here for about 11 minutes, so if you get off the train, stay close. Shelby, Montana, coming up."

The train Malik rode groaned. Steel screeched. He felt a shudder and lurch forward that wasn't enough to let him escape falling back. Brakes hissed and the silver dragon clawed its way into Shelby's train depot.

36

"Shelby, Montana," boomed the train loudspeaker for a fourth and final time. Steel wheels screed over shiny rails. The train shuddered. Full stop.

In the death suite, Erik told Ross: "I got her bags."

His arms bundled a suitcase, a purse and a bedazzled crafts bag as he sidestepped out of the suite. He clunked down the switchback stairs to where Attendant Cari punched in the keypad code, flipped four metal handles and the long steel lever to open the metal door.

Ross slid the body bag's strap over one shoulder.

Offered his other arm to crumpled Constance.

They reached the stairs down as the train car door opened.

In flooded morning sunlight.

Fifty steps down the length of the train toward its rear waited a peeling white paint depot mounted with black letters reading SHELBY. Down that way as he led the funeral march off the train, Erik saw passengers disembarking. Watchful depot workers.

He set Constance's luggage on the wooden platform.

Ross and the broken old woman shuffled off the train.

Mir followed the old woman.

Attendant Cari told the volunteers: "The local stationmaster will help her as soon as he can, but probably not until after we pull out."

Erik gave Constance a condolence touch on her limp arm in that sage brush & dust smelling prairie breeze. Got back on the train.

Ross walked to the luggage pile.

On top of it he *gently* put the baby-sized body bag.

Looked away from where the lonely old woman and her teenager friend stood hugging in the oppression between this *tick* of now and that *tock* of then.

Endless blue sky cupped the small town. Its depot parking lot held five cars. Ross saw empty streets. Vacant lots of *once was*. Across the street from the depot parking lot rose a two-story, flat brick building boarded-up beneath a long red sign with bold white letters: OIL CITY BAR, not "The Bucket Of Blood" nickname that vanished saloon was known by during the town's good years when Ross's father—and his fellow passenger Graham—had been cruising teenagers.

SWAT troopers from the train clustered down the platform, a watchful deployment as a rusted yellow forklift backed away from the open door of the Baggage Car. Ross glimpsed a hand truck, a solo-user, electric-powered, weight-moving machine called a "pallet jack" being rolled back inside that train car's open dark maw. Two civilians in work clothes hopped out of there, gave a nod to the watching local stationmaster and SWAT's L.T.

Two SWAT troopers stood in a Do Not Cross line near the door into Ross's train car and before whatever was going on at the Baggage Car.

Sergeant Michael Carlisle was the closest SWAT trooper to Ross. Sgt. Carlisle brought young trooper David Hale to stand this post with him so the new trooper could "watch and learn"—

—and so the sergeant could find out what, if anything, L.T. told trooper Hale when they went on their pie and donuts runs.

L.T.'s command, thought Sgt. Carlisle, *but my crew.*

He gave a nod of recognition/respect to the civilian helping the old lady. Got one back from Ross.

The Baggage Car's aluminum door rolled down, closed.

L.T. fastened sophisticated padlocks to hold it in place. Tapped commands into a keypad. Worked the mic of a belt radio. Barked an order to the SWAT troopers deployed on the platform.

Blue-uniformed SWATs hustled into the Crew Car next to the Baggage Car. Sgt. Carlisle about-faced to join them, trooper Hale fell in step.

Trooper Hale looked back at Ross, who was older than him. At the teenage girl who was too young for either of them. At the trickling tears woman who could have easily been Trooper Hale's grandmother standing slumped by the pile of her luggage topped by a shoulder bag containing a bulge, a lump.

Trooper Hale wished he knew what more he could do here.

The train whistle blew.

Attendant Cari yelled as if the whole world had to hear: "All aboard!"

Further up the depot platform, Ross saw an obviously married couple slightly older than him who turned their gaze away from whatever was going on down where he stood. The married couple boarded the train. Ross saw a stocky man with tattooed arms and a bad haircut board the train.

Mir stood on the wooden platform of a town she'd never been before and would never be again. The teenager met an old woman's teary eyes with her own shining stare. Hugged the woman whose name and chocolate she'd never forget.

Hurried up the stairs to her mother's forever embrace.

Ross squeezed Constance's shoulder.

Left her standing there beside what she had and what she'd lost. Looking nowhere as she was left in this town where no one knew her name or her pain.

Attendant Cari pulled the train door shut behind Ross.

The whistle blew.

The train lurched, groaned, rumbled forward.

Ross climbed the inside stairs to the top level of this train car and—

Grabbed! Somebody's grabbed me!

Nora. Her cheeks streaked with tears she couldn't deny, her smeared scarlet lips behind her *Shh!* finger as she pulled him . . .

. . . into the deserted death suite.

She closed the door. Latched it. Shut that curtain. Her hand slid into his shirt pocket with its crinkle of cellophane-wrapped lemon drops. Lifted his phone out. Powered it off. Shoved it in a drawer with her own phone. Stuffed white towels over them until the drawer was so full she could barely cram it shut. They both knew she did that to mitigate someone anywhere turning their phones on to listen to what was being said in range of their devices' microphones.

"All my fault!" she sobbed. "Didn't mean to, but I did!"

"*What*, what didn't you mean to—"

"I killed Mugzy," she sobbed. "But I didn't mean to, I . . . I . . ."

Ross felt his life spin as the train picked up speed *clackety-clack*.

As Nora said: "I meant to kill you."

37

hy did you try to kill me?"

"Because we're robbing the train."

38

ho's *we?*"

"I don't know."

39

Graham angled his head by the Observation Car wall of windows to get a better view down to the Shelby, Montana depot's platform.

Something's going on down there, he thought.

Not my concern—or so the odds said.

So going to check—well, that wasn't his ride.

You're either on the train or the train's gone.

The little boy Malik swooped out of his train seat like he was a fighter plane. Arms out like wings, his *zoomies* ran him up and down the aisle in this car where his father kept watch and the ruby-lipped wife sat slumped, alone again.

Graham let go of all that as he sat there and sank into his center.

He didn't keep track of time. *Why bother, it keeps track of you.*

The train whistle blew.

The train lurched. Crawled through the old cowboy town.

Graham stared down from the Observation Car window. Saw Mugzy's beloved standing all by her old lonesome self on the bare wooden platform beside a pile of luggage as the silver train slid past her crying eyes.

Why did life throw her off this train?

His bones recognized that slump of grief and sorrow and despair. He'd seen it more times than he could count. Black-robed widows on Afghan streets. The sobbing children of Beirut. Families lined along a slit trench above rice fields in Asia. A mournful procession in Italy. A dignified walk in Paris. El Salvador. Mexico where the murdered hung from bridges. On a perfect San Francisco afternoon. Cleveland. And Brooklyn, oh that time in Brooklyn.

And Graham knew despair slumped her where she sat. Where she had to be. Where she knew nowhere else to go, no one else to be. Not *doing*: a *done* waiting to be tallied and shuffled on to a *next* she cared nothing for.

Whunk: The Observation Car door slid open.

Graham watched Isabella and her daughter Mir hurry in searching for their father, their brother, for their here and now.

Ulysses realized his daughter's cheeks glistened from no shower.

"She helped someone who needed it," said Isabella as her husband folded their daughter into his arms on this *wobble wobble* ride.

Graham heard Mir's sobbed, babbled, blurted-out story about how on their way to the shower they *saw* and *heard* and *did*.

That family filled cushioned seats. Stared out the windows.

Blood-lipped Suzanne closed her fist over one tiny silver bird.

Let the sunlight outside the windows wash over her face.

The train picked up speed as it passed a clutch of giant gray towers.

"Grain elevators," Ulysses told his family. "Wheat."

Mom said: "Give us this day our daily bread."

Malik pointed into a passing nearby field: "What's that?"

Floodlights ringed a chain-link fence surrounding concrete slabs.

Everyone in his family felt Ulysses tense.

"Missile silo," whispered Major Doss, USMC. "Mushroom cloud atom bombs on top of missiles 90 feet underground. Waiting for someone to push the button. Waiting down there since Grampa was a kid. Dynamite blows the concrete doors off the silos. In the hole, engines ignite, smoke, roar, a missile lifts off the pad . . ."

And Dad said no more.

Graham heard what Ulysses *didn't* say.

Moved to sit on the other side of the Observation Car.

A car-sized wooden roadside sign swayed in the wind at a Scenic Overlook pull-off for the two-lane blacktop highway paralleling the train tracks.

Graham couldn't read the black letters burned into that Tourist Attraction sign about the Marias Massacre of 1870 a few miles south of there when more than 200 mostly women, children and elderly Blackfeet Indians in their camp were slaughtered by U.S. Cavalry troopers. The Indians' chief Heavy Runner was shot dead while waving a copy of their signed peace treaty.

Malik called out: "What are *they* doing?"

Everyone in the Observation Car—the Doss family, Suzanne, Graham—they all looked out Malik's window.

There, walking away from the train tracks trudged a dozen bundled people, women and men, two of them awkwardly muscling wheelbarrows piled high with suitcases. Even the children wore heavy backpacks.

"Where are they going?" asked Malik.

"North," said Graham.

Cool! thought Malik. *North like Stuart Little went in the best book ever written about someone in search of adventure and love!*

Mir said: "All that's up there is—"

"The border," muttered her mother. "Canada."

Ulysses sighed: "Refugees.

"Jesus," he whispered as the train *clackety-clacked*. "Where are we?"

Graham folded away from the window of woe. Left the Observation Car. The door closed behind him with a *whunk*.

Isabella said: "I wonder where he's going?"

Malik shrugged. "He's looking for Mitzy."

40

You're crazy!" Ross yelled at Nora inside the death suite.

She mumbled: "You gotta be crazy to keep from going insane."

Ross snarled: "Fuck your bullshit! Why did you try to kill me?"

"I thought I was just going to fuck you up." Her back pressed against the train windows flowing with golden prairie. "Was supposed to be like before!"

"What '*before*'?"

"Last night. After . . . I dissolved a *deep sleep* mega-Ambien in your water."

The loudspeaker announced that the Dining Car was serving lunch.

"Mugzy," said Ross. "What was in the orange juice?"

"Was supposed to be molly. A dance club drug. Knock you loopy. Make it so I had to—*got to*—take care of you. Manage you. Wasn't supposed to be murder.

"And maybe it wasn't!" she pleaded. "Maybe Mugzy just couldn't handle the high. That's gotta be it! Because the grift is just us robbing the train."

"Who's 'us'?"

"I don't know." She fought her tears. "I'm sorry!"

Ross swept his arm around the crime scene cabin: "This is so over."

He stepped backwards towards the door, kept his eyes on her.

Reached for the cabin's latched door—

—reached back, fumbled with the drawer that held his cell phone.

"No!" she cried. "You can't do that! You can't leave me or—"

He rushed her like a lunatic: "YOU'RE NOT THE BOSS OF *CAN!*"

"If you break way, tell anyone, he'll have to block or neutralize you!"

The man who Nora failed to poison glared at her tear-smeared face.

"Me, too," said Nora. "I'm the data link to him and the grift."

"Who's *him*?"

"I don't know. His handle is Zed."

"Save it for—"

"Who?" said Nora. "You going to call 911? We're on a train in Montana! Who's going to answer? You going to grab Attendant Cari? And tell her *what*? You going to roust the SWAT boss? You've got Ambien and THC in your blood. Probably illegal here lemon drops in your shirt pocket. Who will they believe? Who will they kick off the train? You've got no proof of anything if I say nothing. If you glitch the grift, Zed'll have to neutralize us *both*, even with the program I've got left to run. To stop the grift, vouch for you, I'd have to send myself to prison and paint a target on my back—*our* backs."

The woman who *he'd thought* slumped onto a bed.

Her glistening bloodshot brown eyes looked straight at Ross: "You were never supposed to be here *now*. Why did you have to be who you are?"

"You mean a reporter. Nobody gives a shit about a poet. Or who you fuck."

Nora went cold. Shook her head as she corrected him: "An *investigative* reporter. Who fucked up and glitched the grift in Seattle."

"The video I shot in the station."

"We can't have that out there, *in case*. I thought the new program was just because you filmed me, but probably you filmed Zed, too."

"So you . . ."

"I wiped out your everything while you were asleep."

"You mean drugged. You went through my journal, too."

"I just moved it out of the way. You hadn't had time to write much in it yet."

"Why did you do all that? For what?"

"I told you: we're robbing the train."

"Like Butch Cassidy and the Sundance Kid?"

Nora shook her head. "Don't be so old school."

"What's in the Baggage Car?" he said.

"Maybe millions of dollars."

"*Maybe?* Nobody does all this for a 'maybe.' *What's in the Baggage Car?*"

41

"What do you know about money?" Nora asked Ross.

"What song do you want to hear?" he said. "How money changes everything? How it makes the world go 'round? How it can't buy you . . ."

He didn't say the word his parents' Beatles made sure got heard.

She didn't look at him.

Said: "One thing all our songs forgot. Money *dies*."

Ross blinked.

"I'm not talking about international exchange rates or *adjusted for* values. Or cyber currency where it is *all* ones and zeroes fronting promises.

"Talking about cash," she said. "Greenbacks you stick in your wallet, your purse, the front pocket of your black jeans. All the presidents. Economists talk about a 'cashless society.' Cyber currency. Maybe someday. Not now.

"*Money makes the world go 'round*," she said. "Cash feeds the engine's fire."

She laughed. Not a real laugh. A gallows humor laugh.

"Fire," she said.

Looked at Ross.

Said: "Fire changes everything."

Shook her head.

"Two things you need to know about cash money," she told Ross.

"Number one: *Money wears out.*

"Number two: *Money burns.*"

He blinked.

"Everything wears out," continued Nora. "Even a concrete and steel fortress like a Federal Reserve Bank.

"We've got 12 of them in America. They're not for college savings accounts or loans to get a new car you can't function without. They're for overseeing the local banks. Managing economic policy. Trying to make sure our Beltway Bandits and Wall Street Wankers act nice and play safe.

"There's one in Seattle," said Nora. "And there's one in Chicago."

"Seattle to Chicago," said Ross. "The Empire Builder route."

"Yeah," whispered Nora. "Where this train is going."

She asked: "What do you do with paper money that's worn out?"

Answered her own question.

"All regular banks like where that asshole Brian is president sort worn-out, ragged, torn, scotch-taped bills every month and swap them for brand new printed bills shipped from the mint in Washington, D.C. The worn-out bills are sent to the nearest Federal Reserve Bank. A suitcase full of those *retired* greenbacks can add up pretty fast. And if you have more than a suitcase, more than 10 suitcases, if you have a seven by seven by seven feet cubed steel box . . .

"The Fed banks have giant furnaces. The worn-out bills are crammed into a burn box. Nobody bothers to log serial numbers. They're junk paper, money corpses. The Feds have guards, lots of them—not because they're expecting a holdup, but because a whole crew is harder to corrupt than just a couple badges.

"The guards watch each other and the techs who work the machines. The techs raise the burn boxes full of 'bad' bills over a furnace roaring way past Ray Bradbury's *Fahrenheit 451*. Burns up everything in the box—roaches, rats, trash. You try to look down that hole and watch, the heat'll melt your skull. Inferno shimmers make windows looking into the furnace impossible, too. Plus, there's gotta be a tight seal between where the furnace door slides open and where the burn box on top of it has its door slid open. *Nobody sees* but *everybody knows* that out of that steel cargo box tumbles a landslide of worn-out paper bills that incinerate the second they hit the heat."

Brakes groaned and the Empire Builder slowed.

Ross's eyes locked on Nora as he said: "That's what's in the Baggage Car."

The train engine chugged lower, louder as the silver steel dragon slowed.

"*Yes*," said Nora. "And *no*. It's what's in the Baggage Car *now*. Since that place called Shelby."

Grinding steel pulled Nora's eyes to the train car windows as the Empire Builder slowed into the depot at Havre, Montana, a town almost twice the size of '*that place called Shelby*' 103 miles back west on the tracks.

Nora blinked.

Flinched toward Ross from the sunlit windows showing where they were. Shock rocked her: "*Cops!*"

42

Ulysses and his family stared out the Observation Car window at the Havre train station. *Again* their eyes filled with images of SWAT warriors walking and waiting there outside the train. Unlike the SWAT team from Seattle that rode this train, this new crew of gunners wore black uniforms, and across their backs, white letters read "ICE" and "FEDERAL POLICE."

"This doesn't make any sense," whispered Ulysses.

"What the hell?" said teenager Mir. "This looks like . . . I don't know. China or Russia or some Nazi-land. Mexico that time we went to the beach."

"It's just like in Seattle," said mom Isabella. "Like you said before, Ulysses. Just . . . routine."

"Routine for what?" mumbled Dad. "For who? For why?"

"Look!" said Malik, though no one needed the boy's encouragement.

Their train's SWAT boss L.T. met one of the Havre warriors on the depot platform just past the Baggage Car where L.T.'s men set up a skirmish line facing the other armed force under that sunny blue Montana sky.

L.T. shook hands with his counterpart in the new troops.

"So they're on the same side," said Malik in the Observation Car. "Right?"

The two SWAT commanders exchanged words.

Parted ways.

The ICE boss strolled back to his own shuffling crew of badges.

L.T. marched back to the cordon of his troops.

Gave Sergeant Carlisle a nod.

Sergeant Carlisle checked left. Checked right. Made sure the line of troopers he'd set on post were standing tall.

The sergeant took position beside his greenest trooper.

"Eyes up," the sergeant told that young man named David Hale.

"Yes, Sergeant," answered Hale. "But why? Aren't those guys just like us?"

"You remember Cain and Abel?"

"No, Sergeant. Were they on the team before I got here?"

"Just stay alert, troop."

Civilians roamed the depot platform amidst the armed forces. The Amtrak station's crew. Citizens, some with suitcases. A mailman with heavy pouches slung from his shoulders. Some citizens walking tense, nervous. But no panic. The civilians trusted that they were safe. That everything was OK. And that whatever those two crews of warriors were doing was for their own good.

Though everyone's careful eyes showed all this felt . . . creepy.

"This isn't a coordinated link up, a reinforcement," said the Marine major. "The ICE squad isn't responding to the train SWAT team."

He sensed the stances of the dozen-plus ICE warriors outside this train. Snapshotted their faces, *where* they were looking, *how*. The hands gripping their fully automatic weapons. The sweep of their gazes.

"The ICE objective," said Ulysses. "Their deployment. Sure, posters on the train: *'Watch out for human trafficking.' 'See something, say something.'* But they're not sweeping for specific targets—and 40 miles south of Canada in the middle of nowhere, not likely they're operating from High Credibility intel about dangerous illegal immigrants swarming this depot or riding this train.

"Plus, the verified terrorists out here aren't infiltrating extremist Muslims or foreign agents. They're gun-heavy white militias or whacky religious cults. Conspiracy nuts armed to their teeth against figments of their online intoxications. Any policing of them wouldn't dare be so relaxed. Same with *narcos*. Even if any of that launched this Op, this massive show of force makes no sense. Could trigger a firefight reaction in the middle of an American town packed with legitimate gun owners and kids on the way to school and . . .

"*Presence Patrol,*" whispered the black-skinned Marine. "They're here to show us they're here. Not to *do* a mission, to *be* a presence."

"I don't understand," said military wife Isabella. "Why now? Why here?"

"Yeah," said Major Ulysses Doss, USMC. "Yeah."

Suzanne whispered yet that family heard: "It isn't supposed to be like this."

Malik blurted: "I've gotta go back to our cabin! Go the bathroom! Now!"

His family turned to watch him squirm.

"Don't worry, Dad!" said Malik. "Mom already taught me and Mir what kids like us got to do when we see a policeman."

Then Ulysses' beloved son, the child of a Marine who risked his life for this country again and again, who took bullets for democratic freedom, an American whose lineage went back six generations, 10-year-old chocolate-skinned Malik stilled his *gotta go!* wiggles as he stood in the aisle between rows of lounge chairs. Serious face. Looked straight ahead. Held his tiny arms low. Turned his palms out open and empty for all the world and every Officer Of The Law to see.

But the reaction *gotta-go* Malik got made no sense to him: *Why is Dad trembling and his face, he's . . . WHAT DID I DO WRONG?*

"OK," said dad Ulysses. "If you gotta go, you gotta go. And no worries, odds are, these gunners aren't looking for us.

"But I'm coming with you," the father told the son.

43

Zed stared into the mirror. *So* pleased with what he saw!

The mirror showed the Gods' truth about this train.

This is America. You can be anyone you want. Defy all odds. Any laws.

If you're both superb and willing—nay: *eager* to do what you've got to do.

But who's kidding who. Zed knew the big *do*s are beyond most people.

All those ordinary meat sacks in the streets of everywhere.

Not me *and* not you, Zed told the image in the mirror.

We rule. Even with all life's inevitable unpredictable complications.

Like the nosey reporter.

And the odd silver-haired man.

And now Nora, suddenly rewriting her programmed role.

Or like those police now milling around outside on Havre's depot platform. They weren't in Zed's program. But all he had to do was stay out of theirs.

Improvisation is an operating key to the best coders' programs.

Zed smiled.

Told the mirror: *Only you know and I know the real data flow.*

As he rewrote his program again.

44

Malik raced ahead of his father who got the buzz of a text just after they'd popped open the door to the train car with their suite.

Gotta go gotta go gotta go!

His sneakered feet pounded the train car aisle all the way to the door of his family's suite that was right across from the suite where Mugzy—

Never mind gotta go!

Shuffling from blue-jeaned leg to blue-jeaned leg on the now not-wobbling floor of the suite's tube bathroom, shiny metal everywhere, *hurry up, hurry up, don't catch your peeper in the zipper,* slide it down, fumble it out and aim—

Ahhh.

Sometimes life is all about making it to the toilet in time.

Whoosh went Malik's flush.

He washed his hands even though it had been *weeks* since he splashed or dribbled on them. Washed his hands because that was The Right Thing To Do.

Stepped out of the bathroom into the emptiness of his family's suite.

Whispered: "Dad?"

No reply.

Not that he was worried, *no*, or scared, *I mean . . .*

Zombies On A Train.

They're not real—right?

Malik saw a blur pass the cabin door. Hurried there. Jerked the door open. Looked to his right, the direction the blur—

There! Going down the switchback stairs!

The writer man and the *funny kind of red hair* woman: Malik recognized them as their heads sank out of sight.

Look! thought Malik: *My friend Graham's going down the stairs after them.*

Malik looked left.

Spotted his dad standing back down that aisle where they'd come into this car, cellphone in his hand—his *Don't Touch! Corps* phone.

Malik smelled coffee from around a corner near the top of those stairs.

Then . . . *Oh!* The smells of cool blue sky sunshine. Earth.

The train car door must be open, thought Malik. That's where the writer man and the reddish-haired woman went, Graham behind them. Everything's just down those stairs, *so close.*

Malik saw Dad still On The Phone, texting.

The draft of cool spring air intoxicated the 10-year-old.

He saw his dad pause—

—knew from the way Dad kept his eyes on the phone in his hand that the Must Be Very Important texts weren't silent yet.

"Dad," called Malik from near their cabin door, clearly safe and knowing what he was doing. "Can I go and just like, *feel* the fresh air?"

Ulysses turned away from his phone. Saw his eager son. Looked out the train windows, the Havre depot platform where . . .

Yes, armed troops, but many wearing shoulder patch American flags. Civilians and Amtrak employees milling about. No visible peril. Or *tactical action.*

The phone in Ulysses' hand buzzed Text Message.

He gave his wonderful, obedient, do-right son The Look.

Called down the aisle to him: "You can go to the door but do not—*I say again*—do not get off the train."

The fifth grade boy waved and grinned.

His dad went back to his screen and a message from Gunny.

Malik started toward the switchback stairs—

"Ah, good, it's you!" called out a man standing in the aisle's jog that made an alcove where a counter held a shiny metal aluminum pot of coffee before the aisle became a long corridor past the cabins for the other Premium passengers.

Malik turned to the man's voice.

Thought . . . *maybe* . . . Don't I recognize him?

"Perfect timing." That adult poured coffee into a white Styrofoam cup encased in a brown paper insulated sleeve. "You and Ulysses—I mean, your dad—you're friends of that nice old man Graham, right?"

Malik nodded as the man snapped a white lid on the Styrofoam cup.

"Thanks, thought so, and you're a . . . well, OK, not *really* a soldier yet, but do you know how to get things done?"

Malik nodded: *Of course I do! But it'll be 'Marine,' not 'soldier.'*

"Good, 'cause we can't bother your dad when he's on the phone, and Cari—the woman who's your attendant on the train, Cari? She asked me to get coffee to Graham, but she was in such a hurry—you know how grownups get—she didn't remember that I've got a messed-up leg. Purple heart, no complaints, but going down stairs . . .

"Can you to take the cup down to Graham? But like your dad says—*he's right and he's the boss*—don't get off the train. If Graham got off, hand it to him when he gets back on. If she's around—*Don't embarrass her, right?*—don't mention it, and if she's not, tell him Attendant Cari thought he could use this. Who knows why, right? If you miss Graham down there, just come on back up the stairs, walk the aisle to the cabins, I think he's in . . . Is it Cabin B?"

Malik shrugged.

"You got it," said he who self-identified as a wounded war veteran.

"Remember," said the man as he handed Malik the hot-to-hold, brown-sleeved white cup of *smells like coffee*. "Obey your dad. Do what's gotta be done."

Then that adult turned and Malik watched him limp away.

Malik stood tall.

Yeah! Didn't matter he was just a kid! He was a *get it done* guy.

And Miss Cari *the Attendant* had a great smile that made Malik feel . . .

He didn't know what, but he wanted to make her happy.

Plus, of course, do the right thing.

Malik carried the hot cup of coffee with his locked-steady left hand. His right hand took the railing leading toward the cool of the outside air coming up through the train's open door.

The boy started down those switchback stairs.

Cops!" said Nora cowering beside Ross and staring out the window of the train's death suite at the Havre depot. "They're not in the program!"

Ross said: "You're not in charge of the program."

Nora whirled like a 180 degree *fouetté* turn in the modern dance class she took Tuesday and Thursday nights and yelled: "*NEITHER ARE YOU!*"

She punched her hammer fist toward Ross's chest.

His veteran boxer's arm shot up to block her punch—

—that she pulled short, a refusal of touch.

She hit him with words.

"You're in! You're out! You're on the train! You don't know! Well, let's go take care of *you!*"

Nora blew past where he stood. Jerked open the drawer by the sink crammed with linen and their cellphones. Threw a white towel at Ross's face. Grabbed both phones and stormed out the door.

Didn't look back to see if Ross followed her or not.

She stomped past the alcove where Attendant Cari kept a *smell it* pot of coffee simmering, the same alcove where the night before Nora'd gotten—

Now Nora turned the corner. Stomped down the switchback stairs.

Ross hurried behind her.

Nora spotted Cari at the bottom of the stairs turning from the just-opened train car door to see who was charging her way.

Nora braked beside Cari at the open door to *out there.*

Announced: "I'm getting off the train."

"OK," said Cari to the *kinda quirky* Cabin G woman as the Cabin D man jerked to a halt beside them. "If you wanna."

"I mean," said Cari as the three of them sensed the arrival of another passenger: "Out there kinda looks like The Two Fs."

"No," said Graham as he flowed to the open door. "The Fourth F."

Ross frowned: "Not just *Fight* or *Flight?*"

"*Fight* or *Flight* misses the third F that traps too many people: *Freeze.*"

Then from deep inside the silver werewolf came a smile.

Came: "I've always been a Fourth F kind of soul."

His eyes filled with the heavily armed world outside the train he rode.

And he said: *"Fuck it."*

Graham's eyes pushed Cari.

Who pulled the white stepstool out of its cubby beneath the fire extinguisher. Swung her way out of the silver train car and set the stool on the wooden platform at the train station in sunny afternoon Havre, Montana.

Nora watched Graham stride down the stairs off the train.

Said: "Exactly. *Fight* or *Flight, Freeze* or *Fuck It.*"

Stepped off this train to go her own way.

Didn't look back.

Ross stalked her like an angry shadow.

Coffee-carrying Malik reached the open door in time to see those three passengers who got off the train march away in two different directions.

Like some showdown in a movie! he thought.

The boy eased his head out the train car door.

Saw no zombies.

No castle ghosts.

Malik held Graham's steaming hot coffee as that silver-haired man marched to the right, closer to the new SWAT crew.

The chocolate cherry haired woman marched to the left, closer to the train's SWAT crew.

The writer guy marched right behind her, *so close!*

April's breeze carried small town sounds. The hissing of the train's steam breaks. The chug of its idling engine. A car horn far away on Main Street.

Those sounds plus the distance between everyone else in the universe and this couple on the vast platform of the Havre depot kept what they said secret.

Nora whirled to face Ross. Shoved his cellphone into his hands.

"There!" snapped Nora as Ross grasped his device that connected him to everywhere. "There you are. Here you go. Go tell the train SWATs whatever you want. Or go the other way, tell your story to those cops who came out of nowhere. Call whoever the fuck. Fuck the train and your two-bit gig. You got your phone. You got your poems stuffed down your pants. Get out of here. Get away from *CRAZY* robber *murderer* me. Run. Hide."

"Is that what you want?" said Ross.

Nora's hands flew up in exasperation. She groaned frustration. Growled anger. Turned this way. Turned that. Her face twisted with words she couldn't summon. One instant she looked like she was strangling the wind. The next instant she was waving her arms with silent screams as she marched tight jerky psycho circles under the afternoon's blue sky.

Gunners in each of the SWAT squads tracked her rage between their posts as they stood deployed at each end of that long silver train.

Facing each other. Weapons . . . *sure*, at ease. Eyes open.

Eyes that watched the three passengers who'd burst off the train.

The angry stomping woman and the hard-faced man agitated nearer the train's SWAT crew and the alert eyes of Sgt. Carlisle and trooper David Hale.

The silver-haired man in all black—shoes, jeans and a hoodie he refused to let hide his silvered skull and electric face—he claimed a wide and empty space alongside the train closer to the local SWAT cops, the Boys Who'll Pull You Down.

Graham stood between the two gun-heavy crews of Officially Sane Society on that empty stretch of the depot's gray platform wood.

He stood where every badged gunner couldn't help but see.

Hands at his sides. Draped eyes. Stilled monkey mind.

The silver dragon train hissed.

Graham let his hands float up and out as if to brush the air, pulled them back to his chest, then swept them down as if he'd caught some phantom and was guiding the specter to its knees. He turned and stepped to his right as his arms cradled an imaginary beach ball. Flowed a left step to face the train. His left arm softly rose horizontal in front of his chest to sense what was there. His right arm angled along his side like his palm cupped a rushing up geyser.

T'ai chi.

Sure, an old man stretching from a long ride on the train.

And *yes*, an artistry of "moving meditation."

Plus, a blend of Western motion therapies and Chinese medicine to stimulate the Harvard-studied, neural-pulmonary process called *chi*.

But what Graham chose to vibe in front of The Guns Of Gotchya with his postures and slow flowing turns on that train depot platform revealed itself also as a martial ballet cracking arms, concussing brains and repelling attackers.

All played out as Graham's right to *do*, his cosmic due, his Fuck It *woo-hoo*.

Nora raged in Ross's face.

Only he heard her words.

"*What I want?*" She glared in the face of *the man who she'd*. "What I want is no more of this shit! What I want is outta here!"

Nora stomped back toward the door to get back on the train.

Two gun-heavy ICE warriors stepped out of that car. They'd done their slow *see and be seen* walk-through of the whole train—well, through the lower level, cheaper seats, one slow *here we are* step at a time.

Only Nora heard Ross's call.

"*Hey!*"

She stopped. Turned to face him.

Ross said: "I've got a train to ride, too."

Two heartbeats.

They didn't touch as they turned to face the door to get back on.

Side by side, walked that way.

Graham's parallel arms lay straight out at heart level—*whoosh*: his black soft-shoed right foot swooped an arc brushing his open face-down palms.

Steam hissed under the steel dragon train.

Standing near the door to '*her*' car, Cari checked her watch.

The train whistle screamed.

The Conductor bellowed: "All aboard!"

Graham flowed from a punch to striding toward the door from whence he'd come. He'd practiced his choreographed combat closer to the train than Nora and Ross's real fight, so he was *way* ahead of them in reaching the train door.

Standing in the train car's open door was the smiling 10-year-old boy Malik from breakfast. He shyly offered Graham a cup of *smells like coffee*.

"Thanks," Graham told Malik as he took that warm cup from the boy's nervous hand. "Just what I needed."

Nora saw that happen.

Saw the coffee cup transfer from the boy to Graham.

Saw the ghost of that Snapchat message shimmer in the air:

Don't worry about B father.
U fix the dipshit guy filming
w/his phone. I'll work
Mr. Nosey old man in black.

Charged toward the train door!

Ross chased her across the depot platform in front of all those eyes.

In front of the SWATs from the train, Sgt. Carlisle and trooper David Hale.

In front of the local ICE *Boys Who'll*.

In front of anyone who was looking out the train's nine cars of windows.

In front of Cari, who waited a few steps from where Graham stood on the platform, the cup of handed-down coffee rising to his lips.

Running Nora launched an arms-reaching lunge—

—slammed into Graham.

Their crash knocked the coffee cup from his grasp.

The lid popped off that Styrofoam cup.

Brown liquid splashed the silver train.

The white cup bounced off the platform, under the train, past steel wheels where no one would be foolish enough to risk going for it.

In front of all those eyes—

—SWATs of both sides, stunned Cari, scared Malik, everyone looking out the train's windows—

—Graham eyeballed the man and woman who'd attacked him.

Said what only they could hear:

"We better come up with a great *cover your ass* story."

46

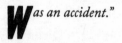as an accident."

47

Malik had to tell Dad the truth:

Was him who handed the cup of coffee to that man Graham for Miss Cari, but Malik didn't spill it.

"Good," said his Dad.

They stood in the upper-level aisle outside their suite as the train picked up the speed of its *clackety-clack* out of Havre, a dwindling prairie city with an underground mall that in cowboy days housed three Chinese opium dens.

Dad nodded to the windows of what had gone by.

"Saw you didn't get off, either." Ulysses rubbed his son's head, knowing that hugging Malik in this semi-private passenger car aisle was *these days* now something the boy simultaneously didn't and did want.

"Mom and Sis are still in the Observation Car," said Ulysses as the phone in his hand buzzed *incoming*. "Give me just a couple minutes and . . ."

Father read Son's look of eagerness crushed.

"Tell you what," said Ulysses. "You handled solo good, coffee cup and all. Why don't you go on ahead. Alone.

"I'll be right there," said Ulysses the father as he watched his son's face beam *Yes!* as Major Doss, USMC thumbed the screen on his cellphone to get the latest *How Bad Is It?* from that day's crisis for Corps and Country.

And for him.

The *whunk* of a train car door sliding open.

Malik—*gone.*

48

Only the three passengers still sat in the Dining Car for lunch as the Empire Builder *clackety-clacked* out of Havre.

Banker Brian shook his head.

Why does that Al guy keep showing up?

Sitting across from me in this empty eating car. Even that snotty maître d' and the waitress disappeared after they delivered *Steak Oh Pover Do Salad* or some damn French that meant *'this sure as hell isn't steak.'* Why the hell would you mix slices of prime cut beef with chopped green plants, tomatoes, cucumbers and—*OK, it was tasty*—raspberry vinegar dressing?

That's not lunch.

Not in America, and this train is still in America, right?

And this guy Al—*Albert*, but Sue can't pronounce it.

There she is, sitting next to him on the other side of the table, that weird bag he's always carrying hanging off his shoulder. He didn't seem like a *purse* guy, but these days, you never know.

Not getting that guy's name right: how embarrassing for Sue.

Typical, thought Brian.

Staring off lost in space, like she is all the time back home.

Up to me to step in and keep her from making a fool of herself.

A-gain.

Embarrassing, but *a man's gotta do.*

Brian coached his play:

Lean across the table like we're all friends.

Say: "Some kind of hubbub back at the station."

Sue still lost in the stars, saying: "Those police. Staring at you. At every-body. Just . . . waiting and you don't know what for or what to do."

"Nothing *to* do," said Brian. "Those guys know who they work for. They're not after folks like us. Not like *that.*"

Sue blinks and like she's coming back to life says: "What happens when '*that*' changes?"

"Why the hell would it?"

"It always has," said Al. "It always does."

"Not when you got guys like me and Fergus Lang around."

"Who's he?" said Al.

Everyone at that table felt Brian sigh as he told himself:

Some people just don't know what they oughta.

Be the good guy, Brian. Talk about something everybody gets.

"Speaking of dogs," he said, "I don't hear that damn yipper dog, what's his name—"

"Mugzy," said Al.

"Whatever. The chatterbox old lady. The yipper who steals off your plate. I always say, you got a dog, you control the dog."

"*Dogs,*" said Sue like she didn't understand what Brian was saying.

"Wow," said Al.

"Yeah, *wow,*" said Brian. "You going to Chicago for business, Al?"

"I'm past business now."

"We're all in business. Buying and selling. Bought and sold."

"Wow," said Al.

"So in Chicago—"

"I get off before then."

"What the hell is before then?"

"Fargo."

"That's about . . ."

"Thirteen hours from now."

"Pretty damn precise."

"Sometimes it's a relief to know how much time you've got left."

"So you'll be gone after dinner."

"I'll be around long enough."

Sue just sat there.

"Getting off this train," said Brian. "Good for you."

Odd, he thought. *Kind of feels good for me, too. Beats me why, 'cause he's nothing to me. Or Sue.*

"Hell," said Brian, "you're lucky to be getting off. I'd drink to that."

That guy named Al blinked.

Blinked again, like he saw something. Like he decided something.

"Good idea!" said Al. "Appreciate it."

"*Ah* . . . That's just what you say, you know? I mean, would if I could, but—"

"Doesn't your wife look out for you? Your heart and all? Carry some *whatever* for *whenever* you can't get what the doctor ordered? In her purse."

"How the hell do you know—"

"We had dinner together last night, just like you told us to—remember? Sitting right over there at that empty table. She was worried about you, had to have the maître d' help."

Albert frowned at Sue: "You got something in your purse?"

"Mini-bottles of Scotch because like Brian says: *'Waste not, want not.'*"

Brian shook his head. *Damned if I know what she's talking about, but hell, that's being a husband.*

Sue pulled three mini-bottles out of her purse.

"I'll get glasses, some ice," said Al.

And *whoa*, thought Brian, he's off to the galley. Finds the maître d'. Gets plastic glasses with cold cubes. Brings 'em back to the table.

Sits down and tells me: "You do the honors."

So hell, thought Brian, I'll screw the cap off a bottle.

Thought: *Lazy maître d' stands there watching me from the galley.*

"None for me, please, dear," said Sue.

She's never been good about handling liquor, thought Brian. Not my thing, booze at lunch, but never act like a wuss.

He knocked a drink back. *Boom!* Empty glass on the table.

Clackety-clack, all the time, *clackety-clack*.

Brian told those two: "Think I'll check out that Observation Car. You coming, Al?"

"No thanks."

"Suit yourself. Let's go, Sue."

"Great idea, dear, but I think I'll stay here. But don't waste what you paid for, remember to take those last two little bottles."

Brian had to stand up to put them clinking into his pants pocket.

"Enjoy the view," said Al before Brian walked away.

"Hell," said the husband and community leader: "You gotta see where you are to know what's going on."

49

Then, *wouldn't you know it*, Brian was only two, maybe three steps away from the door out of the Dining Car and into the Observation Car when from behind him came the sound of running footsteps.

Brian turned to face the way he'd come and saw *that boy*, the youngest of *them*, a kid in blue jeans and sneakers pulling up short and stopping right behind the adult standing in the way between him and the Observation Car.

Kid ran right past where Sue and that guy Al sat side by side at a table.

Brian wondered if they even noticed the passing thunder.

Shook his head to *not* stumble toward some finish of that thought.

Then that kid who was one of the darker chocolate shades of *them* shyly flashed Brian a smile.

Said: "After you, sir."

And *meant* it!

But not in a mean way, thought Brian. Not in a *gimme* or *gotchya* or . . . or a *required* way. The kid just *said it*. Person to person. Kid to adult. Respect. Polite.

Like they were two anybodys anywhere.

Flashing through Brian: *Could have been like the son I never got to have.*

Move on from that! Brian ordered himself as he always did after such thoughts. *You gotta be who you got to be and take that to the bank.*

Still, he felt himself smile back at the bright-eyed boy.

Heard himself say: "Thanks."

And *mean* it.

How come everybody in this hard world isn't like this one good kid?

That thought he'd never before had floated around him like a cloud. Part of him tried to argue that was just the lunch booze, but more of him knew better even if none of him wanted to admit it.

He glanced past the boy to where his wife sat beside a stranger, the two of them now watching to see what he'd do.

"That's OK . . . *son*," said Brian—he just *said it*—he told the boy standing near him. Brian nodded at the stairs down to the level below the Dining Car, the same tube of steel but on that lower level called Café Car where anybody could go. "You go ahead. I'll take a walk down there."

50

You don't know who Zed is."

Nora answered Graham: "Do you ever *really* know who you link to online?"

Ross said: "Or who somebody you meet in person *really* is."

He and Graham sensed Nora tremble.

"Was a brilliant idea," said Nora. "A theory you suddenly saw could work.

"*Where's the money?* How can I stop busting my ass with *gotta-take* gigs just so I can keep running in place? Why me? Why *not* me? What if?"

Graham said: "*What-if*s can ride you to *where the hell.*"

"You had other choices," Ross told Nora.

"Where were they going to take me?" said Nora. "What if I wanted more?"

Ross snapped: "So you could be a poor little rich girl?"

"Should I settle for being anybody *poor*? I'm *me*. The grift, it was my chance to be something more than just me."

"You're a *person*, not some *thing*. Not any black steel box full of cash."

"Fuck the money," said Nora. "I saw a chance for freedom."

"The rest of the world—"

"They're stuck, too!" Nora told Ross. "Rolling the fucking rock up the fucking hill so it can roll back down to fuck us again. I had to program a way to get out of my rock and roll or I was going to get crushed. I had to be able to log in someplace other than that damn chain gang."

"Nice song," muttered Ross with a sneer.

The three of them filled Ross's cabin as the train *clackety-clacked* across Montana's northern border miles of empty golden plains toward North Dakota.

Clackety-clacked past clusters of weathered buildings called towns where no one would ever be recognized much beyond the "city limits" or even truly seen by their neighbors.

Towns where everyone had heard and seen so many trains pass them by they now seldom thought to wonder. Thoughts like that brought only longing for what they knew they'd never know, dreams and nightmares of the unknown that cared nothing about them and who they were. Why think about trains like that?

Ross and Nora and Graham had hurried up the stairs into this train after denies and alibies about the splashed & spilt *call-it-coffee*.

Graham had Nora take them to her cabin, where just as she had for her confession back in Shelby, he took her and Ross's cellphones, crammed them in the sink's drawer with white towels. He led his two younger conspirators out of the cabin, back into the empty corridor of the *clackety-clacking* train.

Nora said: "What about your phone?"

"I don't have one."

He smiled at her shocked disbelief.

"I'm free," he said. "Unlinked. Mind, body and soul."

Graham's blue eyes burned into her skull.

He grinned.

Thrust his arms out wide and crucified.

Leered: *"Want to check?"*

She didn't.

Nor did Ross, who followed Graham's instruction and led their parade down the corridor and into his cabin. Graham claimed the lone chair by the window. Faced Nora, Ross *and* the latched door. Silver-haired Graham rode with his back to the windows full of where they'd been.

That "nice song" sneer sighed the breath out of both Nora and Ross.

She slumped on the edge of the bed close to the windows.

He dropped to *head in his hands* on the edge of the same bed by the door.

Graham's words sliced like a straight razor. "Who set me up with a killer cup of coffee?"

"Process," said Nora. "It's all just keyboard clicking *process*. Surfing to save you from. Get you out of. Like a video game. Or gambling. One click to then and then and then. Correlated searches. Dark web snoops. Spot a similar query. A persistent pattern like yours. Link up. Email to text to Snapchat. No names, only handles. You can be who you want to be. Share anger. Wants. *Oh yeah*s. Back and forth specs and checks. *Did you see*s, everything from how to hack Amtrak to heist movies like *Ocean's 11*. Confirming conjectures into concrete collaboration."

"Like two pimps hustling each other," said Graham.

"At least we weren't somebody else's whores!" snapped Nora.

"Really," said Ross. "That's why you packed condoms."

She felt like she was going to throw up.

Like she *should* throw up.

Refused. She refused. After all *this*, with *next* coming hard . . . she refused.

Snapped: "What, you want me to be sorry for always trying to travel safe?"

Graham said: "You 'traveling safe' got us all here."

"No," said Nora. "What got me here—"

"Us," interrupted Ross.

"What got *me* here," insisted Nora, "was going past *safe* to *smart*.

"What started out by asking *where's the money* went from *how to get it* to *yes we are*—one logical click after another. *Process* to *programing* to *pull-off*."

Memories shook Nora's head.

"We each validated we weren't ghosts. We each broke a law. Did a crime that would flash in the real world as proof of process.

"Remember the afternoon when all the traffic lights in downtown Seattle turned red at the same time?" Nora shook her head. "That was me. My *bona fides*. My proof that I wasn't a cop, that I was . . . who I said I was.

"The ATM in Spokane that suddenly spit out $20 bills? That was Zed. He knew better than to be there running around trying to catch flying-away bills in broad daylight in front of human eyes, not just hackable security cameras."

Graham said: "Who else is in your crew besides you two?"

"Nobody. We programmed the grift so it works with just two."

She shook her head. "But Zed wasn't supposed to be on the train from the start in Seattle. Compartmentalized gigs. No way for cops to link robbers traveling together.

"Zed rewrote the program," she said. "I was wrong about that."

"Oh," said Ross: "*That's* what you were wrong about."

Nora's voice chilled as she told Ross: "I was right about you being trouble."

Ross blinked: "What if we ask the kid who sent the coffee to Graham?"

"No," said Graham. "*One*, odds are the kid doesn't really know, other than gender. *Two*, us interrogating a little boy will trigger his parents, the train crew, probably the on-board SWAT team, and everyone will investigate."

"Or retaliate," said Nora.

"I've got nothing to hide," said Ross.

"How long have you *not* blown the whistle on a coming-soon crime?" said Graham. "Why didn't you do what the law's posters say and *'say something'* to either crew of SWAT badges in Havre, or hell . . .

The silver head nodded to the miles *clackety-clacking* past the window.

"Why haven't you said something now?"

"Zed will come after us if the program fails," said Nora. "We're a threat to him for knowing about the program he's part of. And he knows who we are or enough of that by now. Knew me when I got on the train. And you two . . ."

Graham said: "Sometimes you get on the train or the train gets on you."

"Who the fuck are you?" said Nora.

"Someone who's stuck with you this far."

"Why?"

"It's better to be in the fight than waiting to get hit."

Ross muttered: "Your Fourth F."

"What else?" snapped Nora.

"Guess the two of you will just have to wait and see."

Ross said: "The '*two*' of us?"

Graham said: "Obviously.

"Now," he added in the *clackety-clack*: "How are we robbing this train?"

51

Brian shuffled his journey not *to* the Observation Car but *through* the first level, the regular level, of the rest of the train. He punched the black pad to *whunk* open the door into the next car of coach passengers.

Deep inside him came a whisper: 'You're OK. Nothing's changed.'

Just wobble wobble walk with the direction the train is going.

The people in here, he thought. Down here. On the train's lower level. They look like the people who used to come into the bank. At least you saw their faces.

Kinda miss that, thought Brian.

Now they're mostly numbers in my desktop screen.

Makes it easier to *do*, but kinda harder to *be*.

If he can't see them, how can they see him?

Brian popped open the lower-level door to his car and—

—*there*, by the switchback stairs, that young woman with the long auburn hair and the *killed the cat* face. She slouched against the wall where she could see out the train car door's portal plus know who was coming down the switchback stairs from the Premium cabins, or from the narrow corridor to the Baggage Car.

Can see who's coming from the back of the train toward her, too. Like me.

Maybe she could also sense somebody working their way toward her from where we're going, thought Brian. Nothing much up that way.

A regular door in the middle of this car with a smudged window.

Steep stairs.

The locked Baggage Car door.

Then those SWAT guys from Seattle who *still* nobody'd told Brian about.

Should I talk to her? he wondered.

Better not, thought this older man.

But *who he was* gave him *gotta dos*, so he *polited* her a nod as he eased past her toward the mid-car door and what he didn't know awaited him.

Terri returned the cashmere coat asshole's nod. Wondered if he and his wife still had stuff to talk about. She stared out at the nothing her trip *clackety-clacked* through. Afternoons are long when you're locked into one place like a cabin on a train. Time moves slower.

Clackety . . .

. . . beat . . .

. . . beat . . .

Clack.

Too damn slow and not slow enough, thought Terri.

Back before she stood here, after lunch and before dinner that was still many golden prairie miles away, in that tiny box cabin called *theirs*, Terri'd stopped pacing, blurted to Erik: "I've got to get out of here."

He shifted on the made-again lower bunk bed to stand up—

"Alone," she said, halting his reflexive move to follow her *everywhere.*

Told him: "I just . . . You know how it is."

Erik didn't and his understanding smile was a well-intentioned lie.

"Besides," said Terri. "Haven't you got something to do on your computer?"

Erik's smile froze: *She knows about the mission!*

That will ruin how everything is supposed to work in Chicago!

Naw. She's just going with what she thinks will make me happy.

So he said: "Sure."

And meant it.

Because it was true: Erik hadn't checked Mission Op Status since Terri'd gotten out of the shower.

She left their cabin without another word.

If he'd said anything, she hadn't heard.

Don't check your phone, Terri told herself. Don't swipe to see the time. How long it's been since you came down the switchback stairs, leaned against the train wall to stand by the portal to daylight in a locked door you can't—

Terri blinked: *Someone's clumping down the stairs!*

52

Blonde Cari turned the going-down corner of the switchback stairs.

Spotted the auburn-haired woman from Cabin F standing by the train door.

Locked, it's still locked. No suicides or shenanigans on my shift.

She's pretending she doesn't see me so I won't look at her, thought Cari.

Fat chance, honey, thought Cari. *You're on the train. My train.*

Cari stopped at the bottom of the stairs. Smiled to the woman passenger who looked ten years younger for real and ten years older for glum.

"Are you OK?" said Cari.

Terri shrugged. "Sure."

They both knew that was a lie.

Cari said: "Some days, huh."

Shrugged *bigtime* so the passenger slumped against the wall of the train couldn't help but see and know she wasn't alone.

Cari followed up one truth with another: "Least we're still here."

"Oh yeah," said Terri. "If we only knew how to get somewhere else."

"You're on this train. You got a ticket. We're on schedule."

Terri shook her head:

"That's how I've always liked and wanted and tried to make it. How I thought things worked. You plan. You pick. You position. You posture. You put the right shape and right spin. It makes rational sense and has logic and obvious causes and effects. You can strategize. Figure it out."

"Are we talking about *just things* or *one thing* in particular?" asked Cari.

"Yeah," answered the younger woman.

They both laughed.

The Conductor came from around the corridor on the first level by the locked door of the Baggage Car. Loomed beside the two laughing women.

He was a big burly man. Wasn't wearing his Amtrak uniform blue jacket, just his company white shirt tight on muscles that showed he could have snapped either Terri or Cari like a stick from a tree in the park. No brass name tag. But the cap, the gold braided cap, *that* he wore and let it dip to let them know he'd seen and was watching them even as he quietly padded his *wobble wobble* way toward the next car.

"I'm sorry," said Terri when the Conductor was safely in the next car. "I didn't mean to get you in trouble for hanging out with me."

"*We at Amtrak pride ourselves on our customer service and satisfaction,*" quoted Cari as she stood tall and official. "*Hospitality is priority number one.*

"Or maybe *safety* is number one," said Cari. "Depends on the day and what the bosses say."

"Is he a good boss?" said Terri, who was a pro at spotting hierarchy.

"Doesn't matter," said Cari. "This isn't his usual run."

She added: "The maître d' said that he was some guy who put in for this dispatch and had the pull or came up just right in the computer to get this trip.

"None of us really know him. But then, he doesn't really know me either."

Attendant Cari chanced an unprofessional share with this one-way, gone tomorrow passenger. "He's not my type."

Terri's preoccupied mind triggered her to say: "You mean *man*?"

"I mean *person*. He's too high and mighty for the likes of me."

"Oh."

Terri knew she should stop talking or change the subject, but heard herself babble: "Well, if he's not, I hope you've got somebody who is.

"I mean," she babbled, "for you."

Kept babbling: "I mean, like a man—or a woman—or a *whoever*! Someone."

"I'm a widow," said Cari.

Clackety-clack, clackety-clack.

"I . . . I don't know what to say," whispered Terri. "I . . . sorry, I . . ."

Cari shrugged. "It's just the train, right?"

Like she believed that. Like she had to. Like she hated it.

Cari'd ridden these rails for going on nine years. Left her rented suburban cottage with a flower patch out front and two trees out back for *clackety-clacking* shifts, usually 51 hours straight. She'd learned to read her passengers for what they needed and what she should. Could.

Her soft smile carried her risky *unprofessional* words to Passenger Terri.

"Sometimes you gotta get out of Dodge to figure out where to go.

"Lucky you," she added. "You're on this train now."

Cari shook her head. "But figuring it out is never enough."

53

anker Brian reached the next silver metal door, its window glass blurry as hell, smack dab in the middle of this car where above him ran the row of cabins for him and his and whoever else and Fergus *I fucking know him!* Lang.

Brian popped the black handle pad.

The door slid back.

Oh-oh.

Brian trembled.

There she was.

Marching through the narrow metal-walled canyon of this train car toward him as the door *whunked* closed behind his stopped-cold ass.

No getting around her. No getting past her. No room for anything but her.

Della Storm.

Brian didn't know her name in his head but he knew in his bones that this woman standing 10 feet away who'd seen him, stopped, *smiled*, this woman bossed the scene he was stuck in on this *clackety-clack* train.

Just look at her! he silently screamed.

You had to look at her.

And *oh*, the look of her overpowered him.

Baltimore stripper *shazam*.

Shellac-black hair like Darth Vader's helmet. Cheeks fluffed so pink Brian could smell their freshly powdered cloud from 10 feet away. Mascaraed eyes like two pistols' black bores. Slick pink lips that promised a killer kiss.

Della carried herself like a high school football star sporting high heels. Her crimson dress clung to muscular thighs and around global hips, and jutting out the front of her came two gigantic train-ride quivering breasts.

Even as his heart raced with terror, a whisper in Brian went *maybe if Sue had breasts like that*, but he knew *no*, even that wouldn't change who Sue was. Or wasn't. *What the hell*, he didn't know which and *what the hell*, this late in his life, that didn't make any difference, and none of that would save him now.

Brian *harrumphed* over the *clackety-clack*.

"My," said Della, her husky hoarse voice sounding like she'd kicked the shit out of throat cancer, "that's a mighty big sound for just one . . . little man."

The purple boa around her neck covered any cancer scars.

Della said: "You looking for me?"

Brian swallowed hard.

"Oh," said Della. "Now. Here. When we're alone, now, *now* you see me.

"Or think you do," she said, cutting him with her smile. "Hell, now you can't look away. Pretend you're not staring at what you think you see. What you wanna see. Yeah. I know men like you. A whole lot of men just like you.

"Maybe taller," she said as she took one slow step closer to where he stood trapped in this narrow silvery metal shaft train car corridor. "And younger. But there's a lot of swinging dicks out there like you.

"Unless I'm wrong," said Della.

That slick pink-lipped smile curled.

As she stepped closer.

"I could be . . . wrong.

"Are you the kind of man who likes to cuddle?" said she who could smother Brian in her fleshy embrace. "Who after the sun's gone down or first come up likes to hold a real *flesh and blood* woman close for *her* comfort and care and maybe, only if it comes natural, a tender slice of *un-hun, un-hun*?

"Are you the kind of man who's worth it with all his smell's and silly's and stupid's as the day is long and the night is dark?

"Are you the kind of man who'll hold the weight of a woman worn down by *the day that was* who's going back out there to wear down *the day that will be*?

"Am I wrong and are you that kind of man and not a strong-arming, scared shitless wannabe?"

"I . . . I don't know."

"That's the first smart thing I've ever heard you say."

Della *wobble wobble* clomped right up to Brian.

So close he could feel the heat of her body.

So close he could smell the mint of her mouthwash.

So close there was only a wisp of *clackety-clack* between them.

Della said: "You're in my way."

Brian frantically pounded the steel door pressed against his back. His fourth blow hit the black pad. The door *whunked* open and he stumbled backwards. Backpedaled down the train car corridor. She kept coming toward him one clomping *wobble wobble* step at a time until he pushed himself into the alcove at the switchback stairs, created space for her to pass him by.

Della stopped beside the alcove where Brian cowered.

Tossed her purple boa back over her left shoulder.

That perfumed snake lashed Brian's face.

Della let him live.

Walked on.

Stone cold sober Brian raced back to the door in the middle of the car. *Whunk* and he hurried down that narrow silver metal-walled canyon toward the locked-tight and warning-signed Baggage Car door, turned to his right—

There rose a steep set of stairs.

He grabbed the railing, his heart pounding him up those hard steps.

Thought: *This would sure be a hell of a nasty fall down.*

54

Whunk went the opening door of the Observation Car and Ulysses stepped in only to find his family walking out.

He kept his smile on his family.

Blinked with the passing northern horizon's distant glint of gray off the miles of chain link fence caging the ghosts on the deserted Air Force base outside of Glasgow, Montana. In the days before computers evolved out of War Rooms and into bedrooms, children of Strategic Air Command warriors assigned to that base's Armageddon Duty got used to the roars of jet warplanes taking off in the brightest of days and the blackest of nights.

Ulysses turned to his left. Blinked at that horizon's glint of southern sprawl that ran all the way down to the Montana-Wyoming border where a coal company's bankruptcy would reveal massive amounts of money covertly funneled to "patriotic" and scientific-sounding "independent" groups and TV talking heads who spent years denying climate change and man's role in earth's fate. Now that strip-mined land was a federal superfund toxic waste site.

His wife Isabella said: "The three of us voted to go back to our suite, stretch out before dinner."

"Good idea," said Ulysses.

He popped the black pad on the door to *whunk* it open.

Stepped aside to let mother and son pass.

Turned and put himself between his teenage daughter and the door.

"Better idea," he said. "Mir's going to stick around here with me. There's some things we've got to settle."

55

*H*ow are we going to get off this train?"

Graham's words surrounded the two younger trapped with him travelers.

"We can't run," he said as they sat in Ross's cabin. "We can't hide. We'll all take some hit if we go for help. If we get found out. We're in this together, so we better figure out how to get our own *done*."

The silver-haired werewolf looked at Nora: "That's the new program."

Turned to Ross: "That's the new poem.

"*If*," he said, "*if* Nora's story is real and true. She's obviously crazy, but sometimes that lets you be right. And there's only one way to find out about that and where we are.

"So . . . yeah," said Graham: "We're robbing this train.

"Or at least," he clarified, "going along to see where that ride takes us."

He leaned forward in his by-the-window perch, pressed his energy on Nora.

"Give it up," said Graham.

Clackety-clack, clackety-clack.

Nora sat on the lower bunk in Ross's cabin, her eyes on him and Graham. Those eyes of hers couldn't hide a glint of pride.

"We're not Butch Cassidy and Sundance charging their horses down on a steam locomotive. We're 21st century programming artists.

"Identity theft," she said. "Everybody's nightmare, our specialty. And nobody will ever know it happened."

"Except us," said Ross.

"Yeah," she said. "Except us. And Zed.

"The Seattle Federal Reserve Bank deactivated their burn furnace for their building's renovation," said Nora. "That means all the worn-out money they collect has to be sent somewhere else for '*incinerative retirement.*' Seattle now ships their removed-from-circulation bills to the Federal Reserve in Chicago.

"How do you get a giant steel box of old cash from Seattle to Chicago?

"If you truck it, too many roads. Easy to get detoured. And forget about low profile. Lots of stops for gas and to switch drivers if not to bunk for a night. You'd need an armed caravan to stop Butch and Sundance from riding down on you with motorcycles and machineguns.

"Flying, *well*, the airlines barely carry passengers' bags. Private cargo airlines require public bid contracts and there goes your security. You can't use government planes without planeloads of government hassles.

"But the train? A government subsidized, locked-up in route, only a few stops at remote depots *train* called the Empire Builder? All you need to do is lock the money cube on board and guard it with a squad of SWATs."

"Back in Havre," said Ross. "The other SWATs, the locals. Those 'Federal Police,' ICE. Did they know about the money?"

"Don't think so," said Nora. "The Seattle SWAT team knows, but they wear uniforms with no markings. Stencil 'U.S. TREASURY' or something like that on their black gear and it's like shining a spotlight, saying 'here's money.' The train crew is told they're carrying classified secrets, documents and computer discs. Why wouldn't they believe it? They're all loyal Americans.

"What they're actually freighting through the heartland is a black steel box, a seven-foot-tall cube crammed full of old money.

"We're programmers," said Nora. "We hacked the Fed delivery schedule. Knew when and what train to target. Hacked the Seattle train station and Chicago's train station security cameras so the feed from the afternoon *before* our appearances gets re-looped so none of us are on security films."

And you've deleted what I did, thought Ross.

"We hacked the Baggage Car security cameras, too," said Nora, who sensed Ross's thoughts. "Those out-of-date security cameras can't record sound.

"The top of the money box is flat," said Nora. "Locked with a detachable wireless keypad that confirms the box's identity and sends a constant location signal accurate to within 11 feet. White paint serial numbers on every box.

"Seattle and Chicago, the same drill," she continued. "There's a pallet jack in the Baggage Car, one of those electric-driven, slides-on-wheels with a pneumatic lift. A station forklift delivers the box to the Baggage Car in Seattle, takes it away in Chicago. Maneuvering the box inside the car is done with that pallet jack."

She blinked. "Like I used to use every day in a 'fulfillment center' gig."

"The town where we left Mugzy," said Ross. "Shelby."

"Government surplus," said Nora. "The exact make and model of the money cube. Low bid online. A trash pickup company that actually paid us to pack it with old newspapers for recycling."

Ross said: "So Shelby—"

"A middle of nowhere, whistle stop town. Low paranoia police presence. Where a legitimate freight company delivers a black steel surplus box all painted up and logo'd as commercial cargo for the Empire Builder."

Ross said: "You're going to switch the boxes. Or at least their identities."

Graham said: "How?"

Nora told them.

"Until you two, I trusted the grift's program. Knew it would work. The only thing that had me scared . . .

"*Silence*," said Nora. "We have to be dead quiet when we're making the switch in the baggage car tonight. The SWAT squad in the next car. Somebody's always on-duty, monitoring a screen with the video feed of what's going on inside the Baggage Car. Live action, but no sound.

"What the SWAT guards tonight will be really seeing is a re-looped replay of last night, but if they hear something—the Baggage Car is the next car over—especially if what they hear doesn't match with what they see in their screen . . ."

"One sound and you'll be found," said Graham.

"*You?*" said Nora. "I thought it was *us*."

"We'll see," said Graham.

He didn't look to Ross for confirmation of any damn thing.

Asked Nora: "What time tonight?"

"Late, when we're deep in North Dakota and everybody on the train is asleep. We reverse the SWAT crew's security feed and watch them. What they'll see is the loop of last night's security film. What we'll see is them."

She shrugged. "Hacking the security code on the door to the Baggage Car was a snap. We KISS—Kept It Simple, programmed a second OPEN code for all the train's keypad locks. As soon as this train registers as In Station, Off Run, all the codes and all the hacks and all the reprograms go normal and show that they've been that way the whole damn trip."

"As long as nobody makes a sound," repeated Ross.

Clackety-clack, clackety-clack.

56

Blue sky lit amber waves of grain still called Montana that flowed like an endless sea outside the afternoon windows of the Observation Car.

That view of The Big Empty made most of the train's passengers feel uncomfortably small as the train carried them ever closer to the sun that would (surely) rise over the American Midwest, over predictably civilized cities like Fargo, St. Paul, Milwaukee, and Chicago, that windy city Final Destination now only 24 hours of *clackety-clacks* away from their locomotive's cyclops eye.

Only a father and daughter rode in the Observation Car.

Ulysses led Mir to the last two lounge chairs in that long tube of windows. His gesture asked—not *told*—her to sit in the chair closest to the door, the retreat from this moment that he saw her wishing for as much as him.

He ached to lean closer to her. Ached for himself. For her. For the *who* that they were. Knew she'd needed her own space.

"There's only one right way to do this," Ulysses told his 15-year-old daughter, "and that's to tell you what's going on."

He watched her face go as stoic as it had each time he'd sat down with the family to talk about a deployment that he promised to come back to them from, promises meant as much for him as they were for those he loved.

"Dad, what you said, I get it, I know. I pay attention to what's going on . . ." Mir swept her arm toward the windows. ". . . everywhere out there. I don't want to see . . . But if troops start marching out there, if you're with them, then . . . then I'd . . ."

"You'd be in my broken dream," said her father. "I won't let that happen."

"If you can," she whispered.

"Yeah," said her father, weighted down with centuries going both back and forward beyond his years.

"There's all that and more," he told Mir. "Some of the more I've talked about with your mother. Some of it I haven't told her yet."

He told his daughter about the Nuremberg Conventions, the truths that all Marines—and all citizens—pulled on with their boots.

"What are you telling me that Mom doesn't know?"

"The last text I got from Gunny, when I was with your brother after we pulled out of that place called Shelby. Where you made me so proud, took care of that old woman. What I found out in that Havre town with the second SWATs.

"All of it," Ulysses told her, "phantom troops marching our land, Nuremberg and our politicized service, all of it totals up with all my years in the Corps, from the Naval Academy to now, I could retire. *Yeah*, I know, only 45, but I can walk away with a pension, get a job, and with your mom teaching, the family'd be OK."

Mir angled her head to the world rushing by the windows.

"Except for all of that," she said.

"All of us will always have all of that," said Ulysses.

"But you love the Corps!" said Mir. "You were born for the Corps, you . . ."

She frowned: "What did Gunny just text you?"

"I'm on the promotion list," said Ulysses. "And if I take it, if I let them up me, then I gotta do the job. Take the post. Be even more responsible for . . . If I say yes, I owe every Marine and every American the *semper fi* of whatever they give me."

Ulysses shrugged. "Gunny says it'll be stateside. Quantico. Pentagon. Maybe Paris Island. So my middle-aged ass shouldn't be in danger of getting shot off.

"So either I say a bigger *yes* to being part of the mess out there, or I try to protect my soul, walk away and let it be other Marines' problems."

"You're not a walk away kind of guy," said his daughter. "And your soul goes where ever you go."

"You sound like your mother."

A smile flicked Mir's face. "Sometimes."

Mir asked her Dad: "Do you know what you're going to do?"

"Tell your mom."

"She'll stand beside you. All the way. So will Malik. So will I."

"*Jesus* I got lucky in this life."

"*Eh,*" said Mir. "At least Malik isn't too much of a pain in the ass."

Ulysses saw her brow wrinkle. Read her frown. Knew what she would ask before she said:

"This isn't how we do things. In the family. This isn't . . . You kept me here to tell me—what did you say—*what's going on.*"

Mir blinked: "So, *what's going on?*"

"That's the trouble with telling the truth," said Ulysses. "You gotta go for all you can get to get any of it at all."

Father told Daughter: "I know what's in your purse."

She didn't move a muscle. Didn't blink. Didn't breathe.

"Condoms," said her dad. "I know you've got . . . you're carrying condoms."

She stared straight at him.

"I could tell you how I found out was an accident," said Ulysses. "But that would be a sham because it was an accident I nudged to happen, to fall over, spill out because I worry. I had to know if there was any *what* that I had to know."

"So now you do," said Mir. "Now you *think* you do. Now what are you . . ."

"What I want is to know the true of you."

Mir's chest trembled with her slamming heartbeats.

Ulysses said: "Maybe I'm wrong. Probably I'm wrong. Definitely I barely know anything. But since I found out, I've been watching. Wondering every time you left your purse alone with mom and me. Wondering if maybe you wanted to us to find out, to know."

"No!" said Mir.

But knew they both wondered if that was true.

She took her first deep breath since they'd sat down.

"Are you going to give me the lecture now? Orders?"

Ulysses shook his head *no*: "I'm going to listen."

Then he shut up.

Mir whispered: "I'm not . . . I haven't . . . Not that . . . My friends . . . You know I don't have a guy who I *enough* and who likes me more than *that*, who . . ."

The train whistle blew.

Mir said: "I want to be smart about being me."

"I'm so damn proud of you," said her father.

Mir's face widened in shock.

"Scared and *yikes* and all that," said her father. "But I'm so damn proud of you. Life's coming at you and you're facing it head on. Saying *yes*. Saying *no*. Saying you're not going to be stupid or irresponsible or just trusting stumbling luck. Saying you're going to choose the right me.

"Hold that line," he told her. "No matter what or who or . . . hold that line."

Their eyes filled with a new true of their *who*.

Mir whispered: "Hold the line. You too, Dad. You too."

Neither of them ever confessed that they saw the other one cry.

Ulysses blinked, felt his gaze drop as he said: "Your mother, *um*, when we get back home, she's going to take you to a clinic, for *um*, for more . . . for the rest—"

"AAAHHH!" Mir's eyes squeezed shut and her hands cupped over her ears.

"Please Dad, I mean, *no more*, could you, just don't say . . . please *NO MORE!"*

"Sounds great to me!"

His shoulders dropped. He felt her slump, too.

Heard her say: "Can we just . . . sit here and not talk?"

"Oh yeah!"

They rode like that, *clackety-clack* the only sound for miles of open fields flowing past the windows that filled their eyes.

Until Mir whispered: "There's so much out there."

Ulysses just let that ride.

57

unaway train," said Ross as he stared at the two people in his *wobble wobble* cabin who somehow shared his ticket.

Shook his head.

Shook off that bullshit.

Said: "It's not the train. It's me. How I'm riding it."

His eyes filled with Nora as she sat trembling on the bed.

Ross told her: "You, too."

He looked across the cabin to the silver-haired man in black riding the chair by the windows to *The Great Out There,* told Graham: "And you.

"Who are you?" said Ross. "Tell us who the hell you are, we deserve that."

"Don't be so sure you want to get what you deserve," said Graham.

Nora blurted: "I didn't mean to kill you, Ross!"

Sighed: "Thank God I fucked that up, too."

"Maybe you'll get another chance," said Ross. "Condoms and poison, you're the carrying kind."

"I get what I'm given," said the cherry-haired woman beside him on the bed.

"Try saying *no* to *being given* and *yes* to *choosing it* once in a while!"

"I am!" snapped Nora. "I did! I was! I don't want to spend the only life I'm ever going to have just being someone else's data!"

"The poison," said Graham.

Nora and Ross locked their gaze on the silver-haired man by the window. Who said: "Tell me about the poison."

"It killed a dog," answered Nora.

"But would it kill a man?" Graham's smile tightened like a whip. "Tell us about it. What it was. How you got it."

"What it was isn't what I thought," said Nora.

She gave Ross her full face as she said: "I don't walk around with poison.

"I mean, *yeah*," she qualified, "the Ambien was mine. Who doesn't have trouble sleeping?

"But what I tried to give Ross was supposed to be molly. Looked like molly, clear white capsule. Was supposed to make him goofy high and easy to herd."

"Capsule," repeated Graham.

"I don't know how you buy your drugs," said Nora, "but how people I know buy theirs includes capsules.

"Except for Ross here," she said. "He's a lemon drop kind of high."

Ross felt cellophane crinkle in the maroon shirt's pocket over his heart.

"So you don't really know what was in the capsule," said Graham.

"You're just realizing that now?" snapped Nora.

"Where did you get it?"

"From Zed," said Nora. "On the train. After I Snapchatted a report—

"*Not everything!*" she said, carefully not looking at Ross. "I didn't tell him . . . I mean . . . beyond operating data."

She shook her head.

"After I drugged Ross asleep, searched his cabin, cleared his phone and checked in . . . I Snapchatted Zed. He ran the data on what he wanted me to do. What he said I had to do.

"*Or*, he said, *he threatened* he would have to compute a bigger *do*. He told me he'd taped a baggy with a molly capsule under the stand for the Complimentary Coffee in the alcove just past the line of cabins.

"I got dressed, snuck out of Ross's cabin. I tried to . . . *well*, not tiptoe down the train corridor, that would have been stupid, impossible with the *wobble wobble*, but I was moving *oh so quiet*.

"Until the train lurched. I stumbled out of the alcove with the baggie in my hand. Staggered down the corridor. Mugzy barked, I froze, and that gave Mugzy's poor old woman time to come out of her suite and see me."

Nora shook her head. "Neither of us knew where those moments would take us. What she's facing now."

Graham said: "You tried to dose Ross with the drug Zed wanted him to have. So Zed brought at least one drug aboard. What, for *just in case*? No. That's absurd, so he carried—carries—lots of *whatever* for *becauses*."

The silver-haired man in the black seat by the window saw the possibilities.

"In this *because*," continued Graham, "if a snoopy man, a tortured poet, a fired reporter, somebody with nobody to love . . . If a guy like that dies of a drug overdose, that data computes as its own answer and its situation is probably not much more of a disruption to the robbery program than Mugzy's dying."

"The train's gotta roll," whispered Ross.

"So you carry condoms, Zed carries pills," said Graham.

"Yeah," said Nora, "I think he's also a drug dealer. Dark web, not streets. Back when we were assessing each other, he offered to hook me up with whatever I wanted. I figured it was some kind of test. I would have said *no* anyway—my only highs are legal in Seattle, so I . . . I didn't just decline, I refused."

She shrugged. "Passed the test."

"There was no pass or fail," said Graham. "Either way, he knew you more."

Graham smiled, said: "So what do you—what do *we* choose now?"

Ross blinked.

"Where we are is right here," said Graham. "On this train. We're in a riff that Zed programmed. Obviously, he wants the money in the Baggage Car, or what of it he can claim. Likely, he'll kill if he has to, cost versus benefit, a calculation he's shown he'll make. Whoever he is."

Light filled Ross's face. "He's in the Seattle train depot. He's everywhere on the train. What if Zed is more than just a '*he*'?"

"Nora," said the man who once thought she might be *the one*: "You hatched this online. Made a crew of two. But what if you unknowingly joined a bigger crew that ruled *what's going on* about this train? What if everybody—or most everybody, a few everybody riding this train—what if they're running the program?"

"Who?" said Graham.

"Like the crew," said Ross. "Like our Attendant Cari. The Conductor. The maître d' who tells us where to sit. The waitress. Everybody working the train."

"We're all part of some conspiracy," said Graham. "But I think not that one. Maybe one of the crew is Zed—kind of makes sense—but more? I don't think so. And I don't think all the SWAT crew riding in the Baggage Car are in on it, too."

Graham said: "The bigger the conspiracy, the more it clanks."

"Doesn't matter," said Ross. "This is still all about us. What we do."

"Yes," said Graham. "And I'm stuck in your complications."

"You're a man who lives for complications," said Nora.

The older man shrugged. "Maybe. Me asking about the SWAT team made me step into your mess. But then you came after me."

"Didn't want coffee to be your killer," said Nora.

"Come on," said Graham, leaving his chair to head for the cabin door.

"Where?" said Ross even as he rose to follow, Nora right behind him.

Nora's cabin.

Graham opened the drawer where they'd stuffed their cellphones. Held out the phones for them to claim. Held his hand up to Nora. Pointed to Ross.

Ross got it, turned on his phone.

Thumbed and swiped as the others watched what lit his screen.

Emails about nothing involving this train. Upcoming Seattle concert info that an algorithm wanted to sell him based on a ticket he'd bought through its system months before. News alerts. His cousin from Philly. A rejection for three of his poems by a literary journal. Nothing from his work gig's editor. No texts. No Facebook or Instagram messages.

Nora turned on her phone so they all could see her Snapchat screen:

> Those 2 meats are your
> problem & payroll now.

Then *like that!*

Message gone.

Graham took the phone out of Nora's hand. Took Ross's too.

Turned them off, wrapped them in towels, shoved them back in the drawer.

Led his younger colluders back to the corridor of the *clackety-clack* train where on this afternoon trip, no one else was standing, watching, seeing.

Said: "Now we let the program run until we can take over the keyboard."

"What about our phones?" said Nora.

"Unless you want wherever you are to be known and to risk everything you say being heard by someone you can't see . . ."

"We've missed lunch," continued Graham. "Dinner is coming up, we can't miss that, too. I'm going to go take a nap. You two clear your heads. Go fuck in Ross's cabin. Maybe you'll fall asleep, get some rest. I'll come get you for dinner. We got a hard night coming."

The silver-haired man walked to his Cabin B.

They watched him open that door.

Thought they heard it latch behind him.

Drifted back to Ross's cabin where they most definitely latched the door.

Stood there as the train *clackety-clacked*.

"I never wanted to be a thief," said Ross. "Never wanted to steal my way. Make me just what I steal. Just like all the other crooks out there."

"We aren't—not the plan—we aren't robbing anyone," said Nora. "We're repurposing what was otherwise going to burn up into smoke. *That* was the plan."

Ross said: "Plans.

"My plan was to ride this train. Work the gig that bought me the ticket. Work what I do and do true. My plan was that somehow that would make me lucky or worth something more than a lost lonely life. Let me find the rhyme."

"You're worth . . ." whispered Nora.

Couldn't say it. Tried again: "You're worth . . ."

"Cost," he said. "It's all about cost. What we do to pay to ride the train we're on when we never really know what train it is until it's roaring down the rails."

He looked at the woman who'd dyed her hair to stand in front of him in this *clackety-clack* now.

"I told myself I would have paid any cost to be your *one*, but the *one* you are bought me a ticket to be drugged or worse, locked up in a loony bin or prison or let you get crushed under your own '*plan*' . . .

"Whatever happens," said Ross. "Whatever I choose. Whatever I think I'm going to—*willing to* pay, this train's cost me who I knew in the mirror.

Ross shook his head: "Maybe worst of all, what cost are we forcing on all the innocent people riding this train?"

58

The last dinner on this train.

Everybody came.

Well, except for Constance and Mugzy.

Even Fergus Lang deigned to join ordinary passengers in the 6 o'clock hour as the last of Montana *clackety-clacked* past the Dining Car's sunset windows.

He sat alone at a white-clothed table for four. Paid a hefty tip to do so. The maitre d' split that money among the Dining Car crew.

Fergus Lang rode with his back to the rest of the Dining Car. The maître d' and waitress removed that four-top table's three other chairs. All other passengers could do was ask *why*, and none of them chose to do that as they crowded the remaining tables.

Malik realized Something Was Up right after the waitress walked away with his family's food orders. Mom and Dad and Mir were all . . . smiling at him in their different ways that then & there all felt the same. Like they shared a secret. Like they wanted him to feel . . . They didn't want him to freak out, that's it! They're all in on some knowing and all worried about . . .

Dad cleared his throat, a signal for *eyes on him*, the Marine major.

Ulysses said to his son: "You know how everything changes?"

Malik shrugged.

Felt Mom's and Mir's smiles try to cup him.

"Well," said Dad, "there might a big change coming up for us—for me."

NO not another Go Away deployment where you might Get Shot! rocketed through the 10-year-old son, who knew better than to burden his dad with being a whiny kid who couldn't take it like a Marine.

"Nothing's been decided yet," said Dad. "And this time, we—I've got some power to choose what's gonna be."

"What about Orders?" said Malik.

"This is one of those times I've got to . . . to pick the set of Orders that's right."

"But . . . aren't the Orders always right?"

"The only Order that's always right is to do what's right.

"You know that," Ulysses told his son. "We've talked about that."

"And the Corps," said Malik.

"Son, everybody in this life has gotta be a Marine and do it right, *semper fi* even if they're not in the Corps."

Mom said: "It's confusing. I won't say that you'll get it when you're older. That you'll know what the answer is. But with your smart brain and good heart, at least you'll have a shot at better understanding the question."

Teenage Mir told her brother—

No, realized Malik even as his mind tumbled: *She's telling all of us.*

"Even I'm not there yet, kid," said Mir. "But I'm trying."

"One thing you've got to know," said Dad, promised Dad, ordered Dad: "You're going to be all right. Mir and Mom are going to be all right. I'm going to be all right. Whatever the change. Whatever I need to do."

"OK, Malik?" said Mom.

How the heck should I know if it's OK? thought Malik. *I don't even know what 'it' is!*

Like a hero in some screen, sister Mir told him: "I got your back, Jack."

My back, thought Malik as he rode the Dining Car's *clackety-clack*:

Behind my back as I sit at this table waiting for my hamburger is the table with the dark-lips lady who waves and the man who's always carrying his bag and the guy who yelled at Mom back in Seattle. Don't know how he could be like that and then be OK when we met each other walking through the train. Am I going to understand stuff like that too when I get older?

Brian had to admit that sitting at the table next to the family of them wasn't as bad as it could have been. They kept to themselves like they should, and even if he couldn't hear what they were saying, he figured they weren't trash talking him or the way things should be—hell: *are.* He could tell that because their little boy, the good one of the bunch, the one who . . . Well, that kid wasn't sneaking nasty looks at where Brian sat one table over with his wife Sue and that *damned if he isn't there again tonight* guy Al.

Hell, thought Brian: It's the last night. Let Al sit where he wants to.

Their table also held a vacant chair where Suzanne imagined Constance and Mugzy sitting, but they were gone.

Brian stared across the aisle at solo-dining Fergus Lang.

Man that important needs time alone, thought Brian. He knows I'm here.

"But not for long," said Brian, surprised to hear his thought spoken aloud.

Sue said: "Not for long *what* . . . Dear?"

"Train's almost over—especially for you, Al." Brian nodded to the twilight windows. "Comin' on dark and coming on North Da-*damn*-ko-ta. That's where you get off, right?"

"Yes," said Al.

"Well, hell," said Brian. "We ought to celebrate that!"

He waved the waitress over. Ordered mini-bottles of red wine for all of them. As the waitress walked away, Brian nodded at the half-drunk glass of wine already sitting in front of him.

Told Al: "The little woman here, she already made sure I did what the doctor ordered. Had a hefty one of them Scotches didn't even know she'd remembered to pack. Plus she got me this one here soon as we sat down."

"I remember," said Albert.

Suzanne said nothing.

"But since it's your last night on this train—hell, guess it's last night for all of us—figure we oughta have a drink to say goodbye."

Brian felt something he didn't understand tighten his back. Like he knew something in his bones that he didn't have words for in his head. He picked up the night's first glass of wine. Made sure Al watched him take a long pull to show how a man handles things to that guy who was finally getting off the damn train.

Albert watched what anyone in the Dining Car could see.

The waitress brought three mini-bottles of wine. Brian made a big deal of taking them from her. Being the one to fill everybody's glasses. When it came to his glass, he had to knock back what was left of *vino numero uno* to pour his celebratory drink so the waitress could take the three empty bottles away.

Brian raised his full-again glass, waited until Sue and Al did the same.

"Here's looking at us," said Brian and he downed half his glass to show them all how a toast was done by important men like him and Fergus Lang.

Brian burped. Noticed a couple people in the Dining Car heard him. Felt so relaxed he didn't give a shit about what they thought.

"You know, Al," said Brian. "You never told me what you do for a living."

"The best I can," answered Albert.

"Well, good for you. Me, I run the bank—and make sure the little woman here doesn't run everything into the ground." Brian laughed louder than the conversation needed, but he didn't care. "We all gotta run something."

"Really," said Albert.

"That's the way things are," said Brian, realizing he how smart he was as he drank damn near all the wine left in his glass.

"You must be thirsty, Dear," said the little woman.

"My whole life," came out of Brian before he knew he spoke those words.

"Then can you finish mine?" said the woman who Brian knew, *yeah*, she'd trapped him, but *damn it*, she belonged to him.

He knew who Sue was as she added: "I'm not big enough."

"Oh," said Brian, "like you know—and like Sue here could tell you, Al—I'm *plenty* big enough. If you know what I mean."

He poured the blood-colored liquid from her glass into his.

Leered: "And like we'll see, seein' as how this is the last night in our damn cabin on the train—right, Sue?"

Brian took a long pull out of his glass. Didn't have to watch her to know she got what he was talking about and what was gonna happen now that the wine had loosened things up. He'd packed his little blue pills. Kept his eyes on Al to see if that nobody from nowhere got what was going on *and* gonna go on.

Al sat facing the way the train was going. Stared like he was already gone.

Brian generously shared with them how he and Fergus Lang buddied up back at the BAT convention. Told them more until even he stopped caring what he mumbled. Came time to leave, he took hold of Sue's arm, not so he wouldn't fall on the *wobble wobble* ride, mind you, but so she knew where she was going.

And what she was going to have to do. What they were going to do.

Albert watched them walk away as the train *clackety-clacked* on schedule.

Two SWAT warriors were guests of the Dining Car that night.

SWAT Sgt. Michael Carlisle was one of the treated blue jumpsuit warriors at the insistence of L.T. and the approval of the whole squad.

L.T. first annoyed and then appeased the SWAT team by picking rookie David Hale to be the other trooper to get a hot meal on an actual plate instead of the microwaved rations in the SWAT's crew car quarters by the Baggage Car.

But for the privilege of eating 'with the swells,' trooper Hale also drew the loathed midnight-to-morning solo sentry shift of watching the security cameras' feed of the *nothing happening* in the Baggage Car while everybody else grabbed what shut-eye they could.

Across the aisle from the Doss family, those two guest SWATs shared a table with glum Terri and excited Erik.

The four of them talked salt and pepper. *Yes* and *Please. Thank you.* Looks like a nice night out there. How much more time do we have to go?

Erik smiled through the whole meal.

Told himself: *'Don't say anything that will blow the Op in Chicago!'*

Terri rode the silences of this last dinner with relief, even given her natural nervous paranoia that most people get near cops.

But that night she was grateful that the badges' presence meant she wouldn't have to say much beyond *salt* and *pepper.*

That yellow-eyed train *clackety-clacked* through the American darkness.

Nora, Ross and Graham came to this last supper as a posse. Graham maneuvered to have them seated by the table hosting two SWAT warriors.

Graham nodded for Ross to slide into the chair beside the window, back-to-back with Erik. Made sense: Ross and Erik already knew each other from helping the poor old woman with the dead dog. They gave each other a nod.

So there'd be no mistake, as if he were a polite gentleman of yore, Graham's palm directed Nora to take the chair against the window and facing Ross.

Graham filled the chair beside Ross.

Thus he set himself up to ride the *clackety-clack* with his eavesdropping back against a SWAT warrior, Ross to his left trapped against the window, Nora across from him one chair in from the aisle so he'd have plenty of time to catch her if she bolted from where he could watch her every move.

The Dining Car's door slid open.

The maître d' led the last passenger to arrive to the empty chair at the table with Graham, Ross and Nora:

Della Storm.

Glistening black helmet hair dyed to hide any gray. Blazing dark eyes in a regal face powdered pink around clown lips that glistened neon between flesh and blood. Her audaciously purple dress strained to contain voluptuous curves. The purple boa flowed out behind her as she *boom-boompa-boom*'d to where she sat on the aisle across a virgin white tablecloth from silver-haired Graham.

"*Well,*" she drawled, "look at the four of us. On the train. What a cozy crew are we. Charmed, I'm sure."

None of the three souls she'd joined gave any response to her social proffer.

Della's jaw slackened. Her neon lips glistened as Graham centered her black eyes and she made conversation: "I wonder what the special is tonight."

The waitress told them it was a tenderloin filet.

"Tender is fine," said Della, "but I'm a woman who *tends* to like her meat a little tough. Gives me something to saw into, savor with long, slow chews. After all, we might as well use our teeth while we've still got them."

Ross felt like he'd sucked a whole lemon drop to an unreal stone. Heard himself tell the waitress: "I'll take that."

Nora waved her hand *whatever*, and Ross said: "So will she."

Graham nodded *yes.*

"*Oooo,*" said Della. "A cabal of carnivores."

Nora sat trapped by her side.

Della's eyes turned to Ross across from her.

Purred: "Where are you kids going?"

Ross stared at Nora: "The Windy City."

"Be careful," said Della. "Don't get blown away."

"After all," she added, "you make such an adorable couple, wouldn't want to lose you."

Della turned back to Graham like she hadn't been talking to him all along.

"And what, *pray tell*, about you?" sighed Della.

"I'm here for the ride," answered Graham.

"*Ahh.*" Della smiled slow and hard. "Who doesn't like a good ride."

Della looked at Graham.

Looked at Ross.

Looked at Nora.

Looked at the reflection of the four of them in the now-night dark window.

Said: "I bet you all have some delicious stories."

No one shared a word with her as the waitress brought their plates, four clunks on the white tablecloth.

The smells of burned meat. A whiff from the buttered green beans.

The sounds of steel cutlery scraping white plates.

"My," said Della, clearly trying to make the best of an awkward social scene: "We are so awfully quiet sitting here tonight. It's like we're afraid of the chaperones on our high school field trip bus.

"Did you go on high school field trips? Have to ride the yellow bus?"

The train they all rode now *clackety-clacked.*

Della's eyebrows arched: "Nothing? No one's got a *yes* or even an *un-hun?*"

She smiled in sympathy. "High school. You want to forget it but you can never get out. Days of glory. Days of gory. Seemed so simple then. Like it was all about you and you were the only lonely one.

"And then you had to go on a damn field trip! The annual senior class *'take them out and show them the real world'* safari. Let a few lucky teachers stay behind and get drunk in the teacher's lounge, fuck in the band room.

"I suppose every high school still has something like that," said Della.

She paused and *still* none of her three dining companions deigned to speak.

Della nodded to the night.

"I came from some *out there*," she said, cutting a bite of steak. "Before I moved ever so *big city* far away. A small 'out in the country' nowhere town.

"I don't know where you went on your senior class field trips . . ."

Della chewed her sliced steak.

Swallowed a gulp of water.

Smeared the glass with her sticky neon lips.

She even took the time to slide one buttered green bean into her mouth, chew and swallow it, but no one—*no one*—said anything to stop or divert her story with actual conversation, so she kept going.

"Our big event was about this time of year, spring, when who can think about anything *except*. Our school always rode the two buses full of 12th graders out to the east edge of town for the annual field trip to the slaughterhouse.

"Our year," she said with pride, "was *legendary*.

"Was an afternoon performance. They piled us on the two school buses. Everybody scrambled to sit next to somebody or not get stuck *sitting with*.

"Our boss teacher for the field trip, the *numero uno* chaperone, the man who organized the gig, his name was Pete *yada-yada*. Some boring last name, who can remember. He got his glass eye courtesy of my uncle Jim when they were kids. Shouldn't have listened to my uncle Jim. He told Pete it was cool to shoot his BB gun at the streetlight. Dared him. Bust it out. Laugh city. Turns out, Pete was a pretty good shot. The BB hit the light, ricocheted right back at Pete and nailed him in the eye.

"Odd," frowned Della's pink lips. "I can't remember which one.

"Well, *local boy down*, you know?" Door was open for Pete to get the teacher degree, come back to the old hometown. He taught Social Studies or World History or some such class out of a by-the-numbers book.

"One time, Pete—

"—*no*, that's another story. This is the yellow bus field trip.

"Was a slow day at the slaughterhouse. We missed the white and brown cows clumping down wooden ramps out of trucks into stockyard pens, then one at a time through the chute to the killing floor where some kid's father shoved the business end of a pistol-like pneumatic cow killer smack between the cow's eyes, pulled the trigger and *bonked* a steel shaft right through a skull. No fuss, no muss, no wasted meat.

"So that slow day meant the field trip also missed the gutting, the bleeding out, the skinning—though most of the kids on the field trip got to see the tanning room where hides were leathered.

"One-eyed teacher Pete, he made sure we all crowded into the hanging cooler. An overhead pulley circled the whole room and on out the door down the plant disassembly-assembly line. Full slab juicy pink sides of beef hung from hooks above the sawdust floor where we all got to stand while Pete had some white-smocked butcher lecture on and on about what happened in that cooler.

"Well, needless to say, *boring!* So all us cool kids—*hey*: the cool kids in the cooler! How like, *divine.* All of us hung back in the crowd. Goofing off. Sneaking smirks when Pete and the other teacher chaperones weren't looking.

"All the goody-goody girls were all *eww!* about the slabs of raw meat dangling right in front of them.

"You know me," said Della. "Always up for a laugh.

"I hauled off and gave one of those dangling cow carcasses a big two-handed shove. I was *sort of* aiming for needed-a-lesson Heather who thought she was so *perfecto-mundo*. But the big slab of meat swung round that room on the curving wire pulley line and missed her. Heather was always lucky.

"The dead cow I mega-shoved swung 'round the line and hit the next one dangling there and that hit the next one and the next one and the next one, all of them swinging around the cooler like an assembly line of falling dominos until . . .

"You probably all went to high school with a *Carl*," said Della. "Kind of cute in a *don't look at me* way. A good boy born under a bad sign—his read not too smart, too shy, too poor and dying to please so he could stay out of the trouble.

"*Whump clunk clank* and a giant slab of dead cow swung *whack* into Carl.

"Carl bounced up off the sawdust floor. Got caught flailing around by Pete's one good eye. Pete went all pissed-off-teacher: '*You think this is funny, Carl? You think you can come out here and goof around and get all your buddies to think you're cool and disrespect the school and the butchers here, maybe hurt someone, you think you can get away with yada yada yada!*'

"Poor Carl didn't think anything like that. But all he could do was stand there like one of the sides of beef and take it. Couldn't even get '*I'm sorry!*' out of his trembling lips, shaking hands. I was afraid he was going to pee himself. Stain his blue jeans right there in the meat cooler.

"Pete detentioned Carl then and there, a week behind bars. Then Pete yelled that any of us making one fucking peep, one smirk, one not paying full attention to this field trip tour of what's going on in the real fucking world, any of us doing that, *well*, then he'd slam us on the detention line right next to Carl.

"So my class shut-mouth shuffled on out of that cooler like they were supposed to for the rest of the tour. That leather tanning shed. The stop and chop room for the meat slabs. Whatever else was there and wherever else they went.

"Carl, poor Carl, he stayed behind. Nobody stopped him. The only thing glass-eyed Pete muttered before he stalked out with the tour was that Carl better damn well be on the school bus when it pulled out of the slaughterhouse.

"Well, what could I do but stay behind, too? Hide there in the cooler's swaying meat-hooked slabs of beef. Watch Carl through the swinging pink meat hunks as he trembled with *not the cold* and too cut-up to even cry.

"I waited until everybody was gone on. The cooler door clunked behind them. Left the two of us all alone with the swinging slabs of meat. I walked across the sawdust floor. Took poor Carl by his in-shock arm. Led him safely through the swinging sides of hooked beef. Out of the cooler to a heat lamp examining room they'd nodded to on the tour. Eased us in there and fucked him.

"What every high school boy wants, right?

"Was so sweet. *Then* he was able to cry."

Della shook her black-lacquered head above the white-clothed table full of eaten-off plates, clearly *finally* didn't care about her anti-social, *wouldn't speak* fellow passengers Nora, Ross and Graham with their suddenly pale faces.

"On the school bus ride away from the slaughterhouse, Carl just sat there on a seat all by himself. Stared at the grooved metal bus floor between his shoes. He had such a big day he couldn't even tell me thanks."

Della sighed. "Growing up. We've all been there."

Dessert was cherry pie.

59

T he weirdest dinner, *right?*" said Erik as he closed their cabin door he'd let
Terri walk through first. "Our first 'Date Night' with guys packing guns."

When he looked down to latch the door, the watch strapped around
Erik's wrist told him his heart rate was up and that his current location
was in the Central Time Zone.

From Pacific to Mountain to Central time in slightly more than one
spin of the earth as it circled around the sun in our expanding universe.
On this train *clackety-clacking* deeper into a North Dakota night, Erik felt
off, lost in the spinning tick-tocks, but the high-tech watch assured him
it was the time it was where he was: 7:32 P.M., with Arrival Chicago less
than a true day away.

And nobody knows a thing about that *then* except me, he told himself.

Erik started to reminisce about: *"Remember that time when we had dinner
with your best friend from high school who—"*

—when Terri with her eyes pulled by the night river beyond this train cabin's window said: "OK if I brush my teeth?"

"Ahh . . . Of course!" he said. "Whatever you want."

"We've got two sinks, so if you want—"

"I'll wait—if that's OK."

Terri retreated into the bathroom tube. Rolled the door shut.

The *click* of that lock in a waterfall of blue light.

Shower. Toilet. Silver metal sink. Terri's face captured by the mirror.

She flossed her teeth.

Used mint fluoride toothpaste to brush every tooth. Her gums. Tongue.

Made herself go to the bathroom—*whoosh*.

Washed her hands.

Water swirled down the metal sink's drain.

Terri blinked at her face caught by that blue-lit mirror.

She came out of the tube as Erik moved toward their suitcases. He choreographed his route to avoid any collision.

Terri stood by her pillow. Saw Erik lift his laptop. "Are you going to work or play video—"

"No," said Erik.

At this point in time, Chicago was as Chicago would be. Checking Op Status on his laptop wouldn't change a thing. Plus, he'd gotten no text alerts of trouble.

Couldn't help it, he heard himself say: "Chicago."

Everything changes then, he thought.

Rearranged his luggage because that was a normal thing for him to do. Casually said: "We get there tomorrow afternoon."

"Good," said Terri.

Erik stiffened.

"No!" said Terri. "Great trip—honest! It's just . . . I mean . . . I'm just tired, *really tired*. And it's dark, but that's what it's supposed to be, and tomorrow, you know . . . sun. Standing still. No *wobble wobble* under your feet. In one place."

He said *yeah*.

She said: "So, *ah*, it's getting late . . ."

Not even 8 o'clock in this time now, he thought. But the trip has been long. She was, had to be, *just-tired*.

So he said: "Yeah."

Got his gray sweats. Nodded to the bathroom tube. "I'll—unless you want—"

"No, that's good, I already." She gave him a smile.

He smiled back. Latched himself in the tube's waterfall blue.

Water turned on in the bathroom.

Hurry! Terri told herself. *Be ready so Erik won't see you naked!*

Terri raced to their suitcases stack. Kicked off her sneakers.

Water shut off in the bathroom.

She shoved down her khaki slacks—her panties came off with them, but there was no time to rectify that error. Terri raced down the buttons on her blouse. Tossed her bra. Shrugged her ankle-length flannel nightgown over her head as the bathroom *clicked* open, blue light catching the erotic-dampening, tent-like nightgown falling over her naked back as she saw the bathroom tube sliding open and Erik's politely-turning-away reflection in the night windows.

They stood there.

Clackety-clack, clackety-clack.

"Watched you today," blurted Terri. "Back in that town. You, that reporter guy. The mom and daughter. All of you helping the woman whose dog died."

"Didn't do much."

"But you did something. You all did something."

"Just the chance we had," said Erik.

"No. Not just chance. You're a good man. A really good man." Terri shrugged. "You are. A good person."

Erik said: "Takes one to know one."

They looked away from each other.

"So," she said, "we better . . ."

He said *yeah*.

Someone said: "Last night on the train."

Clackety-clack, clackety-clack.

Terri pulled the flannel nightgown up over her head, *off.*

Erik fought free of his gray sweats.

Wrapped themselves in each other's arms. His muscling mashing hands. Her clawing fingernails. Him kissing her kissing him. Flesh against flesh with hurtling intensity. They're on her bed. He devours her breasts, mouths her stomach but she pulls him up onto her and combat scissors her legs around him, around the imperative of time, *here/now* throbbing their skulls, slamming against each other. Together they came as overwhelmingly as a train blasting out of a tunnel.

No whistle screamed.

No one cried out.

They held each other tight.

Until they weren't.

She settled on his chest where she'd been seemed like for so long.

Said: "We better—I mean, it's getting late, and . . ."

Tired, thought Erik, she's just tired. It's barely 8:30 here, but, *well*, tired, she has to be, she must be.

Soft came her words: "Would you mind if . . ."

"Of course," whispered Erik.

He angel kissed her forehead.

Slid out of that sex-scented bed. Scooped up his sweats. Climbed into his upper bunk and snapped off the light up there as he crawled under his covers.

Terri found her flannel nightgown on the floor. Pulled it on. Snapped out the light by the windows. One last light glowed above her pillow by her plugged-in cellphone. She crawled into her rumpled bed, killed that shared illumination.

Darkness filled this *wobble wobble* box where they lay apart together.

She thought about a sleeping pill—*no*: she had to take this as it was.

Under her bed covers, her cellphone's screen secretly lit her face as Terri quietly did what she had to do.

60

The rumbling train chased its yellow cone of light through that dark night.

Minot, North Dakota—32 minutes dead ahead for a scheduled 9:27 arrival.

Albert stood in the dimness of the closed-doors passageway level under the Premium cabins. He waited next to the Baggage Car door. Alone at the bottom of stairs leading up to where his ticket said he belonged until the train hit Fargo at midnight. Now he was in that *there* like he'd never before been anywhere.

His shoulder bag *clunked* against the train car's steel door to *off the train.*

His mind told him that sometimes the best you can do is give what you can't get. Help someone free her shape from the metal of her life.

Where is—Where are they?

He didn't want to think about that. About what that husband snarled before he led Suzanne out of the Dining Car toward their cabin. About what she might have to do *before*.

ALBERT'S OBVIOUS QUESTIONS
ABOUT THE STAIRCASE MURDER

"How will you get him to come with you?"
"He's got nowhere to go except with me. And I lucked out. Now I can tell him that if we take an after dark walk, circle through the two levels of our car, maybe his new best friend Fergus Lang will pop out of his cabin to say hello."

"What if someone sees you?"
"The more *drunk-man* witnesses, the better—right until we're at the top of the stairs down to the locked Baggage Car. No one's got a reason to be there. The corridor leading there past our cabins is short. I'll either spot witnesses or know they're not there."

"What if someone is *there?"*
"We walk another loop. Can't pass up any chance to see Fergus Lang."

"What if there are security cameras?"
"That computer, I found a public bids' notice to update the train's system. And it listed all the ways the system won't work. I double-checked soon as I got on the train. The few cameras are big clunkers. You can see them. And top or bottom, those stairs aren't in front of any camera lenses.

"And when I'm . . . walking him toward the stairs, *why*, I'll be the nervous, helpful, clumsy little woman. I've lived the life. I've seen the movies. I know how to act and make it look real. *That's* what any security footage will show."

"What if you can't push him down the stairs?"
"Be serious."

"What if you push him down the stairs BUT he just stumbles?"
"A trip or a kick, another push or a pull."

"What if . . ."
"Go on. Say it."

"What if he goes down BAM! but lands alive? Maybe not even bad hurt?"
"I never planned for you to be there."

"But I am, I will be, so what 'if'?"
"These hands hefted cantaloupes to pick the one most likely to please him—as if he ever noticed. These arms toted bags of groceries. Sacks of garden cement and fertilizer. This back pushes his dead mother's damn piano nobody ever plays across the living room to vacuum."

"But if he's only fallen down onto the slope of the stairs . . . ?"
"I hush him into laying still. To let me check to be sure he's OK. Then smash his skull against the edge of a step. Smash him *until*. Twist his head until his fat neck snaps. Until these hands feel his heart as dead as it already is. Deducing what's left on the stairs as something more than what it looks like, more than the booze

it smells like, more than what other passengers saw, figuring out *what really happened* while dealing with a schedule-to-keep train in North Dakota at night . . . Who's going to do that?"

"If there's blood . . ."

"Let there be blood. On me. Smeared from wherever it is on the walls, the stairs. I'm the tried-to-help-him, hysterical wife of a known drunk. No cop in North Dakota will go *TV crime show* on that scene, and if they do, what they'll find in Brian's blood is alcohol proof of an accident."

"What about me?"

"That's up to you. You can walk away now. Get off in Fargo. Go do what you gotta do. Or before you get off, you can be a witness who saw a tragic accident. You could even tell Brian and our Attendant Cari and the SWAT cops."

"What if something goes wrong?"

"It's already wrong."

Now standing at the bottom of the steep stairs by the door to the Baggage Car, Albert thought: *And it's already late.*

A dark silhouette loomed at the top of the stairs.

A woman wearing a knee-length coat, a purse hanging from her shoulder.

Alone.

Her left foot stepped down the first stair.

Her right took the second.

Suzanne.

They met at the last step down. The first step up.

Albert hissed: "Where is he?"

"Drunk," answered Suzanne. "Actually, really, totally drunk."

"Like you want! Only not there. But you can—"

"I can go back and get him. Drag him to the top of the stairs. I'd only need to just let him fall."

Clackety-clack, clackety-clack.

"He's not coming," said Suzanne. "And I'm not going back."

She wore no ruby lipstick.

"Was the little blue pills. They made this happen any and every which way.

"Brian was tipsy when we got back to the cabin. What he said at dinner. What he said so you'd hear it. He made me watch him take a blue pill."

Suzanne laughed—quickly covered her mirthful lips so no one could hear what she had to say. No one except Albert, who stood there, stunned, eyes on her.

"That's when I knew killing him would *totally* work. Those little blue pills take half an hour or more to wind up a man so he *can*. I reminded Brian of that. Suggested we have a drink to pass the time, like we were in some cool movie, and *oh*, he liked that. Scotches for two.

"By the time he'd finished, he could barely stand, let alone . . . But I kept it up like we were *going to*. Sold him that he still needed a little more time for the blue pill to go full power. And so we might as well walk a loop or two to run into Fergus Lang. Show that star he wasn't the only one who knew how to shine.

"I got Brian on his feet, helped him stand on the *wobble wobble*. Turned around to unlatch our cabin door.

"When I looked back, there he was: Shoulders slumped. Mouth gaping so he couldn't stop his drools. Saggy from his eyes to his jowls to his limp dick to his fat ass. Just standing there waiting to take the little bit he could force out of me. Just like he had his whole sorry saggy life.

"And that's when I knew."

Her hand fluttered to a tiny silver bird hung by a shoelace from her neck. "That sad asshole doesn't get to shape all the metal of me."

A quiet laugh shook her shoulders. A wide grin lit her face as she stood at the bottom of those dimly lit stairs outside the Baggage Car.

"All the way up from my heels, every bone in my body, all those damn shit-on lost years and *BAM!* Both hands, I shoved him so hard he flew backwards. Crashed flat on his back on the lower bunk BOOM! Bounced off and hit the floor like a flopped fish but breathing and I knew, no real damage. He didn't even yell. Just laid there. Looked up at me with his gaping mouth. Stunned by what I damn well had done! And he couldn't do a thing unless I made it happen for him. That's where I left him. If he hasn't already, he's soon gonna pass out dead drunk."

She grinned: "Dead drunk instead of just dead."

Suzanne stared at Albert who was soon supposed to make himself die.

Albert swallowed: "What are you going to do?"

"Tell a man named *Al-bear* 'thank you.' Then get off this train."

"What?"

"Next stop. Not *to* the ticket I got, *at* the get-off I choose."

Suzanne told Albert: "Come with me."

They both felt his pounding heart.

She said: "If the fire is what's right for you . . . Wait until Fargo. Do what you gotta do.

"But maybe there's another shape for you in this metal," she said. "Maybe you can find it. Maybe you can make it. Maybe not. Maybe there still *is* a *maybe.*"

"You—"

"I don't know. I'm not expecting. Offering more than asking you to get off with me. For you, that's a *maybe*. For me, it's a *gotta*. I don't know what happens after our shoes touch some Nowhere, North Dakota depot platform in the middle of the night. I don't care where except for being there and not here."

"What if what you do doesn't work?"

"This train already doesn't work for *Suzanne*."

"What about me?"

"You're who was here for me—for *me*, not for who I *was*. You *get it*. Maybe our *maybe* means you go your way, I go mine, never again track together. Don't know *how* we go *if* we go further together. That's all I got."

"But you'll need—"

"I grabbed my purse, wallet, credit cards, phone, toothbrush, old lady meds, took his blue pills just to fuck with him and all the cash except what's in his pants pockets. My hand is never going in there to touch that again. I got my coat." She laughed. "And sensible shoes."

"What should I do?"

"Absolutely only what's roaring up in you right now."

Clackety-clack, clackety-clack.

He said: "Minot's coming up about half an hour down the track."

"*Mi*-not," said Suzanne. "*Why*-not."

Al-bear swallowed—felt himself grin. "I should probably get some things."

"First you better *leave* something."

She lifted the strapped bag off his shoulder. Undid the snaps. Opened the bag. Slowly circled her hand around the silver thermos tube of *IT*. Avoided the thermos's twist-off cap. Avoided the alligator clamp handle she knew was the trigger. Stood there holding explosive inferno in her hand, eyes flitting around the cramped corridor leading from the door marked BAGGAGE CAR to . . .

An easy-open-glass-door cabinet for a fire extinguisher waited on the train car wall near the keypad-locked steel door.

She pulled open that cabinet door. Eased the metal thermos of hellfire in there alongside the fire extinguisher. Pressed the door shut. Nothing for anybody to see who wasn't really looking, and then *IT* would *obviously* be a *Be Careful* find.

She glanced into the lightened bag.

Nodded at small sculpted shapes in there. "I'd like to see those sometime."

Handed his bag back to him. "Go get the rest of what you need."

Smiled unpainted lips. "I'll be at the bottom of the switchback stairs coming down from our cabins. Waiting for Minot."

61

They pulled out of Minot as SWAT officer David Hale came out of a bathroom in the team's crowded Crew Car between the Baggage Car and the Locomotive. Came out of a bathroom up near the front of that train pushing its yellow cone of light through North Dakota's Big Dark.

He joined a huddle of troopers standing in the aisle between their cabins of two-bunk roomettes. They were laughing and joking and being *bros*, the kind of *belong* David Hale had been looking for since he was 10 years old and realized he was the last kid standing on the school's sandy playground.

Now he read the smiles on the faces of the *bros*, knew he was still *Rook*, not one of *Us* until he got them all safely off the train in Chicago.

With no fuck-ups! thought David Hale. Please don't let me fuck up!

He eased into standing *casual* near three dudes: Tom, Tom Fruen out of St. Paul, Jake somebody from somewhere and the trooper named Alice Noah.

"Good thing Alice isn't driving this fucking train," two SWAT troopers who David Hale didn't know had joked that afternoon.

Alice had heard them, shot back: "If I was driving, we'd be flying."

They all laughed—

—OK, maybe David Hale laughed a little too loud, but they all let it slide.

That last night of his first *clackety-clacking*, he left that bathroom the size of an upright coffin and walked into one of those *wow* times that lighten our lives.

Silent but deadly, somebody farted.

"Oh, man!" said somebody as somebody else said: "Name and claim!"

"Come on, guys, it's close in here!"

"Little known fact," said Jake.

Everybody groaned: *'Here we go again with Jake's little-known facts.'*

Groans didn't stop Jake.

He announced: "Cow farts are a major contributor to global warming."

"Do you see any cows in here?" said somebody.

Nick said: "Just a lot of bulls."

Alice said: "Just a lot of bull-*shit*."

"Shoots and scores, *motha-fucka!*" David Wood—*'the other David'*—hit Alice a high-five.

"I only fart twice every 24," said Tom. "Once to get out of bed and greet the day, once when I get back in bed to say goodnight."

"That must rock the socks off whoever's sleeping with you," said Alice.

Everybody laughed.

Especially Tom.

That's when Sgt. Carlisle beckoned David Hale out of his best moment of this *clackety-clack* mission (*so far*) and back to the S.C.—the Surveillance Chair—where radios and cellphones and screens were corded together for two laptop command keyboards. This watch post was set up in the

Roomette cabin right next to the keypad-locked and blackout-windowed door to the Baggage Car.

Sgt. Carlisle nodded to a nearby bathroom. "Saw you up there. You OK?"

"Sure, Sarge. I mean . . ."

Make it a joke! Show him you're one of the guys!

" . . . I mean," said David Hale, "that Dining Car meal was so good I hated to see it go, but you know, when you gotta, you gotta."

"But you're not feeling queasy or train motion sick, are you, Hale?"

"No, Sarge. I'm squared away."

"Good, 'cause nobody wants to pull you off the break-your-cherry."

A SWAT trooper named . . . Pulaski rode the S.C. then. He kept his eyes on the two laptop screens showing movies of what was going on.

The laptop screen on the left showed movie clips from security cameras installed in only about half of the train cars—including the locomotive.

The laptop screen on the right showed one movie only, all day and all night:

The *all* of *nothing moving* and *nothing doing* in the Baggage Car.

Sgt. Carlisle watched rookie David Hale eyeball his coming post.

Hale said: "Run a systems check at shift change, right, Sarge?"

"Got that right, Rook. Now say goodnight. Coming up on the Settle-Down at 10. We're not a bunch of kids, but it's protocol and polite for all us gunners to gear down, quiet down, let who wants to *get to* catch some sleep.

"You got midnight shift, so you better catch some sleep to be sharp. This is one of those rare sometimes that plays as *snooze or lose*.

"Set your cell phone vibrate alarm for 90 minutes. Button it tight in your shirt. Curl up however you can get comfortable. If you're late posting, Pulaski here will come get me and believe me: I will not be happy to see Pulaski's pissed off face interrupting my dreams."

"Got it, Sarge."

That three-striper who L.T. kept pushing Seattle Command to promote (*Fuck the whole college degree thing!*), that Michael Carlisle gave David Hale a smile and the nod: "You'll do O.K., Rook."

But when David Hale went to do what he was supposed to do, walked to his Roomette with its two side-by-side chairs that alligator-opened into bunks, drifting out into the corridor came the sounds of a man and a woman.

The Man: ". . . and I always come a-running."

The Woman: "Yeah, being a bitch is a bitch."

Have to do it! thought David Hale. The mission. And the clock.

He *harumphed* loudly and knocked softly on the then slid-open door.

In his quarters, two comrades in arms:

One, his training officer Jon Nazdin, a badge who had everybody's back.

Two, the Squad Corporal to Squad Sergeant Carlisle to L.T.—Carmalita Vasquez. The squad called her "Karma."

"Hundred percent," she'd tell the troopers under her two-stripes command. "So do it right or I'll be your payback bitch."

Rook David Hale didn't know that Karma was being the trust buddy for poor Jon's woes with his married-too-soon roaming wife.

Jon blinked back his not-tears: "Oh, David! Sorry, we lost track of time."

Karma got to her feet: "Bunk by the window, Rook. You'll have to climb over Jon's sorry ass to get out *when*, but it's better for you to be where it might be easier to catch some *z's* than by the door."

"Don't worry about climbing over me if I'm asleep," said Jon. "I'm used to it."

They left him alone.

David Hale hung his holstered Glock 19 pistol packed & stacked with 14 bullets on the wall where it would be an easy grab in a *clackety-clack* dark train cabin. He left his shoes on. Set his cellphone alarm. He *whunked* the bunk by the window into full recline. Settled his back into the cushion. Pulled the black eye mask out of his other shirt pocket. Had that darkness over his eyes when Jon came back into their cabin, settled in his chair with his phone where he promised himself he would not—*would not*—really, he Would Not text yet another rambling plea to Yvonne that she wouldn't really answer.

Blindfolded David Hale knew it was Jon who'd settled beside him. That made the rookie feel safe, feel right, feel good about his coming midnight shift.

The black eye mask circled him with silky darkness as he heard Jon say: "Don't worry, Rook. You'll rock your first graveyard."

62

The three of them rode the *clackety-clack* night locked in Ross's cabin.

Ross took the chair by the window. He kept his face to the glass and its eerie reflection of him over the rushing darkness.

Nora lay on the upper bunk. Her cellphone rode on her breastbone.

Graham lay on the lower bunk. Faced the door. Near Minot, Ross and Nora heard him slumber with the fatalism of a waiting soldier in a combat zone.

Waiting.

Waiting for the Snapchat *Bzzz!* of the phone between Nora's breasts.

They all carried cellphones now on lanyards around their necks so the phones wouldn't drop/clatter/break on a burgled floor.

Nora outfitted Graham with a burner phone from her suitcase. Loaded it with Snapchat. Ross downloaded that app to his phone. They zapped each other back and forth to be sure the systems worked.

She brought her laptop to Ross's cabin. Ran Ross and Graham through the grift until she convinced herself that they *got it*. Put the silver duct tape roll and scissors on the table of Ross's suitcase.

Her laptop screen played the grift's hack in four windows.

The upper left-hand quadrant window showed the *nothing stirring* Baggage Car lit for the security cameras that fed the SWAT teams' screen.

The upper right-hand window beside the Target Zone view showed the SWAT team's Surveillance Chair watch officer and what could be glimpsed of the rest of the Crew Car beyond his face, a midnight movie starring *rook'* David Hale.

The laptop's lower left-hand quadrant flashed scenes from the few security cameras mounted in the train. The lights-out shadowed Dining Car where no visible ghosts sat at white tablecloth booths set to serve all the right passengers. A random dark *wobble-wobble* aisle. Coach class chairs of slumped citizens.

"These shots we're seeing are real," Nora told Graham and Ross. "But our hack means the SWAT teams' screens and files will fill with yesterday's re-loop."

The lower right quadrant window shined ghostly light forward, ever forward, a perpetual projection over the cross-tied railroad track that this train rode with those *clackety-clack* steel wheels.

"Nose camera in the locomotive," said Nora. "So corporate can see what their train hits that could sue them."

She shrugged: "I just want to see where we're going."

"Where we're at," said Ross.

"We're here and it's now," pronounced Graham.

They emptied their pockets and persons of anything metal that could accidentally *clank* or even *clink* on the Baggage Car's metal floor.

For Nora that meant taking damn near everything out of the black purse holstered to her right hip: The two lipstick tubes. Perfume bottle. Deodorant stick. Toothbrush and toothpaste. Crinkling condoms.

They all knew no surveillance would hear those fall, but seeing condoms accidentally left behind on the post-grift floor of the Baggage Car might make SWAT warriors wonder. One wonder, one check of what was supposed to be the film of the night before and reality would chase them forever.

All Nora left in her belt/purse were charging cords and the rubber & plastic black hairbrush.

Graham made Ross carry his pen and journal, *just in case*: "If a phone breaks or we lose the Snap-*whatever* going through probably the last section of America where Internet is not automatically part of the landscape, best be rigged to work old school so we can scrawl notes to communicate with each other."

Memories drifted in Graham's eyes as if history mattered.

"The nighttime raid *American style*," said Graham, "got perfected back in Occupied Japan after World War II by the Navy C.O. of nightstick cops deployed to keep our drunk sailors and soldiers in line, control black market hustlers, pissed-off survivors of Hiroshima and Nagasaki, lefties, Russian spies, the Yakuza. He was a loveable killer-eyed genius bear named Tom Duval who back in my day bossed a 1970s off-the-books American spy group called Task Force 157. Tom concluded that the best time to launch a raid is 3 A.M."

"We can't wait that long," said Nora. "We got too much to do before the train wakes up."

Ross said: "So Zed picks our *Go*?"

"He gives the signal," said Nora. "We both watch the hack. Make sure the trooper working the graveyard shift back in the SWAT Crew Car is settled in. Seeing in his screens what we want him to see while we see him and that all the rest of his SWAT team are down for the night."

"Down," said Ross. "Sure."

"You want out," said Nora, "we hit Fargo near midnight."

"After that, we're gone grift," said Graham.

Clackety-clack, clackety-clack, knifing through the North Dakota night.

Past lonely lit farms.

Past lamppost-lit small towns like *Rugby, Devil's Lake.*

Past a highway oiled from dead dinosaurs.

This train rode its own highway of steel rails and wooden ties.

Rode its way right into the big time of Fargo with a hiss, a sigh, a soft shudder to not disturb the majority of the passengers who were already asleep.

Nora stood at the window in Ross's cabin. Stared out at the lone streetlight depot platform in darkest Fargo.

No passenger got off the train.

Not even the ticketed-there messenger bag man Albert.

No new passengers got on the train.

A clunk, a shudder, a lonesome whistle, *wobble-wobble, clackety-clack*, the train pulled out of that famous North Dakota city.

Nora saw no one standing on the lone streetlight-lit empty flat wooden platform to watch the train go or yell: *"Stop!"*

Turned from the window to tell the grim Ross and Graham: *"Get ready."*

Graham had to use the bathroom. The old guy curse.

Then Ross had to follow the old guy's lead. A young guy's nerves.

Nora's body commanded itself to *Hold Everything In. Don't let go.*

"Zed is giving the train time to settle," said Ross.

"And to get there first," said Graham.

Nora handed the roll of silver duct tape to Ross, scissors to Graham.

Took a deep breath through her nostrils to be sure they were clear.

Stood tall and feet apart to ride steady in the *wobble-wobble.*

Pursed her lips for a soft kiss.

Closed her eyes.

Heard the silver duct tape pulled off its roll. Heard the snip of the scissors.

Ross sealed her damn lips with a smoothed-down strip of silver duct tape.

Then Nora duct-taped his mouth shut.

She duct-taped Graham.

The silver duct tape meant no one would hear them cry out with a bumped shin or an accidental startle in the Baggage Car, a human sound that might carry over the *clackety-clack* into the Crew Car of SWAT ears.

Three desperados with silver duct-taped mouths on a midnight train.

Staring at each other with all they could not say.

Or scream.

Nora stuck strips of silver duct tape on her belt/purse that was cinched around her waist.

They snapped on surgeon's plastic gloves.

Snapchats buzzed.

Zed posted *Green Light.*

Ross led the way.

They marched through the corridor of this *clackety-clacking* train.

Three passengers with their mouths silver duct-taped and their hands sheathed in *no fingerprints* white plastic gloves.

Ross shook his head: *We look like zombies in search of brains.*

Because *hell,* he thought: If we had them, we wouldn't be here.

They reached the top of the train's steepest stairs. Carefully, *oh so carefully* made their way down to the first level. Stood at the blackened-window, keypad-locked door to the Baggage Car.

Nora tapped-in the grift's secret hack 1-9-4-9 Command Code.

Click! went the Baggage Car's silver door.

Nora punched its black pad.

The silver metal door *whunked* open.

Bathed their silver duct-taped trio with the Baggage Car's glow.

63

Nora. Ross. Graham.

Three zombies with silver duct-taped mouths.

They stepped into the dim-lit Baggage Car. Saw stacked canvas mail sacks and leather pouches. Tagged passengers' suitcases. Boxes from Amazon. A shiny car bumper. A chest-high stack of wooden pallets. A battery-powered pallet jack that looked like a rent-a-scooter with a forklift front.

The train door behind them closed with a *whunk*.

Nora glanced at her cellphone.

In the Crew Car, SWAT officer David Hale stared at the laptop screen he didn't know was staring back at him. Gave no sign he'd heard the *whunk*.

In the Baggage Car.

Two black metal cubes.

The cubes faced each other across the Baggage Car aisle. *Seven-feet-long-every-which-way* twins except for their logos.

Him.

Silver duct tape sealed the mouth of the bad haircut man standing past the cubes by the garage-style slid-down metal doors. Surgeon's gloves hid his hands. A lanyard-looped cellphone rode in the pocket of his short-sleeve shirt. Tattoos swore to the truth of something on arms thick with muscle.

Nora, Ross, Graham flashed: *It has to be him!*

He drew his cellphone. Thumbed commands.

Snapchatted Nora, but they're all together now on the message chain.

> Do your new assholes
> know what to do?

Graham Snapchatted:

> Us new assholes didn't
> come here to take shit.

Four silver duct-taped, plastic-gloved, zombie mimes sprang into action.

Zed and Ross marched—*softly, softly*—to the stack of wooden pallets. Lifted the stack's top wooden pallet, oil-stinking weathered wood. Carried it like a card table between them to the black cube logoed by white paint letters:

> PROPERTY OF U.S. GOVERNMENT
> NO UNAUTHORIZED CONTACT

Zed and Ross stacked pallets against the forbidden metal.

Boosted Nora up there.

She wobbled, tapped the hacked keypad. Its red light winked green.

Graham, Ross and Zed lugged mail sacks—*Quietly!*—away from Uncle Sam's black cube as silver-gagged Nora pointed directions from atop the pallets.

Ross pressed his spine against the side of the cube.

Shot Zed a look: '*The fuck are you waiting for?*'

Zed stood beside the poet, their backs against the cube's black steel wall. They raised their hands to heaven.

On the pallets, Nora grabbed the cube's lid. Lifted it . . .

Over and *open* fell the lid!

Caught by the two men against the wall before the lid could *BANG!*

They eased out from behind the lid. Held onto that stretch of steel so no lurch in the *clackety-clack* would *clang* that metal against its cube.

Nora peered into the cube.

Wrinkled and torn green papers with paintings of democracy's fortresses on one side. On the other side, portraits of dead presidents like Washington who rode a boat to glory and Lincoln who rode a bullet to honor. T.J. who authored liberty and justice for all *except*. Hamilton who knew money and Jackson who knew war. Grant who never lost his battle with booze until nobody cared. All crammed in that black cube along with smiling portraits of a woman-romancing, Paris-stomping, muckraking and moon-tracking bald boy who touched lightning.

The smushed jumble of thousands upon thousands upon thousands of such dream-buying bills filled that steel cube to the brim. Rips wounded many bills, but many could pass across a convenience store counter or a casino chip exchange or slide through a bank teller's cage to get a second chance at cremation. Some bills were wrinkled crumples. Some had scrawled-on phone numbers that might have been true or penned-on cartoons that might have been funny. Some smelled of cash registers. Gasoline. Coffee. Ghosts of blood, sweat, tears and *ta-dah*s.

Nora Snapchatted their picture to the grift's other silver-taped players.

They all—*quietly*—closed the lid on the money cube.

Nora unscrewed the government keypad with its imbedded hack-proof location transmitter accurate to within 11 feet. She passed the government keypad down to Graham. He set it aside as Ross helped Nora off the pallets.

Nora whirred the *silent-enough* nine-horsepower, battery-powered pallet jack across the Baggage Car like she was driving a floor sander or a baby stroller.

First pass failed.

Her skull throbbed.

Second pass, coming in slow and silent, aiming the business end of the pallet jack: forklift prongs, two flat dagger blades of unbendable steel spaced to line up with the gaps between the slats of wooden floor pallets, those two gaps of the wooden pallet under the government's black cube waiting, waiting . . .

Pierced by the blades.

The grift called for Zed to brace and hold steady the steel box, but now there were three sets of male arms to steady the black cube as Nora's gloved hand turned the ball on the pallet jack's control handle and with a groan—

—up rose the wooden pallet holding the black steel money cube.

Nora backed the load-carrying pallet jack in a turn through the Baggage Car, backed the money cube out of the way, settled it on the train car, soft *clump*.

Checked the movie in her cellphone screen:

SWAT officer David Hale sat in his watch officer's post.

Saw nothing going on in the screens of security camera feeds. Watched those movies without sound that showed the unchanging shape of his time.

The robbers in the Baggage Car burned 19 minutes moving the clone cube to where the government cube once sat.

Took them 11 minutes to move the government's cube to its clone's spot.

The train *clackety-clacked* through moonlit shimmers of Minnesota's 10,000 lakes.

The front of the clone cube box where the other cube was branded as government property, a corporate logo of blue sky with white clouds proclaimed:

LONE BIRD SERVICE SYSTEMS

Zed got the boost up onto a new pallet stack beside the clone cube.

Switched the clone keypad for the government tracker keypad.

Graham set that keypad on a mail sack.

Nora and Ross did the *backs-against-the-cube-wall, catch-the-lid's-weight* routine as Zed opened the clone cube, flashed a photo, Snapchatted *what's inside.*

Black and white layers of recycled newspapers. Ripped cardboard. Chunks of this. Scraps of that. A barfed-on college hoodie. The stench of old headlines. Smells of *dead*, maybe mice or even rats, a stray dog—didn't matter, any corpses became soot in the big burn. The clone cube was not as full of trash as the government cube was with money. Maybe three feet of empty rode atop the box load of yesterday's newspapers.

Zed ran his hand along the inside underlip of the clone cube. Found an orange rope taped all the way around the inside walls. Jerked the orange rope free. Pulled up all the slack. The line went tight.

Out of the newspapers rose a bulging green duffle bag.

Zed muscled the duffle bag out of the cube.

Ross *gently, quietly* laid the duffle bag on the train car floor.

Nora checked her cellphone screen movie:

SWAT trooper David Hale, no change.

Graham obeyed Zed's hand signals. Helped that brute off the pallet. Staggered, grimaced under the strain with obvious old man muscles.

Ross pulled a tarp out of the duffle bag.

Nora wrinkled her brow. Shrugged. Shook her head NO to the tarp.

Lifted a white-taped spray can labeled "A" out of the duffle bag.

Sprayed the Lone Bird Service System logo.

No one outside of the Baggage Car heard the *hiss*.

The soaked corporate logo of blue sky with white cloud letters curled off the black steel cube. The white cloud lettering bubbled up off what lay beneath.

The front of the clone cube revealed white letters painted on black steel:

> PROPERTY OF U.S. GOVERNMENT
> NO UNAUTHORIZED CONTACT

Ross pulled out a long, thick mailing tube and a second white-taped spray can labeled "B" out of the duffle. Handed that to Nora.

She took it. Worked her cellphone to Snapchat:

😫😩⏱ ! ! ! 😩

Ross popped the lid off the mailer tube as he and Nora hurried to the clone cube. She shook the white-taped spray can "B."

Zed grabbed the drop cloth tarp. Bustled ahead of them.

Silver-haired/silver-duct-taped Graham hurried to help as he held his cellphone in front of his face, swiped and tapped to exit Snapchat—

Graham's cellphone screen blasted out the jaw-dropped, wide-eyed shocked face of SWAT trooper David Hale.

64

"*What the fuck!*"

SWAT trooper David Hale blinked at the Baggage Car screen's flash:

A horrible *not human* face with a silver mouth.

A monster stared at him staring back and—

Blink!

That screen showed only the logical reality of the empty Baggage Car.

"*What?*" whispered pistol-packing rookie trooper David Hale.

He checked the other laptop screen windows showing this train's cars full of shadows and sleep, nobody moving and nothing going on.

The Baggage Car screen: No monster.

He clicked on this security command's systems check: All normal.

Gag, he told himself. Not the silver strip mouth of the monster, but *gag* as in *joke*, as in: *Let's get the new guy working the graveyard shift!* Like an initiation, a prank to watch him panic. Big laughs.

Trooper David Hale whirled around in his sentry's seat.

Caught nobody lurking behind him. Nobody peeking out of the closed doors to the Roomettes where his new buddies were supposed to be sleeping. He heard snores. Sighs. No stifled laughter. No snickers.

Heard only the *clackety-clack* of here, now.

Thought: If it wasn't a prank . . .

What the hell, a hallucination? A waking dream? Hell, a nightmare.

I was not asleep on graveyard watch! I was not!

'What do you do with what only you saw?' confounded the rookie trooper. What you cannot prove or seem to see again. Tell somebody? Wake up Sgt. Carlisle? Or hell: trigger the alarm. Blast everyone awake. Tumbling out of their bunks. Filling their hands with guns. Running to him to find . . .

The Baggage Car screen still showed him nothing but its boring warehouse.

Trooper Hale shook his head—to clear it, to tell himself *no*.

The voice of reason sounded in his head:

'If you sound the alarm, probably wake the whole damn train. And sure, you'll pass a drug test with flying colors. Pass the psych exam, too. But all that won't matter, because if the squad doesn't see the monster, all their pissed-off eyes will be on me, the new guy who couldn't do a simple sentry post right.'

Clackety-clack, clackety-clack.

Rookie SWAT trooper David Hale sat where he'd been ordered to sit.

Stared at what he had been ordered to watch.

Saw screens that showed no monsters.

65

Silver duct tape gagged, plastic-gloved zombies raged in the Baggage Car.

Ross waved his gloved hands above his head. His wide-eyed glare screamed at Graham what his silver duct-taped mouth couldn't:

"What the fuck did you do!"

Zed mimed his forefinger against his own skull: *"Are you nuts?"*

Graham would have sent a group Snapchat apology, but Nora'd been a blur of action grabbing his cellphone out of the hands of an old man who *of course* couldn't work it. She killed its power. Jerked the lanyard so hard his neck hurt.

I deserve that, thought Graham.

He spread his hands wide and shrugged to the three people: *I fucked up.*

Let them wave their arms in the air.

Let the color fade from their flushed red, silver duct-taped faces.

Then like he's folding in pie crust dough, Graham turned his hands over and down and pulled them in, the tingle of that energy and the motion of its execution pulling the full attention of the other three duct-taped zombies.

He tapped his wristwatch. His hard nod said: *Get over it.*

The other mimes raced to the government's cube, the aerosol spray can "B" in Nora's hand, Ross clutching the mailing tube, Zed scurrying drag.

Zed stopped to spread the tarp on the floor.

Looked back to check on Graham.

Who was coming slow but steady.

Who as soon as Zed looked away—

—rebel mocked & bopped to rock 'n' roll in his skull.

Ross popped open the mailing tube, shook it, pulled out and unrolled . . .

A poster identical to the logo poster they'd sprayed off the grift's cube.

LONE BIRD SERVICE SYSTEMS

Nora re-rolled the poster, face out. Held it that way for a 10-count. When it unrolled this time, the poster barely curled.

Zed stood nearby, tarp on the floor, cellphone ready in one hand.

His other hand commanded Graham to *stop*, stay back where he is.

Ross held the poster open and wide, its back facing out.

Nora sprayed ever-outward swoops of sticky from can "A" over the treasure cube's steel logo:

PROPERTY OF U.S. GOVERNMENT
NO UNAUTHORIZED CONTACT

Zed moved to the side of the cube closest to the door out of here, just off center. He beckoned Graham: *Step closer, follow Ross and Nora, stand closer.*

Zed's V fingers pointed to his own eyes, pointed to Ross and Nora.

Watch them. Keep your eyes on their work. Be ready to help.

Nora used aerosol can B to spray a thick coat of sticky on the back of the grift's fake poster. Knew she had three minutes before the adhesive firms from sticky to stiff.

Zed waited until the spraying stopped. Thumbed commands in his cellphone and from it, an architect's app projected red light beams onto the real black cube. The red light beams created the shape the size of the official government logo showing the exact angle, altitude position and placement for Ross and Nora to glue the grift's corporate poster over Uncle Sam's logo.

That man and woman pressed the grift's lie into place.

Side by side they leaned forward. Their hands smoothed the adhesive-sprayed poster on the hijacked cube. Their arms pressed out to hold the lie in place to dry. Behind and off to the side of Nora, Graham leaned close to watch.

Nora and Ross held the fake corporate poster in place to dry for two agonizing sweeps of the second hand on Graham's old-fashioned watch.

Zed slammed his knee up into bent-leaning-forward Ross's ribs.

"Mmf!" muffled scream as Ross spun off the cube, flopped backwards—

—crashed into Nora as she whirled, ballet-limber bent backwards as Zed's slashing commando dagger missed her throat but ripped a reddening line through the blue denim shirt above her heart. No one heard her gagged scream as she crashed to the floor on top of Ross.

Zed stabbed the dagger at his last target.

The old man with a silver duct-taped gag didn't run away.

Crouched but stayed standing straight up from his hips.

Zed rammed his knife arm toward the old man's core.

Don't catch the arrow, move the target.

Graham folded his left side back, brushed his right backhand on Zed's knife-thrusting wrist—not to try to block the thrust from a younger, bigger, more muscular killer, but to divert-deflect guide the stab slightly off to the side and deeper than the attack wanted to go.

Zed pulled back for control. His halted attack's momentum micro-blink dropped into the *wobble wobble* floor and bounced back up.

Real combat bludgeons practiced technique.

Graham's push up under Zed's rising energy only bounced Zed back a couple steps.

Zed charged back, his left hand reaching to grab the fucking old man while his right uppercut stabbed his dagger.

That wrist got caught in a grip that didn't stop its thrust.

Practiced technique empowers real combat.

Graham folded away from Zed's strike. Blended with/diverted the up-thrusting dagger back with the attacking arm's elbow bending to *thunk!*

The dagger rammed up from and through under Zed's jaw, into his brain.

Wobble-wobble.

The meat of Zed collapsed on the Baggage Car floor.

Muffled screams behind duct-taped gag of Nora as she scrambled to her feet, her eyes on the knife-stuck dead man who tried to kill her, who left her bleeding from the gash of his heart slash.

Graham grabbed her arms. Made her stop. Breathe. Be here.

Pointed to the dagger Zed brought with him, kept hidden *until.*

Pointed to the nearby drop cloth tarp not in her program's inventory.

Pointed at Nora.

Knew she got it.

So did wincing, grimacing, ribs-battered Ross as he struggled—*Pain flash!*—up from the train car floor.

Graham tapped his wrist: *We've got to move!*

He needed blood-blotted Nora to help him roll Zed's body onto the tarp, interrupt the bleeding onto the train car floor.

Graham searched the body.

Found a cash-paid ticket from Shelby, Montana in the dead man's shirt.

Shelby, where the counterfeit cube got on the train to Chicago.

In the dead man's right front black jeans pocket, Graham found a glassine envelope with slots for three pills but holding only one and wisps of white dust. His brow wrinkled as the glassine stuck to his plastic-gloved fingers.

Graham reached under the corpse and found the shirt-hidden, belt-tucked sheath for the dagger.

Found Zed's cellphone, but its screen had gone black. Wouldn't turn on.

He rolled a dead body up in the tarp, just like Zed programmed.

Pulled the wrapped corpse to the pallet stack beside the grift's now relabeled cube. Needed help to boost the corpse up onto the stack.

Their faces flashing pain, Nora and Ross muscled the gift-wrapped corpse up onto the pallet platform with barely a *clunk* from the pallet stack.

Graham muscled the wrapped corpse into sitting against the lip of the pallet . . . pushed the corpse of the man who tried to kill them all.

The dead meat flopped into a bin of yesterday's newspapers. Sank in their junk destined for the Chicago Federal Reserve Bank's crematorium inferno.

From on top the pallet stack, Graham pointed commands.

Nora—pain-shuffling Ross helping as he can—the mailing tube, the—

Graham waved away the dagger and aerosol spray cans labeled "A" and "B."

Mimed both hands blasting out in a big explosion. Like aerosol spray cans exploding in a money-burning furnace and maybe, *just maybe*, causing questions and creating evidence of reality no one is ever supposed to know about. And if puzzled searchers found a wouldn't-burn dagger in the ashes . . .

Nora bundled the dagger and aerosol spray cans into the duffle bag.

Nora and Graham closed the fake cube's lid with a quiet *clang*.

She checked her cellphone screen:

SWAT cop David Hale showed no reaction.

Nora flashed code numbers for Graham on the stack to arm the relocated security transmitter/GPS keypad.

Graham flopped off the pallet stack.

Paused to breathe—he was, after all, an old man.

He and Nora needed seven minutes to rebuild the stack against the identity-switched government cube so she could get a boost up there from the old man and the wounded Ross to install and activate the grift's keypad.

She got down by hanging off the cube like she's doing chin-ups. Helped Graham return all the wooden pallets to their original stack.

With bent over Ross pointing directions, they got the luggage and cargo piled back like it's shown in their cellphones' Snapchatted video.

Or at least close enough to not be noticed by any casual eyes.

Silver duct-taped mouths.

Nora, heart slashed, bloody shirt.

Ross, curled around his ribs' pain.

Graham, face drained. The repacked duffle bag slung over his shoulder.

They stared at the lying box full of yesterday's news and today's murder headed toward tomorrow's flames.

They stared at the lying box full of hijacked dreams.

Stared at each other.

Three silver duct tape gagged zombie desperados.

SWAT trooper David Hale didn't see them leave the Baggage Car.

66

Graham pilfered the First Aid kit in the alcove where Attendant Cari would make a fresh pot of coffee—the sign said—at 6:30 A.M.

About three hours from now, thought Graham.

In Ross's cabin, Graham hydrogen peroxided the red gash above Nora's left breast. Used gauze to cover that scabbing-up cut, sealed it with silver duct tape.

They gave Ross their few over-the-counter tablets for everyday aches and pain. Eased him down onto his cabin's lower bunk.

"Nothing more we can do," Graham told Nora. "Even if he's got busted ribs, isn't much more an E.R. could do either. Better pain meds. Well, better *until*."

The old man helped the slashed woman up onto the top bunk.

He turned to leave—

—they all remembered he couldn't latch the door on his way out.

Nora climbed down from the top bunk.

Latched the door after the man who'd saved her life left.

Turned out the cabin's lights.

In the dark, in pain, climbed back to the top bunk.

Didn't even bother to unsnap her belt purse.

As the train *clackety-clacked* toward some unknown morning.

67

*R*OSS'S JOURNAL!

Nora, on her back, top bunk rocketed-awake in the darkness before dawn.

Ross's journal.

The soft moleskin black book of his poems.

Went down into the Baggage Car last night because Graham insisted on having a backup old-school communications system in case they lost Snapchat.

Didn't come up from the Baggage Car with battered ribs Ross and oozing chest-wound her.

Nora slid off the top bunk—*Don't let the slash's pain make you gasp! Don't wake wounded Ross!*—and piano-played her laptop keyboard.

The Baggage Car, real time *real* view: nowhere on the stacks of luggage or the *wobble-wobble* steel floor did she see that black journal.

Her screen showed her the SWAT's Crew Car, tired but triumphant trooper David Hale turning away from his computer screens to say something to a grumpy Alice Noah. Past her is a glimpse of Sgt. Michael Carlisle, white towel tossed over his shoulder.

There are donuts warming in the Dining Car.

Nora. Not one heartbeat of hesitation. Not stopping to put on her sneakers. Still wearing her robbery clothes from the night before: blue jeans, belt purse, the blue sweater she'd had to have Graham help her pull on over her silver duct-taped wound. She popped her cellphone free of its charger cord and looped its lanyard around her neck. Unlatched the door. Hustled out of the cabin.

The train *clackety-clacked* under Minnesota's soft pre-dawn, a rail-bound silver dragon racing toward Minneapolis-St. Paul.

Nora's bare feet hurried over the Premium car's blue carpet. Careened around the corner and quick-stepped down the steep stairs to the Baggage Car.

This is who I am now, she thought. This is what I've got to do.

Barefoot running to rescue the black journal because the world can't, shouldn't, *won't* live without Ross's poetry: *He doesn't deserve to lose that!*

Barefoot running to retrieve the journal's *evidence of* before any SWAT gunner spotted it-wondered-reported-triggered: *She can't go to prison!*

Nora reached the closed door to the Baggage Car.

Checked her cellphone screen:

Still no SWAT warriors coming her way, though more are awake.

The grift's hacks were still operational. Yesterday's Baggage Car security footage still looped in the SWAT squad's screens. The moment SWAT opened the door into the Baggage Car, their cameras would click to real time broadcasting.

Nora tapped 1-9-4-9 into the Baggage Car's keypad lock.

The silver metal door slid open with a *whunk*.

And *like that*, she's back in where last night she got out.

Nora winced as she got down on her knees.

God, if only I had silver duct tape over my mouth so I couldn't scream!

She got face down between the two lying black cubes, forehead on her right arm, did all she could to keep pressure off her heart-slashed pain.

Like yoga. Dead Dog Down.

She rolled onto her back, sent her cellphone's flashlight beam into the dark shaft gaps in the wooden pallet under that side's black cube.

She wanted to scream *Yes. There it is! The black journal!*

Go for it or get out now.

Nora scooted beside the pallet.

The black cube's wall loomed above where she lay. Filled her eyes as she stuck her hand in the pallet's gap, *pat-pat-pats* the train's steel floor.

Can't reach it!

Nora spun around on her back like some break dancer on a hip hop city's street. Stuck her right foot in where her arm had been too short to go. Kept her leg off the floor of that narrow shaft so she wouldn't accidentally knock the black journal further away.

Her bare foot pressed on the black journal.

The narrow space of the pallet's shaft won't let her bend her knee for a scoot-push to send the journal to where her hand could reach it.

She muscled her good arm on the train car floor. Her lanyard-looped around her neck cellphone rested on her belly. Nora scooted her leg out of the pallet's dark shaft, bringing with it the outlaw journal.

She fumbled herself up to standing barefoot on the *clackety-clack* Baggage Car floor. Felt no trickle from the duct-taped wound above her breast. Grabbed the journal. Stuck it down the back of her pants, just like Ross. Barefooted to the door *outta here.* Tapped the 1-9-4-9 code. *Whunk* the steel slid out of her way. Her right bare foot hit the next train car's metal floor of freedom and her left foot swung to join its partner as she rushed out of—

GAWHK garrote choked her neck!

She gagged. Got dragged backwards, choking, strangling as her back jammed against two hard pillows and her ambusher's right hand pulled her hips tight.

The garrote eased, she gasped, inhaled flowery hair spray and classy perfume as bathing her right ear comes a male voice:

"Hello, Nora."

68

Saw you in the Baggage Car on my laptop," hissed the male voice in Nora's ear. "Lucky I was all slicked up to go grab coffee."

Choking, the purple boa garrote choking her, she gasped not enough air.

The hand on her belly slid up her stomach but *gurgling*, she can't scream.

"My," said the guttural voice in Nora's ear as its hand squeezed her breasts: "Too bad we don't have the time."

Nora's whipped around to facing the alcove wall of the exit door of this lower level of the Premium Car. Images strobe. That wall. The fire extinguisher cabinet. Four safety latches and the big silver lever to open the door off the train. The blurred image of her attacker in the fire extinguisher cabinet's glass door.

Della Storm = Zed.

Black helmet wig, stylish dress, perfect makeup.

Della/Zed tapped the grift's code into the train's exit door keypad.

Red flashed to green.

Strangulation eased, blood and oxygen flowed, Nora struggled against thepurple garrote that's one-handed pulled tight to hold her against Della/Zed.

"Too bad I couldn't boss you with white pills like that junkie my laptop showed getting himself killed instead of killing all of you."

Della/Zed shook the woman held against him by a purple garrote.

"Did you think I'd be dumb enough to program myself onto the bullseye?"

Della/Zed flipped the first of four safety switches on that EXIT door.

Nora hit at the monster behind her. Clawed for mascaraed eyes.

The second safety switch got flipped.

Nora's hands fumbled to her belt purse.

The third safety switch flipped.

Nora grabbed the hard bristles end of the black plastic brush in her purse with her left hand. Her right hand grabbed its grip-grooved black plastic handle—

—pulled the brush apart to free its 3.75-inch pointed plastic black blade.

(Amazon-ordered, $13.95 plus shipping from a national box store discount company with the logo *Always Low Prices!*)

Nora stabbed her woman's self-defense dagger into Della/Zed's skirted leg.

Guttural roar!

Nora got slammed into the wall by the fire extinguisher. The garrote loosened. Della/Zed banged Nora's arm against the wall. She lost her weapon.

Della/Zed flipped the fourth and final switch.

Nora pushed off the fire extinguisher's wall. Slammed her back into the body of the killer who still held the purple garrote around her throat.

Mugzy's murderer shoved her forward.

Nora grabbed a metal thermos from inside the fire extinguisher cabinet.

Della/Zed flipped the EXIT door's long metal handle to OPEN.

A rolling metal *whump* as the door off the train slid to the side and in flooded the windy cool of dawn's early light.

Nora beat the thug behind her with that handgrip-rigged metal thermos.

Broke free, spun around—

—Della/Zed grabbed that thermos.

They wrestled for it. Her killer tossed her back and forth. Her grip wrestled the thermos's screw-top. She spun to pull the thermos weapon from her killer.

But he's stronger. Jerked the thermos from her hands.

The thermos cap spun off as she crashed to the floor.

Goo splattered Della/Zed.

Nora crawled toward the bottom of those steep stairs.

The purple garrote jerked tight. Pulled her back toward her killer. Toward the wind-rushing open door to nevermore. She smelled the pine-scented outside. Clawed the steel floor to stop her drag to dying and saw . . .

Clomping down the stairs as fast as his pain allows comes Ross.

He won't get here in time, knows Nora as she's dragged over the metal floor.

And if he does, lucky for Della/Zed.

Boxer *yes*, but Ross is battered and ribs broken, no match for a monster.

He'll get thrown off the train, too, she knows. Two for one for Della/Zed, leaving only—

Flowing down the stairs comes black hoodie Graham.

Graham stepped on Nora's hand to keep her from being pulled back.

Swung his own right hand holding a Smith & Wesson 9mm silencer-equipped automatic up to be caught by his aim-steadying left hand *phfft!*

The purple garrote slackened. Nora rolled over, saw:

Della/Zed silhouetted by blue sky in the train's open doorway. Ebony wig askew. Makeup smudged.

A small stain on the tight skirt over Della/Zed's leg from Nora's stab.

A second dark stain blossomed northwest of where a heart should be.

Della/Zed's grip on the cylinder's handle loosens. The handle popped free.

WHOMP!

A fireball exploded over Della/Zed. Blew the blazing figure out the door. The purple boa tied on that wrist flapped in the rush.

Just-waking-up passengers on this train were self-involved or deep in their screens as a fireball careened past their windows.

No one saw that hunk of burning hate except 10-year-old Malik, an early riser and with permission he'd earned on this trip, solo in the Observation Car. He wouldn't tell anyone, *un-un, not ever,* that he saw a fire monster fly by the train.

He's learned some things on this trip.

Like, never let anyone know all the crazy you see.

Graham stepped past Nora. Filled the open-to-the-rushing-past *out there* with his body. Used his gun-holding hand to hang on to the inside railing. Pulled the door shut *clunk.* Flipped the steel lever closed. Reset all four safety switches. Stared out that locked door's window to the rushing-past world.

"You're either on the train or gone to nowhere."

Turned.

Wrinkled his brow at stunned Nora and Ross:

"Of course I have a gun!"

Nora shook her head: "He . . . She . . ."

Graham answered: "They're dead."

"Not enough," said Nora. "Not for what they did. Not to just us now, all the way back to . . . high school and addicts and . . . Not enough justice for all of all that."

Graham blinked.

Looked at her.

Looked at Ross.

"You're right," he said. "Sometimes *dead* isn't enough. Isn't . . . full justice."

The silver-haired man with a gun in his hand smiled as he told them:

"My turn."

69

Graham holstered his silenced pistol in a shoulder rig hidden by his black hoodie he'd worn the whole trip. Found the halves of the black brush dagger. Tucked them into Nora's belt purse.

She picked up the black journal.

Gave it to Ross.

"Woke up, saw you in there on the laptop," he told her. "Phoned Graham.

"Old school," he added. "Sorry, got here as fast as—"

"Just in time," she said. "You got here just in time."

"Time for us to get out of here," said Graham.

He gestured to the steep slope banker Brian hadn't been tossed down.

Ross said: "Don't know if I can make it back up those stairs."

"I threw you down them," said Nora. "I'll get you where you need to go."

70

Warm donuts waited in the Dining Car.

Broke-his-cherry trooper David Hale got to go fetch those breakfast treats for the squad.

Whunk and the door to the Baggage Car where everything looked like it was supposed to opened and closed behind David Hale as he walked into the Premium car's first level on his way to get what would win him smiles from *his* whole team. What more could he ask? He stopped outside the closed-behind-him door to the Baggage Car. Pondered whether to climb those steep stairs to the second level or walk through the mid-car door, past the switchback stairs, then through the cars of Coach passengers before he went up to the Dining Car.

And donuts.

He sniffed.

A kind of . . . burning stench, maybe scorched whiffs of perfume like Alice Noah told him she wears off-duty and . . . *naw*, not gunpowder.

That's some serious shit somebody's smoking, he thought.

Maybe. Or maybe not.

What could he tell anybody about what only he got to smell?

Especially when there were donuts.

71

"S t. Paul-Minneapolis, Twin Cities, next stop. Nine minutes."

The Conductor hung the mic back up on the rear wall of the Dining Car. He tugged his uniform's blue vest so it wasn't riding up. Adjusted his shoulders in his blue jacket. Checked the feel of the blue cap on his skull. He did all that automatically, without conscious thought, with quiet pride.

The Conductor headed toward the front of the train for his morning walk-through. He'd already had his black coffee. Yogurt. Said *no* to the donuts that would make tugging his vest down over his belly a mockery of proper uniforms.

A well-muscled handsome young man raised his hand off the white-clothed table where he sat alone in front of a hearty breakfast of scrambled eggs and bacon—with *two donuts!*

The Conductor stopped beside the young man: "Can I help you?"

Erik vibed excitement: "Just checking. Are we on schedule?"

"We'll get where we're going on time."

"Thanks." Erik kept his grin on the Conductor until that man of authority had walked on and wasn't watching him.

Not that it mattered, thought Erik. He knew Terri was back in their cabin. Said she needed time to pack and clean up, shower—*I mean, after last night, well* . . . Plus their train was almost there, *gonna get there*, as scheduled, 3:55 on this Saturday afternoon. Erik one-hand, cellphone-thumbed the message:

CONFIRMED GO FOR CHICAGO!

No one in the family sitting across the aisle from Erik's table paid attention to his texting. Even if their eyes glimpsed him working his cellphone, they didn't "see" him doing that—or rather, they saw him doing what then had become synonymous with *being there*, servicing a screen that rode your hand, everyone's hand, and thus just a natural part of *what was*, so there was nothing to truly see.

Mom Isabella and teenage daughter Mir chatted chopped sentences neither of them had to explain when they said things like: "That's so Aunt Roma."

Mir smiled at her dad: "OK, going to see family for Spring Break was a good idea."

Softened her smile to say: "So was taking this train."

Malik said *zero* about the earlier this morning's Flying Fireball Monster.

Carefully ate his donut the '*right*' way. Nibbled all the way around the brown crust of his plain donut like a careful chipmunk. Only after he'd nibbled off all the donut's brown crust his teeth could reach and revealed its crumbly yellow insides did he draw a deep breath tantalized with the ovened doughy aroma.

Then he picked the spin. For Malik, that was always counter-clockwise, turning the crust-consumed/yellow-revealed donut for one bite at a time until he celebrated and mourned that he was at last down to the hole.

His dad had long since lost surprise at how his son ate donuts—and pie, especially cherry pie like they'd had for dessert the *clackety-clack* night before. Malik *as usual* gutted his slice, devoured the cherry filling, swearing that the fruit-kissed crust is the best part so you save it for last.

Ulysses sat at that white-clothed breakfast table with his family. Sat in front of his fried eggs and bacon and banana—he gave his donut as an extra treat to Malik. He smelled coffee cooling in his cup.

He rode that train, eyes on windows of greening spring and souls' cities.

Whunk pulled Ulysses' gaze to the coming-into-the-Dining-Car rumpled mess of a man who hated him and his family because he didn't look like them.

Banker Brian shuffled into that so-damn-sunny Dining Car.

Didn't see her.

Where the hell are you, Sue?

His skull throbbed. He slumped in the nearest chair on an empty white tablecloth four-top. His mouth tasted of vomit he'd sent into his cabin's blue-lit bathroom tube by dawn's early light.

God, don't let Fergus Lang see me like this! he prayed.

Water, his mind whispered. Please, water. And coffee. Lots of coffee. Don't even fucking mention food.

But if you could, if you would, you should tell me: *Where's my wife?*

The train groaned. Shuddered. Stopped in the Twin Cities with the tiniest of lurches, but even that sway dizzied Brian and *whunk!*

He swooned around to look behind him . . .

. . . but it was only that silver-haired weirdo coming into the Dining Car, walking to the kitchen area, talking to the maître d'.

What if everybody said *'Who's Sue?'* when Brian asked? What if they looked at him with eyes that cut him down for losing his wife? What if, what if—

Brian's head hurt too much to think anymore.

Malik watched his friend Graham fill to-go clamshell boxes made from dead dinosaurs, conveniences that wouldn't decay in a landfill.

Graham wore his black hoodie like a monk's robe. Wore it, Isabella was certain, to cover his aged body from the morning's chill. He walked past her family on his way out the Dining Car door with a soft nod and a tired smile.

As the door *whunked* closed behind Graham leaving the Dining Car, Isabella told her family: "Looks like he didn't get much sleep."

Malik shrugged. "Maybe he found Mitzy."

72

Graham opened the door to Ross's cabin.

Ross sagged in the window chair. Nora slouched on the lower bunk.

"I brought you breakfast," said Graham. "No coffee, not yet. We have to wait a couple hours, Wisconsin, cut it as close to Chicago as we can, so we should all try to zonk out, get a third wind."

He set the plastic boxes of food on the mirrored sink.

Set the bulging duffle bag on the bed beside Nora. "I grabbed all the electronics in Della's cabin. Can't let badges click into any of that."

Graham reached into the grift's duffle. Lifted out Della's laptop. A plastic bag of cellphones. Sheets of paper-clipped documents. Makeup jars that could have hidden something quickly scooped up with perfume bottles and a hairspray spray can. Pulled out a foot-long opaque plastic pill box containing foxholes for squads of stone-me soldiers.

Graham opened the medicine box for Ross and Nora to see.

"Those white pills. They're like the pills in the glassine bag I found in the junkie's pocket back in the Baggage Car. He was serving his demons of *right now*, not a complex program to some *if-then*. My bad for not putting it together then and there. *Sorry.*"

Ross and Nora blinked.

Graham kept going. "Also—you'll love this, Nora—that bag was sticky, like it had been taped to something for someone to find."

"Like what Della gave me for Ross," said Nora. "Tape something somewhere on the train, Snapchat whoever for pickup, and still nobody sees who you are."

She pointed to a foxhole of large capsules dusted with pink powder.

"Those capsules are like the one Della left for me. But the powder, looks like he dumped one, probably refilled it with a crushed-up white pill."

"With what killed Mugzy," said Graham. "What would have killed Ross."

Nora snapped pictures of one of the white pills and the intact capsules. She tapped her screen.

"The white one is a mega dose of Oxycodone," she said. "One pill is maximum dose for six hours, two at a time is a fatal overdose."

She held up a pinkish powder capsule.

"The capsule Della left for me was full. But just one of those crushed white Oxys wouldn't have filled it. And one pill would have only grogged Ross up, so . . ."

"Give him more," said Graham. "Drop him into overdose city. Grind up a few white pills, pack that powder into a dumped capsule to pour in his orange juice. But what are those capsules when they haven't been dumped and chumped?"

"Like I thought, like I was told," said Nora: "*Molly.* A wild party drug like ecstasy, maybe a blend of them. Date rape if you use it that way. Drug somebody super suggestible, crazed and flying but nothing you can't control. A kind of incapacitation. Would have made Ross a puppet for me—but that wouldn't have lasted the whole rest of the trip, so instead, Della—Zed zeroed out the target."

Graham looked at the pain paled man riding in the cabin's lone chair.

"Ross," he said, "we can cut an Oxy in half, smaller. Your ribs—"

"No," he said. "I gotta do what we gotta do with what I got."

Graham breathed in all that this cabin allowed.

A slow smile stretched his face like an opening window.

"Sometimes it all comes together," he said: "This is what we're going to do."

Told them.

"*That's* the program you want to run?" said Nora, eyes wide, jaw dropped.

"It's absurd!" said Ross. "Whacko! Complex! It'll never work!"

"You're crazy!" said Nora.

"Crazy flew out the window of where we all are a long time ago," said Graham. "And nothing works if you don't make it. No doubt there'll be improv along the way. But like Nora said, quick and easy doesn't always deliver justice. And you both owe me for saving your lives in your grift where you'd trapped me. So now . . . now it's your turn to work my mission.

"Unless," said Graham, who wore his black hoodie unzipped, "now you two want us to ride some other train."

Clackety-clack, clackety-clack was the only response.

"Then eat," said Graham. "Rest as you can."

He left the cabin.

Nora latched the door. Knew that wouldn't stop his return.

"We have to pay what we owe," said Ross.

"We don't have a gun," said Nora.

They ate whatever breakfast mush they found in the plastic boxes.

Ross slouched in the window mounted chair as the Midwest clattered past.

"Do you want to talk?" she said from the lower bunk where *they'd*.

"What's there to say?"

They rode silent in the *clackety-clack*.

Nora stood. Walked to Ross. Handed him his black journal.

He threw it back at her.

She caught the journal.

Stumbled back to slump on the lower bunk.

Couldn't read his face. Couldn't . . .

She flipped through the journal to the last written-on page.

Ross had scribbled the date on the top of the page.

Wrote: *"On train, pulling o/Seattle station."*

The poem on that page showed no crossed-out words or rewritten lines.

Like he cellphone photo snapped the perfect shot with his first *Click!*

THE ROAD

How can I walk straight

when all my fevered soul seas

is the curve of her ways?

Nora looked up from what he'd watched her read.

What he'd written before.

The pain of his broken ribs and that poem's battling ghosts trembled him.

As the train they road *clackety-clack, clackety-clacked.*

73

Onward, ever onward *clackety-clacked* that train.

Through rolling fields.

Past white paint homes.

Past high steel walls caging junkyards stacked with rusting cars.

Past razor wire chain link fences penning men in orange jumpsuits.

Past sidewalks stacked with furniture, mattresses, baby carriages.

Past teenagers walking by the tracks, out of sight of parental eyes, waving at strangers *clackety-clacking* past, going somewhere else.

Past a man raking leaves in his front yard. Strapped across his back is an AR-15 rifle akin to the weapons carried by Ulysses' troops and the Taliban.

Rumbling through Red Wing and Winona, don't forget Tomah.

Through a tunnel to a Main Street of colorful awnings, empty sidewalks.

Through the last of 10,000 lakes to . . .

Ah, Wisconsin's wondrous green.

A land famous for golden beer.

A state where pro football gladiators are proudly owned by their fans.

Where locals elected one Republican Senator who fought against rich monopolies and for women's rights *and* one Republican Senator who lied about his war record, smeared innocent Americans with fake news plus Big Brother witch hunts and persecuted homosexuals with his gay hatchet man who then went on to mentor a *"reality"* TV star/multiple bankruptcies, inherited-wealth ga-jillionaire who became a President of the United States.

Onward, ever onward, this train tracked through Wisconsin, a state that one Presidential candidate didn't visit and lost the election while the other candidate came there and conquered the country.

Wisconsin, home to Frank Lloyd Wright who built architectural wonders and to an excitable boy named Ed Gein who built trophies out of his murder victims' bones. A fertile geography that birthed Laura Ingalls Wilder who used Guttenberg's machine to deliver stories about a little house on a prairie under a sky without airplanes and Orson Wells who made art with what flickered on the first screens Americans watched for fun, for relief, for enthrallments of who & how they thought they had to be.

Onward rumbled this train with its crew and passengers.

Attendant Cari frowned as she had to make a rare last afternoon pot of coffee in the Premium car's alcove. *Must have been a long night.*

The Conductor and maître d' sat in the after-lunch Dining Car, counted and tallied. The weary waitress watched as she sat with her glass of lemonade.

The Doss family rode in their four bunks suite.

Teacher Isabella vacation-worked her lesson plan for *East Of Eden.*

Mir texted with her friends about what they'd do that summer.

Malik held open his new best book ever *Dandelion Wine* even as he watched the windows in case there were more Flying Fireball Monsters.

Ulysses stretched out on an upper bunk above those he loved. Listened for the beating of his heart within the *clackety-clack.*

Banker Brian moved around his cabin in head-throbbing, nauseous slow-motion, stuffing yesterdays he and Sue brought onto the train into the roller bags she'd pulled through the Seattle train station. *Gonna make damn sure I got it all, she'll show up to get it right, all she has is coming with him, she'll see.*

He heard a knock on the door.

Whirled to see her finally come back to—

Saw that weird silver-haired guy in a black hoodie.

Who waved.

Brian tried to wave but woozy made it not worth it. He let that weirdo in. Gave the guy what he wanted. Mumbled him out the door.

Got back to being alone.

Brian's golden topcoat hung on a hook, swayed gently with the ride.

In another cabin, Erik powered off his laptop while his digital watch counted down.

Terri circled in a *wobble-wobble* walk through the *clackety-clack* and failed to blot out what she'd done the night before.

SWAT Sgt. Michael Carlisle watched his team in the Crew Car pack up and square away. Knew trooper Alice Noah kept her eyes on the screen showing that black cube in the Baggage Car.

He'd after-breakfast walked through there, and something—one of those sixth sense *somethings* good sergeants get—something made him wonder.

He stood as still as the *wobble-wobble* allowed. Let his eyes patrol the Baggage Car's *clackety-clacking*, oil-dust smelling, secured confinement.

Everything looked like he remembered, *but . . .*

Nothing seemed changed in the security footage he then scanned with Alice Noah and David Hale, *but . . .*

David Hale—who the sergeant knew was nervous because he'd worked the graveyard shift—Trooper Hale said: "Is there a problem, Sarge?"

Got the *"You never know"* response that kept David Hale on his toes for the rest of his forever.

And they were all four hours out of *last stop, final destination* Chicago.

Nora took a shower.

Not much of one. It hurt to raise her left arm, but: *"Stinking from last night won't work."* She'd gone to her cabin. Got the little black dress and rhinestone heels she now wore in Ross's cabin as the clock ticked 127 minutes left.

Ross sat on the lower bunk. Watched her put her brush back together. Sheathed the dagger so it was now just a handle she held as she shaped the hair she'd chopped and dyed on the Wednesday night before this Saturday afternoon.

A lifetime ago, thought Ross. Hers. His. *What are our lives now?*

Heavy breaths came from Ross as he watched Nora's no-nail-polish fingers uncap a lipstick tube. Twist it to snake out the neon pink nub like Della/Zed wore, not the electric crimson that the real Nora preferred. She leaned forward over the sink, closer to the mirror as she chose the color of her kiss.

She sent her hand into the black purse on the sink. Her fingers lifted out the bottle of perfume she'd worn with Ross.

"No." He said *no.*

She looked at him.

He got off the bed. Fished the bottle of Della's perfume out of the duffle bag. Gave it to Nora. Stood by her as she sprayed herself with a professional's scent.

She turned to give him a full face-forward view: "Can you see it?"

Nora's cherry hair framed her face with its black mascaraed bloodshot eyes and her slicked lips. Her black dress's V neckline showed cream skin. The heft of her breasts. The crease between them scented with Della's *come-hither.* The tight black dress showed the twin nubs of no bra.

"I don't know what you want me to say," whispered Ross.

"The truth. You can see it, right?"

"Not what it is, but . . . The dress, the way it clings to you, *yeah*, you can see the bulge of the duct tape bandage."

They stood face-to-face on the *wobble–wobble* train.

Nora worked her hands near her heart. The little black dress slid off her shoulders. Fell to her hips. Trapped her arms at her sides. Revealed her naked flesh and the silver glisten stuck over its wound.

Her chest rose and fell but her eyes never wavered from Ross's.

She said: "Rip it off."

74

Fergus Lang wore his blue pinstripe suit and power red necktie as he reigned supreme in the chair by the window to his world, the *out there* he didn't give a shit about beyond its due to him. His flaxen hair was perfect.

Somebody knocked on the curtain-closed door of his Cabin A.

He hadn't bothered to latch the door after that blonde broad who worked for the train had come in to get his order for a Red Cap for his bags at Chicago coming up in—he checked his gold Rolex watch—less than two hours.

Is the knocking on his door that small-timer from a nowhere bank?

Fergus bet that stooge's hometown bank was on the menu for New York financial giants. He knew all of them that mattered, the ones that gave him money to get what he wanted or to get Uncle Sam to cover his losses, *so what*, he was Fergus Lang.

That smalltime banker on this train, *'Brian'* something or other. Except for being honored to be there, he didn't bring anything to Fergus Lang's table.

Fuck it, get it over with, get Mr. Smalltime gone.

"Yeah!" yelled Fergus Lang, *why get out of the chair.*

The door slid open . . .

. . . and there she was:

A black dress babe who he knew right away had dolled up for him, a hot pink lipstick smile as she slid the door shut behind her.

Carried no purse.

She wore no purse carrying any protection or secrets for Fergus to fear like a recording cellphone or whatever the guys he hired used to *get the goods on.*

What she did hold in one hand were plastic glasses, exactly three ice cubes in one *like there should be,* the other with *who cares.*

What she had in the other hand was a can of the right diet cola.

All *slow,* all *go,* she said: "I thought you might like to share the last one."

More than an hour and a half left on the train, thought Fergus. Plenty of damn time.

"I've been wondering when you'd show up," he told her.

Didn't get out of his chair. *Let her come to him.*

"I've been wondering when you were going to ask," she said.

"You've seen me on TV. Read the magazines. I'm not one for asking."

"Oh, I know what you're one *for,*" she said. "But you should know who I am."

"Oh, I know who you are." Fergus leered. "So what's your name?"

"You can call me Candy." A slow pink smile. "And you can call me thirsty."

She swayed toward him on the *wobble wobble* train.

Came right up to him, the wet-his-whistle last can and glasses in her hands.

He gave her his famous *best in the world* grin.

She frowned. "Oh, that's unfortunate."

"What the hell you talking about?"

"You've got train breath. I can smell it before I even get a step closer."

Fergus blinked.

Nobody says they notice, everybody says, FUCKING SAYS I don't have, no, I'm fine, perfect, I am, no I am, really, you've got to PLEASE—

Her face brightened. "Good thing I come prepared."

Call-me-Candy turned away from him. Took the glasses and can with her. Bent over to set them down on the rumpled lower bunk that nobody'd bothered to make so it was ready. Bent over and pointed that *gimme* heart-shaped ass of hers right at him. Turned back and pulled something out of a slit on that black dress.

Shook a strip of cellophane with two yellow lozenges in front of his face.

"Best breath upgrade ever," she said. "Best suck for the best blow.

"It's your pick," she said.

Fergus pointed to one of the yellow lozenges.

She ripped the other cellophane square open—

—winced like maybe her arms weren't that strong.

Her lizard tongue slid out for that yellow lozenge. Took it in so she wasn't setting him up with something she wasn't doing, too. Gave him a smile, a *yum.*

Ripped open the other cellophane. Her hand brushed his cheek. His mouth opened, and following the re-emerging of her tongue, his slid out for her to put—

Lemon, turns out it's lemon-tasting!

He let the lemon lozenge *clickety-click* around his mouth to kick that train breath out of his life forever—or for at least as long as this was gonna be.

She better get to it, he thought. More than an hour left, *but still.*

She turned, gave him the ass again.

Only so much dawdling he was gonna take.

POP! Fizz, trickle.

She let him watch her pour his diet cola into the glass with exactly three ice cubes. Handed him his glass. Filled hers from the same *so-it's-safe* can.

The lemon thingy *clickety-clicked* in his teeth.

She smiled, *clickety-clicked* too, showed him he was safe.

"Maybe I should spit it out," he said.

"No." She raised her glass of cola. "They're an interesting combo."

Her hand holding her glass found the back of his hand raising his glass.

Their touch, *oh yeah*, Fergus felt her tremble like she should.

Candy said: "What shall we drink to?"

Fergus told her: "How about to you being lucky to be here?"

"To my luck." Her voice was flat. "And to yours."

She drained her glass.

So of course Fergus drained his glass, the swirl of lemony cola—

Gulped! Choked! Swallowed the whole damn mouthful of everything!

"What a man," she said, "you didn't spill a drop. But let it settle in you before . . . well . . . before we go."

"You're not going anywhere *until*," said Fergus Lang.

"We're all here *until*," said the sultry babe.

She took the glass out of his hand.

Stared at him.

Gave it a *clackety-clack* beat.

Fergus loosened his red tie.

Stood in his handmade shoes on the *wobble wobble* train.

She said: "What is it you want?"

He felt the slow wonderfulness of his grin, told her, *oh he told her,* told her: "Whatever I want is what you're gonna give."

She's standing right in front of him, so close so he smells the lemon of her breath and her big dollars' sweet perfume as she whispers: "Here it comes."

WHAM!

She punched Fergus Lang in the balls. Grabbed them. Squeezed.

His mouth opened to scream.

She slammed the heel of her palm up into his chin. Knocked his head back.

Fergus Lang fell onto his luggage. Flopped to the train car floor.

Saw the devil in a black dress *whir* open his cabin door.

75

Graham stepped past Nora to breach Fergus Lang's cabin.

Sniffed: "Do you think lemons might be overkill?"

"I hope so," she said.

Felt a lemon river ride her where *whoa* she was going to go.

Nora reached her outstretched hand to Ross in case he needed or wanted help as he eased into the cabin carrying the grift's duffle bag.

"What the hell!" Fergus Lang flopped on the floor amidst his luggage.

The ga-jillionaire rumbled to his feet. Stabbed his forefinger at Graham.

"We had a deal!" said Fergus Lang. "First night on the train, you come knocking to me. We had a deal for you to keep that Goddamn reporter off me!"

Ross blinked.

Remembered:

First night on this train. He's lemon stoned. Naked. Kneeling on the floor of his *clackety-clack* cabin. Nora's bare thighs straining wide on his shoulders. That intoxicating smell, that wondrous taste, her moans and out in the hall, *knocking*, a muffled word that sounded like . . .

Lang. As in Fergus Lang.

Ross thought: *We miss so much of what goes on all around us.*

The silenced pistol flowed from its rig under Graham's black hoodie.

The gun's black bore *thunked* Fergus's third eye.

Graham told the rich man: "Turns out, I work for somebody else."

His left forefinger touched his pursed lips: "*Shhh*. Don't tell anybody."

Then—

Like it's the new fucking national pastime! thought Fergus.

—Graham kneed Fergus Lang in the balls.

Fergus's jaws gasped open.

Closed around the barrel of a silenced pistol thrust inside his mouth.

"Can you hear me?" said Graham.

Fergus's nods wobbled the pistol up and down in Graham's hand.

"You know *who*, right?" said Graham. "*Who* you fucked over and pissed off enough to send me here? Explosive diarrhea for your bodyguard so he can't travel. An elevator accident for your *goes everywhere with you* Harvard flunky. I think Mugzy the dog and his old lady got their last-minute cancellation cabin. But you *know* who would have hired me to do all that to get us here."

Mouthful of gun Fergus's eyes widened and he nodded *yes*.

Gagged as Graham shoved the barrel deeper, growled: "*No . . . you . . . DON'T!*"

Graham leveraged the pistol to stand Fergus up on his toes.

Eye to eye, told that terrified tycoon: "You don't know *who* because there's more than one *who* you've ripped off and pissed off enough to want you dead."

The black hoodie assassin leaned back as he held his gun in Fergus's mouth.

"Let me give you a hint," said Graham. "Of all those who want you dead, my client is the craziest. The most sophisticated. Clever. Creative. Dramatic."

He shrugged: "Why else would this contract have come to me?"

Nora unzipped the duffle bag on Fergus's bed.

Ross stood by the bag, his eyes locked on the man with a gun in his mouth.

Who got told by his obvious assassin: "You have no idea how lucky you are."

Fergus Lang's eyes widened . . .

. . . an odd glaze flowed through them.

The wobble of the gun barrel in his mouth blinked Fergus to totally there.

"Do you know why I'm not going to kill you?" said the man who could.

The Obvious Hitman angled his head toward The Devil In A Black Dress.

"She convinced me that whacking you isn't worth the karma," said Graham. "Sure, I'd love to get those *great job* points, but I've got better things to do.

"So our problem now," said the Obvious Assassin, "is business. You know business. A deal is a deal. If I don't deliver the goods, I'll get the bads."

The murderous metal pipe shoved the roof of Fergus's lemony mouth.

"And you're sure as shit not worth that," said the old man with the gun.

"But the good news for you is," he said, "a deal is a deal *unless and until* something goes wrong. And if *what goes wrong* isn't my fault, *is their fault*, then there's wiggle room for a contractor like me to walk away. So *if* I give you a fighting chance to live, I've got to have a sellable *what went wrong* or I'll pay.

"Are you following me?" the man with the gun told his hostage. "Can you see how it all makes sense?"

Fergus Lang blinked *yes* as he felt the swoon of this new real. After all, he was the master of deals, and like he'd famously told the BAT convention: *"If it ain't a deal, it ain't real."*

Real Real Real ran around like a train inside of Fergus's skull.

The Obvious Assassin said: "So, you want to make a new deal to get us both out of the old one? Or do you want to pay your tab?

"You can trust me." The Obvious Assassin nodded at the Nosey Reporter. "I kept our first deal. Kept him off you and what you're doing on this train. The only story he can get to smear you now is if you end up dead."

One look at Ross and Fergus knew that was true . . .

. . . but *damn:* What weird eyes that nosey punk has!

Fergus heard the man holding the gun in his mouth say: "Nod once for *yes*. Or nod nothing and I'll let your enemies' beautiful plan kill you."

Fergus bobbed his head as best the gun allowed.

"Not a word," said the Obvious Assassin. "Not a sound."

The gun slid out of Fergus's mouth.

The Obvious Assassin directed him to sit on the bunk, hands on his knees.

"You gotta give those motherfuckers who want you dead credit," he who worked for them told Fergus Lang. "They are devious and their plan is brilliant."

He lifted a small glassine envelope into the cabin's sunlight.

Wobble-wobble, clackety-clack trembled that translucence of *swallow-me*s.

The Devil In The Black Dress said: "Why are there two instead of one?"

"Who could be sure how much of what we put in the glass actually got into him?" said the old man. "Better safe than sorry. But I dumped out half of what's in that capsule like you used, so it's really only an extra *half* dose.

"And the white pill is the white pill. Within the non-dangerous dosage, not like what's sometimes found in orange juice. It'll all blend well with your lemons."

Graham's right hand pushed the pistol into Fergus's sore groin.

Graham's left hand gave Fergus the glassine envelope.

"Take them," he ordered. "They'll keep you alive. And lucky for you, that banker's got a drinking problem. I got him to give me this."

Graham handed Fergus Lang a mini-bottle of Scotch.

The pistol stroked Fergus's cheek just like The Devil In The Black Dress.

"Use all the booze to swallow both pills. Numb the attack. We'll check."

He did and they did.

Clackety-clack, clackety-clack, the train is 55 minutes from Chicago.

76

"Your attention please! In eleven minutes, arriving Chicago's Union Station. Final destination. Thank you for riding the train. Watch your step and be careful on the platform. Eleven minutes. Last stop, Chicago."

Fergus Lang lay flat on his back on his cabin's lower bunk dressed in his blue pinstripe suit and loosened red tie. Silver duct tape bound his feet. Circled his hands closed as if in prayer. A silver strip covered his mouth.

His eyeballs swayed with the *clackety-clack*, the *wobble-wobble*.

Held warped images of two men who rode in this cabin with him.

Graham pulled off Fergus's red necktie, cinched it over the prisoner's eyes. Told the prisoner: "Here comes the Assassination of Fergus Lang, Act One."

Blindfolded Fergus heard a long hissing *Pssst!* Felt *wet* spray up his body from his shoes to soak his socks, wet his pants. Hissing soaked his suit jacket, his shirted chest, his arms. *Oh YUCK* his neck is soaked, his face! Up into his hair. Down over his nose—*Don't breathe it in/smells like flowers!*

"Roll over!" commanded the Obvious Assassin.

The prisoner obviously obeyed.

Got sprayed on that side, too, right down to his handmade Italian shoes.

Graham returned Della's hairspray can to the duffle bag that now held Fergus Lang's phones and wallet with all his credit cards and I.D.s. Graham had already confiscated Fergus's wads of cash—including $1,000 hidden in those handmade Italian shoes.

Graham cut the silver duct tape off Fergus's ankles. Cut his hands free. Ripped the tape off his mouth. Unwound the red necktie from his eyes.

Fergus's eyes tracked that red necktie dangle from the Obvious Assassin's left hand while that hitman's right hand held the whisper pistol.

"Get up," said Graham.

Fergus did—

—*wobbled*: Him. The train. Both. He heard himself snicker. *Wo.*

Graham crammed most of the red necktie in the left side pocket of Ross's leather jacket, put its skinny end in Fergus's left hand.

"You drop that," said Graham, "your ass is lost."

Fergus wanted to say *What?* but having something to hold onto felt good, helped him know where he was: Standing right behind that Nosey Reporter. He held tight to his end of the tie while that Nosey Reporter tucked a black book down the back of his pants under his leather jacket.

Graham showed Fergus's wild eyes the silenced pistol holstered under his black hoodie. "You yell or cry out for help or even talk to anybody but us . . .

"Plus," he added, "you probably already know that they own the cops."

Of course they do, thought Fergus. That's all how the smart guys always tell each other it is. The walls on this train bent around him like magic.

Graham slid the duffle bag over his left shoulder. Swung Ross's computer bag onto his right. Told the tie-linked, disabled duo:

"Let's go."

Screech of metal on metal, shudders of *slowing down* as that trio's parade followed the Premium passengers blue carpeted corridor toward the steep stairs.

The door to Ross's cabin whirred open.

Out stepped Nora wearing her jacket, blue sweater and black slacks from the day she'd boarded this train. She waited while the parade passed her by.

Fergus whispered: *"What happened to the dream girl?"*

"She woke up," said the Nosey Reporter leading him.

"Wo," said Fergus.

Nora lurched into line. Her two hands pulled a stack of roller bags and other luggage—hers, Ross's, Graham's. She flashed on the memory of the meek ruby-lipped wife dragging roller bags through the Seattle train station.

Keep going, Nora told herself. *For Ross.*

For you, too, she heard herself say. Pushed that thought away.

They took the steep stairs. Easier for her to bounce and drag what she carried down them than down and around the switchback stairs.

The bottom of the steep stairs on the train's first level.

Their ride shuddered. Groaned. Steel whined. Brakes hissed.

Inertia surged them toward the Baggage Car door . . .

. . . rocked them back in their shoes.

The train whistle blew.

"Your attention, please! Now arrived, Chicago, last and final stop. All passengers must leave the train. Take what you brought with you unless you have made arrangements for Red Caps. Be careful when stepping down onto the platform. Now arrived, final destination, Chicago."

"Let's get out of here," said Ross.

"Outta here," chorused Fergus Lang, holding on to the red tie.

Graham said: "We've got to get out in front of everybody."

Nora tapped the grift's code into the EXIT door's keypad. Flipped the four safety switches. Pulled the lever in the gray metal door from CLOSED to OPEN.

The gray metal door in train car wall slid away.

Blinded them with a portal of sunlight and blue sky.

The duffle bag and computer bag strapped from Graham's shoulders *plus* the weight of the decades he carried made him awkward as he bent to get the white wooden step-stool out from under the fire extinguisher cabinet that earlier held its own refutation. He grabbed the vertical hand-rail by the now open door. While holding the stool with his other hand, managed to swing out and off the train *backwards* like Attendant Cari always did. But as Graham lowered himself to position the step-stool close to where it should be, instead of an Amtrak professional, he looked like a bumbling, black-hoodied, silver senior citizen.

He turned from where he'd landed—

—stood face to face with three SWAT gunners.

77

L.T.

Sgt. Carlisle.

Trooper David Hale.

They'd swung off the train from the Crew Car as the Empire Builder chugged and groaned its way into Chicago's station following a last-minute track change due to equipment malfunctions in the switching yard that was nine years overdue for routine infrastructure upgrade.

That last-minute switch surprised the waiting Chicago Federal Reserve Bank's SWAT squad and cargo handling personnel—including the forklift crew and motorized transport dolly assigned to secure removal of a labeled and keypad/cyber-identified black cube from the Baggage Car. The Chicago SWATs split up to escort the slow-moving forklift and scramble to the newly designated track where were no guards there to meet the arriving train.

Once L.T. realized that, he grabbed Sgt. Carlisle and the closest trooper for a movie-worthy, swing off the train to secure the platform *until.*

Safe on the Chicago train station's platform, L.T. and two troopers found themselves face to face with the silver-haired *T'ai chi* civilian.

Who blinked.

"We made it!" he told the hard faces of those heavily armed guardians.

"I mean," continued the old man, speaking to L.T. but with his eyes also meeting Sgt. Carlisle's as the old guy reached back to help a woman who'd clearly over-packed for this trip off the train: "The ride was great—*Did you see those mountains?*—and the service . . ."

He gave the SWAT gunners a shrug.

"The service," he said, like a kindly old person anywhere, everywhere. "The service was great. Like it was, you know, back in my day."

"It's today," said Sgt. Carlisle.

L.T. told the old guy: "And you're not supposed to be here."

Trooper Hale's heart-attack training flashed through him as the old guy freaked: *"You mean this isn't Chicago?"*

The reddish-haired young woman who'd made it off the train and onto the wooden platform dragged her burdens toward the distant doors into the station.

"This is Chicago," said L.T. as he spotted the journalist who'd annoyed him back in Seattle step off the train followed by a disheveled blue suit who shuffled as close to the journalist as a nervous lover. "But this isn't a designated exit."

"The door opened."

Sgt. Carlisle stepped behind the shuffling-away, flaxen-haired, blue suit who looked familiar as he rode the back of the writer guy who was trying to catch up with the luggage-laden woman. Sgt. Carlisle peered through that open door up into the train. Saw the Baggage Car portal still secured.

"Look," he heard the old man tell L.T., "I did what you're supposed to do when a door opens. Went through it to where I'm supposed to go.

"Truth is," said the old man, "when you get to be my age, you can't always, and when you gotta go, you gotta go, and once I was packed up and down those steep stairs and saw an open door . . ."

The silver-haired man in the black hoodie nodded past the other now open doors on the train: "Figured I better make it into the station 'quick as I can."

L.T. blinked. Gave him a nod.

Away he went with an urgent old guy shuffle.

Sgt. Carlisle stepped beside his commanding officer to watch the old guy go.

"Want to do anything about that, sir?" said Sgt. Carlisle.

Hurrying toward them came Chicago SWATs and the yellow forklift and the motorized flatbed transport for what was securely locked in the Baggage Car where L.T.'s own disembarked team now formed a protective cordon.

L.T. said: "No. We're off the train."

78

"Keep walking!" hissed Graham as he caught up to Nora pulling her luggage on his left and on his right, the duo of Ross leading wild-eyed Fergus Lang clinging to the red tie between them.

They marched past Attendant Cari as she set a white step-stool on the platform at the other—the approved exit—door of the Premium cabin car. She smiled at them and would have even if the old man hadn't given her a huge tip.

But Cari frowned: Had the Conductor not known the other door of this car was not supposed to be opened for passengers to disembark? Just like him, new to the run, asking nothing, doing what he pleased.

Footsteps clunked on the train car steps behind her.

As Cari turned to deal with her rule-following passengers, Graham spotted a quartet of Red Caps waiting on the platform.

"Wait," Graham told his trio.

Fergus bumped into Ross's back. Fergus's giggle quickly changed to *Oh-oh*.

A wad of Fergus's cash filled Graham's hand as he hailed the Red Caps: "Are any of you here for Fergus Lang?"

A gnarly Red Cap raised his hand.

So did the arriving passenger in a blue suit.

Graham handed the senior Red Cap a $100 bill that smelled like Italian leather and sweaty feet: "He'll need all of you."

Hundred dollar bills found the other three Red Caps as Graham said: "Get Mr. Lang's bags out of his cabin, Cabin A. Get his friend Della's out of Cabin G."

He saw Attendant Cari help dazed golden topcoat Brian off the train.

Told one of the Red Caps: "He's on Fergus Lang's tab, too."

A Red Cap headed toward that paid-for customer.

"I forget," said the old man to the gnarled Red Cap: "What's the best hotel?"

The gnarled senior Red Cap ventured a famous name.

"Yes, that's it. Load it all in a taxi and send it to that hotel. Make sure the desk clerk holds it for Fergus Lang or sends it to his room, doesn't matter."

Two more hundred dollar bills got tucked into the Red Cap's shirt pocket.

"Will that cover the taxi and the doorman at the hotel?"

"Oh yeah," said the Red Cap.

"Then go. Don't bother any of us with any problems."

The silver-haired man in the black hoodie marched his three companions toward the inside of the train station.

Wide-eyed Malik was the first person in his family to get off the train, right behind that man in the golden coat who acted stunned when a Red Cap took his bags, told him: "Compliments of Fergus Lang."

Who's that? wondered Malik.

And where's that guy's ruby-lipped wife who liked to wave?

Grown-ups, thought Malik. Who knows what they do.

He turned to help Mom climb off the train.

Felt himself blush as blonde Attendant Cari gave him a grin of approval, of recognition, of appreciation for Doing What Anybody Should.

Malik watched a squad of SWAT troopers quick march past toward the Baggage Car like they were being chased by that yellow front end loader.

His sister Mir stepped onto the platform. Their dad stepped off the train carrying heavy bags. Through the crowd of passengers and crew members and station workers, Malik saw his buddy Graham hurrying into the train station.

We never got to say goodbye, thought Malik.

In the train that brought her here, Terri surrendered to the weight of her bags. She slouched out of their cabin ahead of all-grins Erik.

Erik's babble followed her as she clumped along the blue carpeted corridor to the switchback stairs and the door open to the train's final destination:

"Smells like a great, cool spring day out there, doesn't it? The weather app says so. Sure, oily train smells, metal and how come that steam doesn't smell? Gotta be some wind, it's Chicago! Windy City! Looks like everybody's getting off OK. Don't fall down the steps—just joking, you can do it, you're amazing, you can do anything. Do you want me to help? No, OK, cool, *yeah*, you look great! Wonderful. How are you so smart and beautiful at the same—"

Attendant Cari looked up from where she stood on the sunlit wooden platform of reality at the bottom of the stairs Terri clomped down.

That look: Terri knew Cari would lend a helping hand if she could.

Terri's shoes made it to the *no wobble-wobble* ground on her own.

She stared at the blonde widow. "Thanks."

Without batting an eye, Cari said: "It's what we do."

Terri rolled her suitcase toward the dark windows' giant arc above the doors into the station from the tracks of trains.

Behind her came the sounds of Erik babbling to Cari, getting back: *"Thanks for riding Amtrak."* Terri wished she'd had more money for the tip

Erik gave Cari, who would budget part of that cash to buy a glass vase for the purple lilacs that were supposed to bloom in her suburban Seattle rented cottage's backyard any day now, *any day.*

But right then on that Saturday afternoon when she was still in Chicago, Cari's passenger Erik said: "We got here on schedule!"

Cari told him: "We all gotta make things work as best we can."

Terri heard Erik roll his suitcase after her.

The bag Terri rolled behind her weighed nothing.

The bag she rolled tore her apart with its weight.

Terri rolled past that perfect family of four rearranging the luggage they'd carry from the platform onward, ever onward. The Mom who so clearly loved her husband and The Dad who so obviously loved her back. The eager Son who was the goofy kid brother to that *so much life ahead of her* teenage Daughter.

We never got a chance to talk, thought Terri as she rolled past the Daughter's looking-up eyes. *I've got so much to tell you and so little to say.*

That teenage woman smiled at the older *'used to be her'* who now rolled her suitcase on to great things Mir could only imagine, hope.

Terri rolled her suitcase onward through the crowd of fellow passengers from other cars and coach fares who she realized she'd never really seen and would never ever know. Past the Conductor who glanced at his cellphone screen to be sure his mom who'd just moved into the assisted living facility on the outskirts of Chicago was doing as best as could be while she waited for his visit.

Terri rolled onward through the sounds of voices. Laughter. A baby's wail. The rumble of suitcases' wheels. Shouts of men and women and SWAT warriors shifting cargo and baggage onto carts. The cool breeze escaped from some greater wind outside the station brushed her cheek, stirred her auburn hair. Sights of where she was became misted by what she'd done as she faced the wall of the train station where she had to go, that gravity pulling her closer, ever closer.

79

F our pros in black suits moved into position in the center of the dome-roofed main hall of Chicago's Union Station.

They had their axes.

They were ready.

Just another gig that didn't pay enough for the prep they'd had to do.

The upright bass plucker was a come-out-of-a-conservatory kind of guy with magic hands and a whiff of crazy that the far younger saxophone stud who rode his sound up from the ground of the Southside, *man*, he dug the *gots it* old guy. They both liked working with the acoustic guitar slinger who played better than she sang and as she struggled to find the *wow* in the songs she wrote, got up every morning and checked her emails and text messages for that one *I heard you* revelation that would up her to the big time.

"Which way should we face?" the bass player asked the fourth black suit, a grad student in film school Field Director who'd followed all the contracted orders to put this whole thing together, YouTube channel and all, his digital camera charged and ready, with a sensitive mic clipped to its side.

The Field Director positioned them with their backs toward the gates for the arriving trains: "That way I can see when it's time."

The smartass bass player went: *"And a one, and a two."*

Even the Field Director had to laugh.

Chicago's Union Station is a busy place on any given non-plague-ruled day, and that April Saturday afternoon created a teeming crowd of comers and goers, of strollers and snackers, of waiting-fors and walking-throughs for the Field Director to *not* film, that wasn't his job today, *damn it*.

He watched them walk by. Those here for the trains. For shelter on their way to the gym or work. The twirling embrace of two people the day after they'd first each said: "I love you." Most of the people the Field Director saw streaming though the train station were talking on their phones or walking while staring into their screens at nothing he'd ever filmed.

He was a tall man—terrible basketball player. He peered above the heads of the streaming crowd. Motion caught his eye back by the wall of gates.

Some silver-haired freak in a black hoodie was leading his own trio of players back behind giant opaque plastic tarps draped from the floor-to-ceiling scaffolding of the station's never-ending repairs and renovations.

The Field Director frowned: *What are they doing back there?*

80

Graham said: "The Assassination of Fergus Lang, Act Two."

He and scarred Nora, battered Ross and tie-holding Fergus stood inside an eerie chamber made by walls of blurring plastic tarps and the crisscross scaffolding built up to the curved ceiling of the train station. They were boxed in with thick smells of cement, broken bricks, construction chemicals, dust. The translucent walls of their shelter rippled gray light.

No one else was in that chamber with them at 4:17 on that Saturday afternoon. Workweek construction teams had left behind crates of this, stacks of that. Deeper into the scaffolding stood a truck-sized green steel box full of the renovation's rubble and random trash. From outside came the sounds of the bustling station, track announcements, marching charging feet.

"Lucky find of privacy," said Graham. "Better than a bathroom stall."

The whisper gun filled his hand.

Fergus snapped to full focus on that black bore staring at his face.

"Drop the tie," ordered his Obvious Assassin.

Fergus did.

"Get behind him," the Obvious Assassin told the Nosey Journalist. "Put your gun on him."

Ross blinked but moved behind Fergus Lang. Pressed the bottom of his 20th century fountain pen into the stoned man's spine.

Fergus straightened with that obvious pressure.

Graham holstered his whisper gun.

Handed the duffle bag to Nora, dramatically ordered: "Glove me."

Lemon-stoned, she still was able to unzip the consolidation of the grift's gear in the duffle bag. Found the box of plastic gloves like they'd worn the night before in the Baggage Car. Like she was a nurse in a TV drama's operating room, gloved the surgeon standing in front of her.

"For my protection," the Obvious Assassin told Fergus's ears.

Graham reached into the duffle, pulled out the aerosol spray can wrapped with white tape sporting a black "B"—the fixative that stuck the fake corporate poster to the real treasure box's black steel.

Told Fergus: "Grab that cross bar of the scaffolding over your head so your arms spread out like a Y."

"*Why*," sighed that wide-eyed man as he reached toward heaven.

Graham pulled the stoned man's tie close to his nose. "Smell that?"

Nora inhaled, too: Purple boa Della's flowered hairspray.

"That was Act One of your assassination," said Graham. "Remember?"

The choking flaxen-haired man hanging like a Y from a scaffolding cross pipe nodded *yes*.

Graham shook the fixative aerosol can B. A rattle of marble inside metal.

He sprayed fixative over Fergus Lang's Italian loafers. Soaked the outside and then sprayed up each of the blue suit's pants legs and jacket sleeves. Sprayed the man's crotch and ass and back, his arms and hands clinging to the overhead cross bar, sprayed him from his toes to his no-tie neck.

"Let go," ordered Graham.

Fergus released the overhead pipe.

"You know the monkeys?" said the Obvious Assassin. "The hear no evil, see no evil, speak no evil trio of statues? Cup your hands together like them. Cover your eyes, your nose and mouth."

"I'm a monkey," whispered Fergus Lang as he obeyed.

Graham sprayed the monkey's wrists and hands. A sticky needle mist showered Fergus Lang's thick neck and jowls. Soaked his flaxen hair.

"Look at me."

The monkey's sticky hands fell away from his open eyes of terror.

"That's Act Two, the trigger dose.

"North Korea," said Graham. "Remember them? Their whacky dictator?"

"*Ahh . . .*"

"Remember his brother he assassinated? In Kuala-Lumpur. At the airport after he got off a plane. Two women take turns spraying wet onto him. Covering him in time release, binary contact poisons.

"That's how *who* you fucked over and pissed off ordered your hit. A big show assassination after you got off the train in this hog butcherer town. Send a message. Make an example.

"But killing you wouldn't be true justice. So I'm giving you a chance.

"You're soaked with the two poisons. Your hands, your face, more death soaking through your clothes—you can feel it, can't you? Feel it . . . sticky. After it stiffens, you'll be a stiff. The two pills I gave you will stop the poison if your heart keeps pumping them through your system. You've got to keep moving. Never slow down. Fight the stiffening until it wears off.

"My work-around on your contract hit is that I can tell the people who want you dead that *obviously*, it wasn't my fault. That their sprays didn't work. But you and me, we'll know the truth: if you live, it's because I let you."

Graham jerked open the plastic wall to reveal the bustling train station.

"This is Act Three of your assassination: you escape, you get away.

"But remember: They're out there. Watching. Could be strangers. Or your staff. Could be the cops. But no matter *who* they are, you've got to save yourself."

"Save myself," said Fergus Lang.

"To stay alive, you've got to run," the Obvious Assassin told Fergus. "Run to fight the poisons. Run to keep the antidotes pumping through your veins. Run to keep *them* from catching you."

The doomed man stared into the train station of his assassination's escape.

The silver-haired werewolf kicked Fergus's ass: *"Go!"*

Fergus Lang rocketed away like a scrambling flaxen-haired chimpanzee.

Graham let the obscuring plastic sheet drop back in place.

"Nora," he said: "The grift's hack of this station's security cameras?"

"Still operating. Showing yesterday's arrivals, not what's happening now."

"Kill the hack."

She thumbed and swiped and tapped her cellphone screen.

Graham tossed his plastic gloves into the dumpster. Tossed the aerosol spray cans in there, too. And the dagger.

Ross said: "What did you just do?"

"Justice," said Graham. "And it's *we*, not *just me*. We made an asshole's nightmares come alive. Turned them loose on him. My original plan was a simple trigger squeeze, but this, the justice you both say you want and you both should appreciate. This is more than just me. It's *us*: a hit, a program *and* it's poetry."

"You got Fergus Lang stoned out of his mind and he doesn't even know it!" said Nora. "Scared the shit out of him! Made him run wild out there! He'll have a heart attack!"

Graham shrugged with his reply:

"Assuming he has a heart, if he collapses, ER bloodwork will show he's using opioids like he's made millions of dollars pushing. Plus the illegal party drug molly, along with marijuana that may or may not be legal, who can keep track. The booze from that mini-bottle is a bonus.

"He's got no money, no I.D.s, no phone, a blown mind, blood full of trouble and a story so crazy who'll believe him? He won't be a North Korean *whack* escapee, he'll be a talk show joke *whack job*. Even if he gets to his people first, he's never going to be the same. His *real* is now a crazy lie that he didn't spin. A compulsive narcissist like him, how long will it take for that to come out?

"Especially," said Graham, "if a redheaded hacker cruises for official reports to leak and a freelance journalist out of Seattle busts a story or hypes it to a colleague? How long before Fergus's own people dump crazy, broken him? Before Wall Street turns on him? Before his actual *hard-ass, cold-heart* enemies *really* move on him?"

Graham smiled: "If you can't kill a big lie, birth a bigger truth."

"There's no murder contract," said Ross as Graham adjusted their bags.

"We sold a man a scam he knows could be true. Made him feel it in his bones, thanks to modern chemistry. You saw his face: he *got it*. There are real *who*s out there, power players who do, can and will issue murder contracts. Mining tycoons in 1917 tried to pay a Pinkerton detective named Dashiell Hammett to kill a labor organizer who was in their way. Hammett turned down the contract, but other contractors didn't and lynched the labor leader from a downtown street car trestle in Butte, Montana.

"Fergus Lang knows he's pissed off powerful people like that. Hell, he's one of them, only not so smart. He knows there's more than one of his crowd who'd pay to drop him if it suited their bottom line."

"Hack's off," said Nora. "The station's cameras are running live."

She stared at Graham: "Who are you?"

The silver werewolf said: "I'm the *who* you never see."

His smile softened: "Or . . . *I was*.

"Supposed to be I was gone. Out of the shadows. Off the go-to list only seen by our official good guys *before*. Now . . . *Thanks*, but disappear into real life. Into this world now."

He repeated himself with angry disbelief: "In *this* world! Where a jil-lion of us stopped looking out the windows and got sucked into our own mirrors and screens, and that turned the wrong people loose. The people I used to hunt."

The three of them stood on solid ground behind walls of translucence.

A light beyond time lit the face of the man who'd brought them there.

"After all the shit I've done for our best hearts and minds I'll be damned if I'm gonna let the assholes win."

He shrugged to the man and woman who could be his children.

"You do what you can . . . *right?*"

Ross said: "You're a mad *ronin*."

"What?" said Nora.

"Good for you, poet," Graham said as his smile curved around Nora like a sword. "Japanese."

"Like *haiku*," whispered Nora from memories and dreams.

"You are a delightful surprise," said Graham while Ross watched.

"*Ronin*," said Graham: "A masterless samurai."

But he shook his head: "I take no man for a 'master.' I never did. For me, 's about the 'why,' not the 'who.'"

He smiled: "And a 'mad' *ronin*?

"You mean 'mad' like *angry?*" said Graham. "Who isn't? So me, *oh yeah*.

"Or do you mean 'mad' like *crazy?*" His smile slacked and his eyes drooped but never lost their burn or their focus on Nora and Ross. "I go back and forth about my opinions on that for you two, but for me . . . *oh yeah*."

Nora said: "So because of all the shit rising in the world—"

"And who makes it," interrupted Graham.

"—you decided to murder Fergus Lang?"

"You spank the asshole you can reach. Do it loud and hard if you want people to work figuring out and fixing what the asshole did to deserve getting spanked. Every crime must have a punishment—right? Plus, maybe you get some of his fellow assholes to pucker up and not dump their loads on us."

Graham's face turned to a stone the opposite of Nora's lemony rock 'n' roll.

"Murder's always the easiest solution. Not always my style, mind you. A drop usually lacks a . . . finesse. I am—"

He corrected himself. "I *was* known for my finesse.

"Then you two and Della/Zed came along and complicated everything."

His smile focused on Nora while Ross watched amidst the muted buzz of the train station beyond the plastic tarps.

"And you, amidst your Bad Ass big moment, talked about *justice*."

Graham gestured to her with his empty left land while his empty right hand hung down by his side and unzipped his black hoodie. "You were right. Some assholes deserve more than just a bullet."

Graham smiled: "Murder is easy but mockery makes a better mess."

"Finesse," said poet Ross.

Programmer Nora shook her head: "This was fun for you."

"Well," smiled Graham, "turned out to be. Thanks to you two."

"Now," he said, nodding to their confinement of opaque plastic walls, quoting the most popular song with American troops during his generation's Vietnam War: "We gotta get out of this place."

81

Where the hell do I go? thought golden cashmere-coated banker Brian as he shuffled deeper into the Chicago train station cursing the injustice of it all—including his booze foggy aching head.

He shuffled past a bunch of black suit band guys, and *yeah*, was good that the Red Cap—*Jesus, thank you, Fergus Lang! Always a class act!*—*yeah*, good that Brian didn't need to drag those two roller bags like he was an ordinary Joe, *but what the hell*: The incessant *rrr* drone of metal rollers on the train station tiles behind him! Like his bags were chasing him, not following him.

Coming from the Red Cap behind him: "Are we getting a taxi, sir?"

How the hell should I know? thought Brian. Where the hell is Sue? She's supposed to know what to do. Go to the hotel, she'll be there, all sorry and shit—*no*: doesn't make sense. If she wandered off the train in the middle of the night, just like her lately, she'd be scrambling to catch up on the next train. And if she wasn't coming . . .

Anger and fear took turns pushing Brian back and forth.

Wait here. She'll catch up. Nothing to do with anything else but her being *just Sue*. That fucking North Dakota Al's got nothing to do with it. Get to the hotel, convention tomorrow, everything like it's supposed to be and Fergus Lang, oh man: *I know Fergus Lang!*

Brian could hear approving sighs, feel looks of respectful awe.

"Sir?" said the Red Cap.

Brian stopped on the sunset hued tiles of this train station floor. Wobbled like he still was on the train. Through the bustling crowd saw *no Sue*.

Saw that family of *them* walking in from the outside depot platform.

"Check the bags," said Brian, his wave an order for the Red Cap to lead the way. "Then show me some out of here, front of the station, fresh air."

Mom Isabella led her family out of the traffic of people using the gates to platforms of waiting trains. Scanned the streaming crowd for her sister's face.

Her daughter Mir stepped next to her, said: "Where's Aunt Roma?"

Her husband Ulysses said: "Do you want to text her?"

"While she's driving like a bat out of hell to get here on time because—"

"Because she's Aunt Roma," said Malik, who, even at 10 years old, knew. He looked up at his mom, fidgeted: "I've got the zoomies."

"Anybody would," said Dad Ulysses. "Been a long ride."

Isabella sighed. Scanned the vast crowd in this huge station, still no Roma, no obvious *stranger dangers*—but you never saw them *until*.

"I got him," said teenage Mir. She told her parents: "Maybe we'll find Roma."

Mir's touch on her little brother's shoulder let him dash off into the crowd, spinning circles to help him obey Mir's: "Stay where I see you!"

Isabella watched her loves slide into the streaming crowd of strangers.

Felt the man of her eternity step beside her, shoulder to shoulder as they faced what's out there.

Ulysses said: "You've got to be the first one to speak my new *who*."

A hurricane of *what*s and *when*s, *how*s and *why*s, of smiles and sorrows and exhaustions of just soldiering on and through and to, of the grims and the glories of getting to be who she'd chosen to be, of the kids' experienced crestfallen excited faces, of loss and learning and leaving it all behind while carrying it all ahead, all that swirled Isabella in that train station, rocked her standing beside the man she loved who deserved and accepted, needed to, *should* for all the rest of us and *had to* for the integrity of him who'd finally decided on his next move.

His decided move that she guessed.

Isabella said: "Congratulations, *Colonel* Doss."

Ulysses said: *"Semper fi."*

They held hands.

Stood tall where they were.

Terri rolled her bag into the final destination train station. Erik suddenly hurried to roll past her into the station's crowd. Up ahead in the traffic flow, Terri spotted four standing-there black suits. Saw one of the black suits raise a camera and *knew*, knew and knew that knowing made everything worse/didn't matter.

Yelled: *"STOP!"*

Felt herself rise up closer to Erik, her eyes ignoring everything except his puzzled expression as he stood near that quartet of black suits, his right hand closed around DON'T FUCKING THINK IT, speaking as fast as she could, filling the roar of *now* with the echo of her voice.

"I can't do this anymore!" cried Terri. "This isn't, this can't, it maybe never was, never did, this won't ever work and I'm sorry, *so sorry*, but it's over. We're over. I can't be with you and pretend it's all one wonderful big picture. And you can't be with me trying to build the pieces back into what's supposed to be. And you're the most amazing man who's *exactly* who I'm supposed to want to spend my life with, but I can't stay with you for one more fucking minute!"

Sobbing, she knew she was sobbing and slaughtering at the same time.

Words kept tumbling out of her:

"Last night, texted Anna, she's double parked outside, and I'm sorry and I'll . . . I'll send you money for the train tickets and . . . and . . . and I gotta go, I'm *gone*."

Rolled her suitcase away as fast as she could. Rolled to a run. Rolled past the Field Director who panned the flow of a woman fleeing into a crowd . . .

Gone.

Came the voice of the bass player behind him: "I think the word is *cut*."

The Field Director slowly turned in the train station streaming with curious faces. Lowered the camera. Grimaced at the stunned handsome stud who'd produced this whole elaborate . . .

Well, call it a debacle, thought the Field Director. Least we got paid in advance. OMG, what a thing to think *now*!

Erik knew nothing beyond what wasn't happening.

No music. No *on his knee*, tears of joy, squeals of '*Yes, of course!*' filmed and forever posted in the big picture *wow* of The Way Things Are Supposed To Be.

This magic moment gutted him like an alley knife spilling who he was onto the tiles of this horrible forever place.

A ghost of him pushed a small velvet box back into his front pocket.

Mindlessly filled his grasp with the handle of his roller bag.

He wandered off to the city of broken hearts.

The saxophone player said: "That poor shit earned his blues."

The guitar player who now wasn't going to get to sing softly as words were spoken and her colleagues played said: "We had to learn that damn cheesy pop fluff he thought was their song for nothing. Suit up. Get here. Set up."

"For nothing," said the sax player.

"Fuck that," said the bass player. His colleagues felt him rise as he repeated the most famous introduction in all of jazz: "*Let's take a train.*"

And *like that*, everything happened.

The band launched into Duke Ellington's up-tempo masterpiece from the era of black & white movies, "Take The A Train":

Bummm, da-da-dah dutta, bah, da-da-dah.

Passersby looked away from where they were going or their screens of where they weren't to see what was happening where they were, where white stone columns styled from the ancient civilization that birthed democracy held this train station's sheltering stone ceiling below the forever sky.

Graham, Nora and Ross eased a discreet path around where Ulysses and Isabella stood together waiting for Aunt Roma.

Slid through the crowd along the edges of that train station's vast center court as the band played from the heart of this center for transitions.

A woman screamed.

A ripple surged through the crowd.

A handmade Italian shoe flew into the air above everyone's heads.

"Stop!" yelled a cop's voice.

A pair of blue pinstripe pants sailed over the starting-to-panic crowd.

The black-suited quartet played: *"Da-dah, dat da datta . . ."*

Duke Ellington done proud by a bass, sax, and acoustic guitar held by a woman who started to scat the sounds of the music: *"Ba-dah, bump ba butta . . ."*

AND HERE HE COMES!

Heart-pumping, bare feet thumping, sticky feeling not letting his skin go stiff, fought free of all the *gonna kill you* sticky clothes, flaxen hair stuck straight out in sprayed glory, flesh a-flapping, penis a-flopping, *buck naked* comes running for his life Fergus Lang.

Barreling through the train station crowd.

"Get out of the way!" bellowed the voice everyone'd heard on TV. "You're not gonna get me! Nobody's gonna catch me! You can't kill me!"

And he's running, a cop chasing him, a white-shirted stationmaster, too. Travelers jump out of the way. Mothers with baby strollers. Fergus runs past that kid and his sister from the train *get out of the way!*

"Is this real?" said Malik at the sight of a naked floppety-flop, middle-aged White man running amok through the train station.

"Yes," said his big sister Mir with absolute certainty.

"Sure," said Malik, who'd already seen zombies on a train, ghosts in a castle and a Flying Fireball Monster.

When the first note sounded of his black-suited quartet *taking the train*, the Field Director'd swung up and red dot turned on his camera, through which he now panned the crowd and *what the hell was he getting on video!*

Fergus Lang ran a circle through the center of the train station, huffing, puffing, panting, wheezing *whoa look at me go!*

Ran past a bookstore/news stand.

Whirled and ran back to the store.

Grabbed a magazine off its out-front rack.

Held it above his head as he ran, yelled: "I'm on the cover! On the cover!"

Threw the magazine at an Amtrak staffer grabbing for him.

Made the guy duck as the magazine whacked a toddler in the eye.

All of that caught on camera.

'Keep running!' screamed in Fergus's skull.

Cops to the left.

Cops to the right.

Bam! Fergus stopped cold in his tracks, hands out from his sides. His face snapped this way. Snapped that. The cops froze in their tracks, too. Music played like some Marx Brothers comedy mania as Fergus dodged to the left, dodged to the right, took off running toward the station's front door of sunlight.

The band played on as the Field Director's camera and a hundred cellphone screens streamed *look at that famous buck naked madman go.*

Standing in the eyes a-staring, jaws a-gaping, history-recording crowd, Graham told Ross and Nora: "I think we're done here."

He nodded toward an exit sign: "Let's take a different door."

Back on the platform by the train that got them here, Sgt. Carlisle stood beside Trooper David Hale as he watched the rest of their team storing weapons and gear in the undercarriage of the blue bus to the borrowed barracks where some of the guys said there'd be pizza and beer and maybe a pass to some local bars' action, or at least beds that didn't rock before the next day's deadhead return to the city where it rained a thousand days a year.

The Chicago SWATs now held mission control over that black cube on the back of a flatbed truck rumbling through the windy city to an inevitable inferno.

Sergeant Carlisle asked David Hale: "You have a good trip, rook?"

"Nothing happened." *'Cept my mind trick about a silver-mouthed monster.*

"You mean nothing happened that was *ours*," said Sgt. Carlisle. "Something's always happening. But when that adds up to we don't gotta do what we're bottom-lined trained and sworn to do, *well*, that's a good trip."

Those two sworn men stood there with all of that.

Sgt. Carlisle nodded, said: "Let's go. We're on the bus."

No more a rook David Hale angled his head to the silver dragon sleeping on the tracks beside them, another chrome machine that moved him through time and space, but a vehicle where he'd been somebody, meant something.

Trooper David Hale grinned: "I'll miss that train."

Outside that train station, Aunt Roma frantically looked for parking.

Outside the train station shuffled a man in a golden cashmere coat.

No sign of Sue. Brian's head throbbed. He heard a *clink* in his coat pocket. Knew that *clink*, knew it was more of what she'd left him.

The hair of the dog, thought Brian.

Brian wobbled as he pulled from his coat pocket and twisted off the cap of an airplane-sized Scotch—*Should have flown. Gonna fly home. Gonna get, gonna be, gonna make it alright, the hell with her*—turned his face up to glug the booze, heard a ruckus back in the station as he stepped off the curb, turned to see—

WHAM!

The Chicago Transit Authority bus slammed into the man in the golden cashmere coat. Knocked him 21 feet to smear the city pavement D.O.A. Investigators bagged broken glass from the bus. Broken glass from the dead man's palm. Broken glass from inside his pockets. Detectives' calls to the driver's license listed hometown's police department confirmed the dead man's ways.

But what the primary Chicago cop never logged in his Final Report was how when he *finally* got the next of kin/suddenly wealthy widow named Suzanne to answer her cellphone somewhere in the Midwest, the cop heard some man ask *'What's going on?'* as the cop notified her about the tragic accidental death of her husband who the city attorneys were certain left her no grounds for a law suit against the CTA because the tox screen and evidence indicated that he'd been impaired by alcohol when he stepped in front of the bus.

What that homicide cop could have sworn he heard after the formalities and the widow's gracious goodbye was the sound of stunned laughter.

Nora. Ross. Graham.

They walked to the river.

Across an alley from the station. They heard the sounds of city traffic. A bus's frantic HONK! Sounds from inside where they'd been.

The wind was cool and wet with nature's stream and the tears of this town. They smelled hard cement. Gray sky. Broken ribs Ross beside knife-slashed Nora.

Graham said: "You two better get to an E.R."

"How about you?" said Nora.

"If I go to a hospital, they'll wheel me straight to the morgue."

They stood on a surface that didn't wobble. That made no *clackety-clack.* They stood on the ground beneath their feet.

Ross said: "We made it."

"Together," said Nora, looking at him.

"In a stupid, wrong-headed, lying plan," he told her.

"Wasn't stupid, just wrong. Now my head's on right."

"You tried to kill me."

"No. I tried to save you. Like you tried to save me."

The wind blew.

"We both did a lousy job," said Ross.

Looked around where they were before he looked back at her.

Said: "Was any of us *real*?"

"You saw my tears because I felt *true* come alive in my lies."

"What about now?"

"Now is what I want to know. And do. But not alone. With you."

He stared at her misted blue eyes. Her chopped and dyed lies.

Shrugged: "Who else would believe who we are? Everything else—"

"We'll make everything else. Best as we can. And make it all true."

The cool wind blew.

Graham said: "And then there's me. Plus, of course, *this*."

He held up the duffle bag looped over his left arm, looped over a whisper gun waiting inside his black hoodie.

"The grift," said Graham. "All Della's electronics. Her laptop. Her cellphone. All Zed programmed that he didn't share with Nora. Hard copy printed pages of pick up and deliver shipping manifests and order codes and contracts for a black cube and a shortage space leased in the outskirts of Chicago."

The three of them stood looking at each other in the chill of that Saturday afternoon river wind.

Graham smiled: "So what happens now?"

Came the lonesome whistle of a train.

ACKNOWLEDGMENTS

Special Thanks To:

Henry Allen, Amtrak's Empire Builder, Hal Bernton, Jamie Binns, William Boyle, Ray Bradbury, Clarisse Callahan, Michael Carlisle, Jessica Case, Agatha Christie, Leonard Cohen, S. A. Cosby, Jeffery Deaver, John Dos Passos, The Drive By Truckers, Bob Dylan, Alison Fairbrother, John Fitzgerald, Bonnie Goldstein, Desmond Jack Grady, Jane Grady, Nathan Grady, Rachel Grady, Keir Graff, David Gutman, Alfred Hitchcock, John Lee Hooker, Stephen Hunter, Warren Iverson, Craig Johnson, Angie Kim, Sinclair Lewis, Joe Lansdale, Ron Mardigian, Jon Nazdin, Alice Williams Noah, George Orwell, Alan Pulaski, Bob Reiss, The Rolling Stones, S. J. Rozan, Cari Rudd, Hank Phillippi Ryan, Carl Sandburg, Yvonne Seng, David Hale Smith, Bruce Springsteen, John Steinbeck, Roger Strull, Richard Thompson, Paul Vineyard, E. B. White, Holly Wilson, Josh Wolff, Warren Zevon, You.

ABOUT THE AUTHOR

James Grady's first novel *Six Days Of The Condor* became the classic Robert Redford movie *Three Days Of The Condor* and the current Max Irons TV series *Condor*. Grady has received Italy's Raymond Chandler Medal, France's *Grand Prix Du Roman Noir* and Japan's *Baka-Misu* literature award, two *Regardie's* Magazine short story awards, and been a Mystery Writers of America Edgar finalist. He's published more than a dozen novels and three times that many short stories, been a muckraker journalist and a scriptwriter for film and television. In 2008, London's *Daily Telegraph* named Grady as one of *"50 crime writers to read before you die."* In 2015, the *Washington Post* compared his prose to George Orwell and Bob Dylan.